A man catches lobsters, a criminal is murdered, a disturbed boy cries for a decent childhood, a singer smiles in fear.

Stepping through a tragi-comic twilight world of karaoke clubs, dirty deals and people trying against the odds, to make a life, **Sharks** is not so much a who-done-it? thriller as a who-got-done?

When even poverty can be worth more than a few bob, illegal money lender, Jimmy Tollan and his cohorts ruthlessly run the lives of too many. Gripping, real, moving, yet comic and ultimately hopeful, **Sharks** is a thrilling story of our times.

Mike Hildrey is chief investigative reporter on Glasgow's Evening Times. Winner of numerous press awards, he has spent many years exposing greedy criminals, smart-assed conmen, worthless government schemes, ruthless landlords and countless wideboys. He is married with one son and considers himself a top amateur journalist who should have been a professional gardener.

sharks

SHARKS

MIKE HILDREY

Argyll
publishing

© Mike Hildrey 1996

First published 1996
Argyll Publishing
Glendaruel
Argyll PA22 3AE

The author has asserted his moral rights.
All characters and situations in this novel are entirely fictional.
Acknowledgement is made for permission to use extracts from:
New York, New York (Kander/Ebb) to International Music
Publications Ltd;
Step Inside Love (McCartney/Lennon) to MCA Music Ltd;
and *Only the Lonely* (Orbison/Melson) to Music Sales Ltd.

British Library Cataloguing-in-Publication Data.
A catalogue record for this book is available from the
British Library.

ISBN 1 874640 32 7

Origination
Cordfall Ltd, Glasgow

Printing
Caledonian International
Book Manufacturing, Glasgow

This novel is dedicated to
all those who encouraged me.
They are
Mark, Brenda, Norman, Jess, Angus, Ron, Marian,
Lorna, Linda, Bob, Jim, Bob, Willie, Chris, Brian, Jean,
Jocelyn, Rod, Ian, Austin, Bev, Sam, Lesley, Chris,
Lewis, Paul, Lorna, Martin, Billy, Ally, Frank, Jane,
John, Clifford, Jonathan, Joe, Tricia, Russell, Derek and
Russell. Some of you cannot be identified, so for
diplomatic reasons, I have left out everybody's surname.
You all know who you are. I thank you individually and
collectively.

Contents

1 The fisherman

THE ENGINE was choking, missing the beat, with an irregular cough.

He had the usual choice, turn back or take a chance. There wasn't a lot to be weighed up. The tide, the catch, and the weather, which, more often than not, was the deciding factor.

Not today though. The sun shone warm enough to defy the steady chilled wind. Matt was sweating under his one-piece waterproof suit. The wind and sun burnished his weathered face.

He was alone on the sea, twenty two years of age, in command. The boat, the oldest in the motley collection which still ploughed daily out of the tiny stone harbour, was his mistress.

She was yellow, and a sort of mottled blue where he'd painted her with whatever was left from other jobs.

Her official title was KY 186. Her name was printed on her bow. *Safe Haven*.

He called her Oystercatcher.

He wasn't the owner. He was more than that. He was custodian and sort of captain.

He loved the sea with a grateful passion. The depth, the waves, the smell, the changing colours, swelled his soul.

And yet there was a niggling doubt about his right to work the grey seas breaking off Crail.

He held his nerve as the engine coughed while they

stuttered along the coast toward Anstruther. There were another one hundred and sixty creels to lift. He was under pressure for the job was important. Every trip was crucial to his livelihood and his lifestyle. The cash from every take went three ways, for he was feeding a few mouths – himself and his mother, the boat's owner and greedy Oystercatcher herself.

Oystercatcher gave out midway between the Isle of May and the rocks opposite the old caves between Anstruther and Crail. She wouldn't restart.

He tried everything. Choke in, choke out. Changed the filter. Checked the connections. Dried the leads. Engines were all the bloody same. Temperamental.

Oystercatcher's engine was a 1975 model. The boat had been kept alive with regular stripping and painting. Her worn engine was tired. She was nearly thirty years old and she wouldn't start.

The last thing he wanted to do was call for help. He had another hour and a half before the tide would turn.

Matt gave her ten minutes to cool down. Maybe she just needed a rest to allow the fuel to ease down.

He unzipped the top of his suit.

He could see the cormorants on parade, drying out, out on the rocks. Dozens of them, like soldiers at ease, the wind and the sun easing the heavy sea water out of their dark plumage. They were part of the jagged rocks. Part of his broken childhood.

They'd been there on those rocks when he arrived in Crail fourteen years earlier. Lifting their enormous wings, stretching their powerful necks, jagged tough predators. It wasn't so much what they did, diving and hunting, as the contribution they made to nature's wild jigsaw. He was pleased to be a working part of the sea, the harbour, the boat, the lobsters, the winter and the summer.

He didn't wait long, and when he pressed the starter

the motor spluttered into life.

The sweat on his chest was turning cold. He zipped up his suit and moved Oystercatcher closer to the shore where he lifted more creels. Two contained lobsters. The cormorants flopped off the rocks moving steadily away from his presence.

Just as they'd done all those years ago when he nervously walked out at low tide to get a closer look at them.

When he was a stranger.

When he was a boy.

When they did a runner. A million years ago.

He felt guilty. A grey intangible guilt. He had done nothing wrong. But there was a bug eating at his soul.

He turned Oystercatcher seaward toward the horizon for the deep sea lobsters. The big colourful ones.

2 The chips were down

THEY READ the extensive menu several times. Something to do, for they were without thoughts or conversation.

They moved to the till at the drafty door. Luigi, working alone, salted, vinegared and wrapped the chips, taking their money as they all exchanged a curt thanks.

They made their way past the drooping privet hedges beneath steel-shuttered houses. Light crawled out of the few occupied homes.

They shuffled past unlettable flats, through the smashed community, carrying the weight of an ugly environment.

Nobody hurried in Garthill.

Behind the Black Inn the older boy succumbed to the temptation of the heat from the newspaper.

He was too eager. As he tried to unwrap the newspaper all three packets of chips fell to the ground. One burst open and some hot chips spilled out. He was distraught.

"Aw Jesus," he muttered anxiously. He picked up the two intact wrappings. Then kicked out angrily at the burst packet.

In the half light filtering from the caged back window of the pub his eyes followed the chips. They landed next to a white hand.

He thought it was a plastic hand. A dummy hand. Then he saw it was attached to a body. A dark huddle lying on its side. The incessant penetrating drizzle had darkened the hair. The boy hesitated, straining his eyes to see more. The side of the face was smeared with dirt.

The eye was open and frozen in fear. He sensed that he was looking at death rather than a collapsed drunk.

He absorbed the image without picking out any more details. He had seen enough. He was in shock and speechless until fear broke through. "Oh fuck."

His pal responded, "Whit?"

"There's a deid body."

They were frightened, unable to respond to the situation. It was as much the setting as the body that frightened them, for the backyard was a dirty unpleasant place. A dog shit of a place.

They went home to tell of the body at the back of the Black Inn. Was it a man or a woman? They weren't sure. Probably a man. Trousers and shortish hair.

Neither had noticed a baseball bat in the couch grass.

The loss of a some chips was no longer a cause of stress. A neighbour called the police.

3 Catching a crab

FROM FIVE yards away Jimmy Tollan's son spotted a crab crawling into the dark seaweed at a rock's edge. He'd never seen a live crab before. He stepped quickly across the wet sand and peered at the glistening seaweed fronds.

Nothing moved. The boy was eight years old. He had rarely been out of Garthill. The scheme was ingrained in him. He knew about high rise lifts, telephone kiosks, ice cream vans and spray cans. He was almost streetwise. The musky smell of urine, detergents, cigarette smoke and frying fat was a base to his senses.

This was different. The wind carried the mysterious seaweed aroma into his eager nostrils.

What a week. Crail, Fife. A quaint fishing village. The cobble stones. The fishermen. The creels. The boats. Painted. Red, white and green and blue and yellow. He looked out to sea, sucking in the cold wind tempered by the sunshine.

This would be something to tell the teacher about. Turning he waved to his parents standing high above on the stone rampart. Through the sharp wind he heard his father's bogus effort to show concern. "Don't get cold son. Keep away fae the waater. Whit are yi daein?"

The boy cupped his hands round his mouth and bawled into the wind. "A crab. It's alive. It's moving. C'moan doon Da."

Jimmy heard, and so did Rita.

"Ah cannae hear. Ah cannae hear whit yir saying Matt. Cannae fuckin hear yi, son." The wind carried Jimmy Tollan's lie.

Matt knelt down and pulled the seaweed apart, searching for the crab. He gingerly lifted the seaweed fronds away from the rock and spotted the crab. It was big enough to grasp. He stood up, ecstatic, slightly nervous. His heart was pounding with excitement. He hardly looked at the crab.

With the creature held high in his right hand he raced across the bay toward the chunks of weather-worn pink-tinged granite stone that formed the harbour. He stumbled up the worn steps and rushed along the centuries old pier to stand breathless in front of his mother.

She stepped back. "Dinnae bring that thing near me. Do as yer telt. Throw it away. Tell him Jimmy. Get that away."

Jimmy laughed. "Ah'll protect yi darlin," he chuckled, putting his arm round Rita and looking down at the boy. "Matt. Throw the fuckin thing away."

Matt's fingers tightened on the crab shell. "Naw. Ah'm takin it back to the caravan," he murmured.

Tollan stepped forward. His hair ruffled in the wind. His hand shot out knocking the crab to the ground. As it landed his right heel drove down breaking the shell. He placed his foot beside the broken shell and pushed it off the pier.

There was a small splash. That was that.

Rita knew there was still good food to enjoy, that she could curl up with Jimmy in the spacious caravan and watch the TV, while Matt would potter around in the rocks at the cove.

Later some sex. No. A lot of sex. Jimmy was good in bed, gentle, considerate, and caressing. A control freak. Afterwards he would talk of his love for her. He held her body and he held her attention. Then more sex. In bed he was a good man. Sleeping with Jimmy was a thrilling cosy adventure.

But that was not enough. She needed more than that. He crushed the crab and their week away from Garthill. The destruction happened every time they tried to get away from their bogus existence.

The neighbours knew where the money was coming from. They avoided her eyes when she got into the Audi outside the maisonette. Not once had she heard them speak against her man. The judgement was in their eyes and in the number of times they stopped talking when she met them at the shops or on the way to school with Matt. Their eyes accused her of being a money lender's woman. Their unspoken words echoed in her head. "The rest of the scheme is payin' for that motor. In fuckin interest. We paid for yir summer tan. You bastards should be in jail, no driving about in that motor."

Jimmy had been in jail many times. Assault, robbery, theft, breach of the peace, fraud. Rita hated the very words. So much dirt. So many crushing words, conviction, extortion, indictment, summary, remand, all jumbled together by police, lawyers and Procurators Fiscal to create a brutal image. Of her lover.

That last case was saturated in shame. Illegal money lending. He was publicly branded a loan shark. Four years, or was it less? Two years for money lending. Fourteen months for attempted extortion. Six months for keeping the Monday books. The sentences to run concurrently. She never really understood what it all meant. All she knew was that Jimmy never stayed in jail for as long as she expected. Even if he did get four years.

That last case nearly finished them. There was so much shame and no hiding place. Her love for Tollan was almost obliterated. The judge's words on the news the night Jimmy was sentenced at the High Court . . . "You are an evil man. You preyed on the poor and the vulnerable forcing them deeper into debt. Elderly people were forced to live without heating. You are a heartless evil man. I have no alternative, nor would I wish to have, but to send you to prison for . . ."

The heavy spray from waves breaking on the stones at the base of the harbour wall dampened her face. From behind Matt said, "Watch oot ma. There's mair big waves comin."

Jimmy took her hand as they walked across the cobblestones to the car. The harbour was therapeutic. Strange how she felt. Lobster creels, rope, rusted mooring bollards, the bright fishing boats. The seagulls. The black ducks in the corner of the harbour. A little something extra had been squeezed into her mind. Into her very soul. This was good. Jimmy had brought her here. That added another notch to her reluctant love for him.

He could afford to buy their brief escape from the scheme. Not that there was anything wrong with the scheme. The people were good. The shops were useless but close at hand. The scheme fitted her like a cheap dress and despite the shame of her relationship she got along well enough. Her association with the notorious loan shark was merely an affliction. Somebody had to sleep with him. She was his woman. So fucking what? Rita respected her background standing confidently on her own ground in that tormented scheme, where drink and drugs heightened the dull pain of distress.

After all everybody had a skeleton in the cupboard these days – a son who was a hopeless junkie, a violent husband, an alcoholic partner. Her burden was that little bit more difficult to live with, in that they were accused, from behind closed doors, of being parasites on their own people. Their scheme, like hundreds of others, was built to house familes unable to afford a better quality existence. The residents lived with the dirty activities spewed out by poverty.

Crail was special. She could feel the oxygen in the air. The freshness stimulated her senses.

In Garthill she rarely looked at the sky. Here she felt and saw much more. The wind throwing clouds across the sky. The air, the movement. The birds bobbing in the sea. The coarse sand. The bouncing whiteness of the waves. She heard things, the change in the sound of waves, the calling birds, even the wind's changing discord. She noticed the look on wee Matt's face as he ran across the bay, wet sand on his knees and a sparkle in his eyes.

Jimmy had chosen to spend the money on her. It could so easily have been wan of they ither lasses. Yea. One that had borrowed from him. The truth slammed into her conscience.

Jimmy didn't make his way directly to the car. Without a word of explanation he walked to a strange little entrance in the corner of the cobbled square. The sign above read, Fresh Lobsters For Sale. Crab Salads For Sale. She followed and before she could stop him he bought three lobsters for twenty quid. Jimmy paid cash.

"A treat fur tonight. Different fae steaks, that's fur sure," he said. "Hiv yi ever had them?"

Before she could say no, he added, "Ah hiv. Ah had them at Roganos. Tasty. But a right cunt tae eat."

How was she going to cook them? Boil them, yes. There were no big pots in the caravan. Steaks would have been better. Easier to cook.

Rita didn't want to reject the lobsters. That would hurt Jimmy. He was not kidding himself that he was the big spender. The lobsters were a gesture. A reward for her loyalty and for their sexual enjoyment of each other. Love can be a matter of chemistry for a long time.

Stand by your man. That is crap. I love him and that's it. The denial of her blind loyalty was understandable. For in truth he was using her. He used everybody. The poor for profit. The young and strong as enforcers at thirty pounds a beating. The addicted for profit. Rita was more than a satisfying sexual partner. She was a vital cog in the machinery of his life. Without her he had no base. He hardly loved her. She was his sex, his partner on holidays, his cook, his bogus raison d'être.

The car crept smoothly up the narrow street between the ancient fishermen's houses huddled tightly together against the elements, exactly as they had been built centuries ago. The harbour they left was quaint, picturesque, historical. A sheltered bay where time had stood still and the geographic reason for Crail's very existence.

Crail was a magnet for those fortunate enough to know and enjoy its wild charms. Cynical locals quietly nicknamed their town God's Waiting Room. A bit unfair for the incomers tried to respect the local traditions.

Jimmy Tollan remembered Crail from his childhood,

a one-day bus outing that his mother dragged him on when he was ten years old. He might have decided to spend his ill-gotten gains on a caravan on the West Coast at Largs, or one up in Argyllshire. The advert he noticed in the paper was for an almost new caravan on its own site near Crail, East Neuk, Fife. Remote, distant from Glasgow, and as he vaguely remembered, a nice place, the sort of place Rita and the boy would like.

Jimmy was here because it was a haven, a safe house, to escape from the pressures of business in the scheme. A drop-out retreat should either the police or the relatives of clients, be showing too strong an interest in his activities.

The Audi moved powerfully along the coast toward Anstruther. Jimmy was relaxed. They were only four hundred yards out of the burgh when he took a turning to the left staying in first gear and driving cautiously on clutch control down a rutted farm road. He was relaxed. The local polis had no interest in him. No smart-ass cops checking him out. There were, as far as he knew, no outstanding warrants to worry about.

The spectre of jail was never fully removed from his thoughts. But at the moment there seemed to be little chance of detection. The business was running smoothly and without any pressing problems to consider, he allowed himself the thought that he could do another sentence without too much grief. The last had been relatively easy.

Getting parole had not been too difficult either. Rita helped.

Ahead a tractor pulled out of a field onto the farm track. Jimmy stopped to allow it to move out of dirt flying range to the farm where he had chosen to buy the caravan. The setting, overlooking the rocky bay, was breathtaking. The vista opened up with the Isle of May breaking the seascape.

"Ah've never thanked yi properly for sticking by me. Yi helped wi everythin," said Jimmy. Rita remained silent. She didn't want a conversation about jail in front of Matt. Jimmy mistook her silence for a mood, slipping his hand onto her thigh and stroking lightly but sensually.

"Come on, we're havin a good day. Don't fuck up. Ah'm no drinking. We'll stay in the caravan. Tomorrow we'll go out fur a meal."

All the reassurances a woman could want.

She remained quiet. So she could listen. "Yi never quit on me. That's a big plus fur yi."

Rita closed her ears to his words and related to her own thoughts.

Oh yea. You are so fuckin right on that one Jimmy. The social worker coming to the house when she was raising the boy perfectly decently. Matt was dispatched to the shops for bread, cigarettes, an Evening Times, crisps and ginger. That would save her going out later.

The social worker, or parole officer as she thought of him, was easy to talk with. His eyes explored the room and its contents. The thirty inch TV, the video, the drinks cabinet, music centre, in a freshly painted and pictured lounge. He absorbed the scene without being judgmental. There was nothing unusual in visiting a home where big money had been spent. Several of his clients matched Jimmy's wealth.

Mr Anderson had readily accepted Rita's offer of tea and biscuits, and settled in for an hour's gentle inquisition about her relationship with Jimmy, his attitude to work and to his son, and his chances of staying out of jail when released from Penninghame at the end of training for freedom.

The car eased past the tractor as it turned into the farmyard. She could see the caravan now but the sight didn't break her thoughts. Her mind was locked into the relationship with Jimmy. She liked the money. Loved his body. But what a bastard. Evil. A real pig. Sometimes she hated him for what he was. Yet she remained his partner for he was the father of her child. And he was sexually attractive.

Rita had known exactly what to tell the easy going social worker who was only doing his job reporting the surface view of her relationship with Jimmy Tollan.

The report was not shown to her. Nor to Jimmy, who would have been more than satisfied with her contribution. She backed him on every front. The right message was being directed at the parole board members, who might grant him a few months off the sentence, enabling him to get back to his lucrative business before anybody else took his clients.

Jimmy was a superb actor. He could assume any persona instantly. In prison he assumed the role of a contrite, friendly, individual who was determined to put his criminal tendencies behind him. A performance of Oscar-winning magnitude, which was more often than not successful.

He was that peculiar mixture of a man, a confusion of bully and coward, friend and foe, dirty and clean. He was relaxed yet unhappy. He gave little of himself, and was therefore a difficult man to sum up. A closed book.

"A sad bastard," was the summation of those acqainted with his ways.

He stood five foot eight inches tall and was physically rounded in every way. His head was round, like a ball, with dark brown eyes, so dark that you couldn't see the pupils. His dark hair rounded over his head fitting neatly over the top of his ears and down the nape of his neck. Well groomed and moulded to his head.

Beneath the dark ball eyes was a small neat nose linked to a full-lipped mouth by two lines. He even had a cleft in his strong chin – God's thumb print. The only blemish to his face was a small jagged white scar coming off his left cheek and onto his jaw, where a boy had cut him with a thrown slate. The roundness of his face was set on a strong muscle-defined neck. He had a square chest set high in a finely proportioned body. Jimmy walked strongly driving himself forward on muscled if shortish legs.

He was blessed with a good body and an attractive face. But what he gained in physical presence he squandered in a fearful cunning aggression, born of stress. The stress of panic.

"Ah don't have a Da." The words had tripped of his

tongue hundreds of times. He hated having to say them, for he had no picture whatsover of his father. Nothing on which to focus anger, love, or even interest.

For years he burned with curiosity about his father. Jimmy had nothing to explore. The man had left before he was born. Gone to some distant corner of London, never to be spoken about.

Jimmy was left to field the childhood questions. "Is yir Da working? What does yir faither dae? Whit team does your Da support? Has your Da got a motor?"

His father was a blank space. There was no voice, no size, no face, no eyes. The seed of his life was only his mother, who said not one word about the absent partner. He was fatherless and the stranger would not return.

Jimmy rebelled against people around him. He used them to fill the void finding a powerful role as the scheme's money man – the friend who was big enough to lend cash and strong enough to demand his rights, the interest on his loans.

In a tight corner he could assume any role. That came naturally. In prison that meant becoming a new man. A committed family man determined to go straight, to support his wife-to-be and child.

The prison and social work services swallowed his act easily.

Parole-Home Background Report for Review
This Report is based on several interviews with Mr Tollan in prison and with his fiance Rita Fullerton at her home.

They live apart but intend to marry.
They have a three appartment council house in Garthill on the first floor of a maisonette style block with a veranda.

The Offender
Mr Tollan has been extremely co-operative during all interviews. He is enthusiastic about all vocational training courses within the prison.

He states categorically that he has no ciminal associates.
He does not see parole as a certainty and appears realistic
about his chances of an early release.

Criminal History
Mr Tollan has an extensive record of crime. His early offences
were in the nature of breach of the peace, minor thefts, and
assault.
He later progressed to more serious offences including, fraud,
assault with intent to rob, and armed robbery. He has had ten
sentences of imprisonment.

The assessments were made by professional senior social workers whose job was to support and direct offenders back into the community. To help. To guide. To advise. To be a there. To be firm but caring. To oversee Jimmy's return to so-called normality. To understand and to make the judgements that would assist the flawed father to settle to a decent home life and, miracle of miracles, encourage him to seek employment or cope with unemployment.

They stood little or no chance of guiding him into a job. The ease with which he could make big money in the poverty-wracked scheme was too powerful. The punters needed his money, and with the cash an adrenaline shot of fear.

Jimmy's need was even greater. He had to have a position in the scheme of things. So he and Rita played the parole game to the limit.

Mr James Tollan and Miss Rita Fullerton have a steady
relationship. They intend to marry in the future. They have
an eight year old son.
Miss Fullerton has a daughter by a previous relationship. The
daughter stays with her former partner who is now married.
Mr Tollan says that he cares for the daughter as for his son.
Miss Fullerton confirms this. They have been engaged for
several years.
They have a strong commitment to each other.

The home is clean and well maintained.
Miss Fullerton is on Income Support.

As were hundreds of people who borrowed from Jimmy. The irony was there. Then again it depended where you were coming from. Jimmy Tollan was a central figure in a bigger money game.

To the poor he was first a pal and then an enemy capable of exacting a punishing price if they didn't keep paying. To the police he was a ned, an evil bastard. To the lawyers he was the chance to defy the odds. Reporters used him as a good story. He was part of a social worker's caseload. His family were embarrassed by the blacksheep who blackened their name.

During his last prison sentence he had made sure that the screws saw him in a favourable light. At forty-one years of age he was too old for the macho bit. The other prisoners accepted that he had nothing to prove anymore. He had cried on that first night back in Barlinnie Prison, for ten minutes only. He held his shaky nerve, just. There was never any danger of suicide. He settled down to do the time and get out as soon as possible.

The screws' report was more than favourable. Indeed it was a glowing testimony to his total acceptance of prison, to his full participation in everything that was supposed to be good for him. Rehabilitation appeared to be his sole concern.

The official parole report on prisoner 96-859 from the establishment of HM Prison Perth was comprehensive.

Response to Prison
Report by Voluntary Training Instructor Thomas McBain.
James Tollan has been a good and willing worker. He shows a pleasant attitude to everyone in authority.
He is a keen volunteer on a woodwork training course.
Mr Tollan mixes well with other inmates. He mixes with the better type of prisoners, avoiding contact with troublemakers. He conforms to the system.

He seeks out the staff for open discussions about his progress.
We recommend him for parole.
B Hall officer William Davies reports: His cell is kept clean.
He is one of the better types in the hall, and would appear to
be keen to seek employment when released. He spends a lot of
time reading. He is ready for parole.

Jimmy eased the Audi smoothly through the open farm
gates, past the long barn and up across the sea-sprayed turf
stopping at the smart caravan near the gorse bushes. Matt
was first out of the car, racing down the hill to the pebbled
cove in the hope of meeting the farmer's daughter. The girl
who wore wellies all the time might be there.

4 A friend and a mum

The place was deserted except for two cows on the high tide line. They lifted their heads in unison and tottered up the tightly turfed bank. Matt watched them for a while and then walked along to the rocks at the side of the cove. Maybe he could spot another crab. Boredom was setting in when he heard the call from Jocelyn. Good. The girl in the wellies.

"Hi Matt. What are you up to down there?" she said, making her way across the coarse sand and onto the bed of rounded pebbles. She was carrying a small toy spade and a red plastic bucket. Jocelyn was sixteen years old and bored with her older brother's company at the isolated farm. She had seen the car passing the farmyard and had come down to the beach in the hope of meeting the boy from Glasgow. She came prepared to be a mum.

They pottered about for a while collecting baby crabs. After that Jocelyn selected interesting pebbles, which she dried on her skirt and held out for him to study. Soon they were talking. What more natural than to ask what Matt's father did for a living.

"Ah'm no sure," he replied cautiously.

In truth Matt was unsure. He had an idea that whatever he did was meant to be a secret. Even without the full knowledge his father's relentless addiction to crime was carved into his subconscious. Already Matt carried an indelible scar.

The kindly girl dug into her primary school education and tried to help him answer her friendly question.

> *Daddies work most every day,*
> *They say goodbye. They go away,*
> *By car, by bus, by railroad train,*
> *By trolley, subway or even plane,*
> *Every morning, every year*
> *A lot of Daddies disappear,*

> *And every child would want to know*
> *Exactly where those Daddies go.*

The gentle approach solicited no response from Matt.
Jocelyn was working in the dark. Unaware of the blockage.
He was tired after a long day in the car and then in the
biting sea wind. At home he spent most of his time in front
of the TV.

Matt wanted out of this. He was too tired to find an
excuse to go back to the caravan. He couldn't be bothered
with the climb up the hill and had neither the strength of
body nor the will to leave a situation he was finding
uncomfortable. So he suffered in resentment of his weak
position.

Jocelyn took his silence as enjoyment of the children's
poem. The rest of it was coming back to her. She spoke out
loud and clear in the peace of the cove caressed by the gentle
breaking waves.

> *It's Dads who make our newspapers,*
> *Our books and magazines,*
> *And Daddies who produce the shows*
> *On our television screens.*
> *There are acting Daddies,*
> *Painting Daddies,*
> *Singing Daddies too.*
> *Dads are circus acrobats*
> *And keepers in the zoo.*
> *Dads make puppets,*
> *Dads play ball*
> *Dads play music in a band.*
> *One Dad is a magician,*
> *Hiding rabbits in each hand.*

Matt was irritated. The poem had lasted too long for him
to maintain concentration. On top of that he knew what
she was pushing for. The little boy was facing out to the
sea. Watching the waves break on the wet pebbles as the

29

tide ebbed. His eyes absorbed the scene, a fishing boat in the distance on the grey sea, seagulls breaking and floating in the blustering damp wind.

He had heard every word. Jocelyn had positioned herself so that the wind hit her shoulders first. She wanted him cocooned from cold. A friend and a mum.

His words plunged with the brutality of a knife into her stomach. "Fuck you. Don't ask me whit ma faither does. Fuck off and leave me alain."

He was nearly crying. He stood up, bent down and grabbed a handful of the white and black pebbles they had carefully collected while wandering the beach. His arm moved back. He hurled the pebbles and turned away up the hill, through the gorse bushes to the caravan. At the steps he looked back to the bay. Jocelyn was still sitting as he had left her. Thinking.

Matt stepped into the warmth of the caravan, seeking some of the easy cheap love and care to which he was accustomed. The TV was on. Hymns from a crowded church. Posh people. Men in dark suits and mustard yellow ties. Women with stupid yellow, pink and white hats. All of them balancing a hymn book in their hands and gazing upwards to the pulpit. Their lips mouthing their praise to God. He'd switch channels later.

Something wasn't quite right in the caravan. The lounge was steamed up from water boiling in a pan. He saw the mess in the kitchen corridor. Scattered across the floor were broken lobster shells. Bits of claw, white flesh and dark mottled shell.

He looked in his parent's bedroom compartment. Rita lay face downward on the bed. He touched her, the curve of her bottom encased tightly in blue jeans. She twisted round. Her voice was a whimper.

"Oh Matt. It's you. The bastard's gone."

Matt understood. His eight most formative years had given him the experience to understand this scene. Jimmy and Rita. They'd had another fight. Jimmy had left. That was the route his father always took. To leave.

In years to come Matt would hate them both for his childhood. Later, from a distance, he would try to love them by understanding them. Or maybe simply because he wanted to love them.

While she gathered herself he switched channels without finding anything suitable. Nothing good on. Songs of Praise. An appeal for charity. He left it on The Money Programme.

They were prattling on about nothingness. Later Jeremy Beadle would be on.

Rita came through. Tired but controlled. She had toughened out on these scenes and lived with hardened internal scars.

"Switch to something else Matt," she said totally uninterested in the analysis of a financial wipe-out that cut the foreign reserves, smashed the value of the pound and meant that half of the families in Britain would have their spending power decimated.

"We're awright Matt. He's left plenty money."

Tea was the next event.

"Do you want some French bread and chips? Ah've got those big eggs from the farm. And Ah've got two loaves. Ah brought tomato sauce with me."

Once the debris was cleared from the floor Rita perked up no end. Matt put on his pyjamas and warmed up in the cosy caravan. Rita slipped into her nightdress and the nice thick dressing gown Jimmy had bought her last Christmas.

They had a smashing night, watching the telly. A mother and son at rest. Rita missed out on her sexual pleasures with Jimmy. The consolation was that there was no trouble. The bastard was gone.

Matt fell into a deep sleep induced by a long confusing day in the sharp east coast winds and softened by new images . . . crabs, pebbles, ducks and fishermen unloading their creels in the harbour. Rita left him on the couch, covering him with two blankets and then drifted off to sleep in the tiny caravan bedroom lulled by the swish of waves lapping on the squared East Neuk rocks.

Jimmy Tollan's anger had abated by the time he crossed the Kincardine Bridge. He cruised down the M80, choosing from his favourite tapes, the theme tune from Once Upon a Time in America and Frank Sinatra. The crooner cheered him.

> *Start Spreading the Noos,*
> *I'm leaving today.*
> *I want to be a part of it,*
> *Noo York, Noo York.*
> *I want to wake up where the city ,*
> *Doesn't sleep . . .*

Glasgow was fast asleep except for the odd cop car cruising in the soft darkness beneath the high rise blocks and solid warm tenements. He was a hungry unhappy shark in the empty half darkness of the city. Jimmy went to a snack bar for a hamburger.

5 The karaoke kid

THEY WERE looking up at him, waiting for his performance to begin.

"Go on wee man. Gie it laldy."

So he did. Tightening his hands on the microphone he filled his lungs. Confidence was the name of the game.

> *Dad dad da ra ra*
> *Dad, dad da ra ra . . .*

He sang, with a vengeance.

> *Start spreading the noos.*
> *I'm leaving today.*
> *I want to be a part of it . . .*
> *Noo York, noo York.*

This was the gemme. His soul sang. The throat was oiled with a good few swallies. He was relaxed. He was operating. Happy. The voice just warbled. Nae other word for it. It warbled. Sweetly.

He could ask it to do anything. The audience loved this one.

> *Start spreading the noos.*
> *I'm leaving today . . .*

Everybody in the pub was Frank Sinatra. He was giving them that feeling. Their eyes, gleaming with alcohol and admiration, thanked him for his efforts. He was better than a jukebox.

He reigned supreme.

King of the Karaoke.

This was his night. Saturday night in the Black Inn. The best night of the week. At last, Celtic had won. His maw was content after a wee win at the Bingo on one of her rare excursions from the safety of her home. The pub was trouble free, and he still had enough money for three more pints. Johnny McPherson was in his own little Paradise.

"Stay up son. Gie us mair." The words carried from the back. He knew the man who called. He always wanted another song from Johnny. The request came as a mixture of amused warm appreciation.

Johnny was a small jocular man with a badly broken face and constantly laughing eyes. Coarse flesh lumped across his cheeks like putty clinging to a collapsing structure. The nose, cheekbones and jaw were out of position while his forehead seemed awry, giving the impression at first glimpse of a broken vase, badly glued together.

Sober or drunk he lurched. Like a grotesque wooden puppet he jerked his way through life on a two badly healed legs. He never tired of confirming that his bones had been broken by the balanced drive of a well directed baseball bat.

Strangely, Johnny was a happy man. In conversation he smiled openly. He laughed freely with a hardened affection for he was genuinely keen to spread some humour around. He was a nice man to know, easy company, making no demands of anybody. The jokes, more often than not on himself, lacked wit.

Johnny lived in the dark shadow cast by Jimmy Tollan. Though he danced to the loan shark's tune, he never once cried. He always owed. He was always behind with payments.

He was the laughing victim, casually recounting stories of massive criminal injury payments. The rewards from beatings at the hands of the men he tapped. The cash was handy, helping to pay off the very loan sharks who had had beaten him up. A serious joke.

"Ah paid them a right few bob. Kept the rest fur masel. That's the gemme. Eh?" he bragged with a wry broken smile.

He sneaked in and out of the scheme, hiding behind a newspaper on the top of the bus. Watching for his

opponent's car. Leaving his mother's house by the back of
the close. He paid when he could. The rest of the time he
ducked and dived. Lied and begged.

And often sang.

That Saturday night at the karaoke was little different
from the one four years previously when he first suffered.
He was almost home that time.

This time he was seven lurches out of the pub when
his left leg was smashed from beneath him. Instant terror
hit his mind. A flood of cowardice. The pain came later
after the awful realisation that he couldn't get up.

Then another blow. His nose and cheek cracked with
a crunch. Now he felt the wet hot blood on his face. The
pain came through, jagged, hurtful stabs, followed by the
voice.

"Yi had yir fuckin chance. We gave yi plenty time. Yir
no the only wan. But yir fuckin us aboot."

Oh good, he wasn't the only one. Johnny, terrorised
from the stabbing piercing pain, found the fleeting mental
space, to see the joke.

He could smell the man's aftershave and began to see
his leather jacket and the heavy toe of the baseball bat.
Messed with blood.

The bat moved out of his vision. Crack. More
consuming pain. His mind whitened.

He heard the distant noise of the big TV as the
mounting pain crept out of his left leg and into his mind.
Somebody had come out of the pub. He pressed his arms
down on the wet pavement and lifted his head. On the
opposite side of the street he saw the man in a leather jacket
placing the car key into a smart red Audi. The man carried
the baseball bat in his left hand.

A voice from behind broke his concentration. "Fucking
arseholes? Whit the fuck happened tae yoo, yi stupid
bastard?"

The man moved round in front. "Aw Jesus pal, yir in
a fuckin bad way."

The man bent down over him, grasped him under the

armpits and tried to lift. "Come on. Gie us a haun. Staun up pal."

The pain intensified and with it, his fear. At last he heard himself speaking. "Leave me alain. Gonnie get yir hauns aff. Ah cannae get up. Ma leg's fucked."

The man made no response.

Then the voice again friendly. "Right mate. Ah'll get an ambulance."

A few more joined him from the pub. They all had the same thing to say. The voices kept coming at him. "You'll be awright soon."

The blood from his face was soaking into his T-shirt. Spreading dark red across his trousers. Wet. His life was ebbing away. It was surreal. He could see people around recoiling. He was more in control than them. He tried to avoid looking.

They lifted him gently onto a stretcher. Pain became fear and turned back into pain.

He was in the system. In hospital they took a blood sample then shot something into his other arm. The prick was nothing, then a mild strange freeze. Nothing more. He remained awake.

They cut his trousers and gently moved the blood-soaked cloth away from the wound. They X-rayed his legs and the side of his face.

His clothes were removed. All of them. And a gown thing, made of cloth that looked and felt like paper.

His heart seemed to beat poorly. His sight was clear. He could see the ceiling tiles – some were new, whiter than the others. They placed him on a trolley, folding up the comforting sides.

And they pushed him down a corridor. To theatre. The trip seemed to take hours. Every event was frozen in time. Nobody spoke except to say, "You'll be allright."

He passed others. He was to face the scalpel before them. For the first time he thought of Jimmy. The fuckin bastard.

Then he was inside a green tunnel. The trolley seemed

to be on tracks. The tunnel walls covered in silvery looking pipes, black cables, thin, connected to machinery. Ahead he could see the flapping plastic doors. Presumbly the men with scalpels lurked behind there.

A friendly face leant over, introducing himself as Vinnie. He had on a small green turban-like hat, the same colour as his gown.

"Is this a life or death case mate?" That was the best Johnny could come up with.

"You'll be fine. Where are you from?"

"Garthill. Injun country. Where are yi fae yersel?"

"Maryhill."

"Cowboy country. Dae yi know Tommy McFadzen." The man showed his smile.

"No. I'm going to give you another jag."

He did. Another man materialised on the other side of the trolley, with a smile, and all in green, to say that he was the anaethestist.

"Ah thought he wis," said Johnny, his eyes moving back to the Maryhill man.

His last thought for two hours. The time disappeared like a lost jigsaw piece. He awoke from nothingness on the way into a ward. He was moving, until the trolley stopped beside a bed. They lifted him onto the bed and told him to have a wee sleep. He didn't notice that his left arm was connected to a drip.

He awoke at two the following day. His eyes drifted round the ward, his mind focussed on Jimmy Tollan. Another three days. That's all he'd needed to make a score payment. Three more fuckin days. Jesus. Fuck him.

"How are you doing?"

The voice was upbeat, chirpy. It came from a boy in the opposite bed, who was holding a book and smiling in friendship.

Johnny tried to answer. But his mouth wouldn't open properly. There was a blur in his left side vision. A bandage. And wiring or something.

"You missed breakfast, and lunch too. Good today.

Chicken soup, braised steak and potatoes, and stewed apple and custard. Not bad at all." The boy's face was framed against a metal headboard.

The nurse appeared. Had she known he would waken at two? Telepathy.

Her eyes picked his name off the tag above his pillow. "You slept right through, John."

Yes, he was in hospital, in a routine he knew from past experience.

"If you need any painkillers press the buzzer. That's it there. The doctor will be round to see you later."

In the afternoon. Must be serious.

"Do you need the the toilet."

He nodded gently.

She returned with a cardboard disposable bottle. The spout was far too big for his cock. She pulled the curtains for his privacy. It took all of three minutes to get the right angle. Not easy when one leg was immobile, and one arm was linked to a drip. He filled it, while dealing with the quips from behind the curtain.

"Nurse. He needs some help. She'll hold it for you. The bottle, I mean."

The nurse was on his side. "Need a bigger bottle, John?" Her voice trailed away as she went off down the corridor.

His left cheek was one enormous bandage. His left leg wouldn't move. His jaw was clamped to his neck in a strange contraption.

The consultant arrived with an entourage. They clustered inside the curtains while Johnny learnt the full horror story.

"You're doing very well. You gave me quite a night. There was a bit of work to do."

What did that mean?

"We've reset your lower jaw. The cheekbone was fractured. They should both set well. We've fitted a metal frame to hold your jaw and cheek steady. It will heal faster."

His voice brimmed with professional confidence. It

was friendly, carrying in the ward.

"Your leg required a bit more work. There's a pin down your femur bone. It is screwed to the bone on both sides of the break. The operation worked fine. We may have to go back in at a later stage to take the pin out. We'll talk about that later. You'll be up and walking sooner than you think."

Their eyes smiled at each other. The consultant had engendered the feeling that recovery was to be a team effort. He was good at his job, in both the theatre and the ward.

Johnny kept his angry thoughts till after lights out. The pain killers kept him calm as he cursed Jimmy.

Three days more, and twenty pounds would have saved him from another climb back from the edge. The ward loved him.

6 Kissed a girl

JOHNNY remembered hospital as fun. He liked the nurses and they enjoyed his relaxed patter. "Any chance of a wee swallie," quickly registered his priority in life.

They even overlooked his drinking. Booze brought in a quarter bottle at a time by his pals.

"A lost cause worth drinking to," was his line. That worked in the warmth of the friendly ward where he rapidly won a 'character' status.

The nurses were sexy. They looked good, smelled good and were ready with a warm smile. They were 'real dolls' in every sense of the words, cracking mature women. Not that they would sleep with him. If he could remember what to do. He hadn't kissed a girl, never mind the whole bit, since Marie locked him out. He just never went back to her. That would have been a waste of time.

His sardonic humour nipped in. "Aye. Her time. Eh?" He allowed himself to face the truth about the girl he loved. She was beautiful. She never gave him any hassle. She was a fuckin great kisser who tried to make their sex life perfect. She was passionately pleasurable. They had plenty of friendly orgasms. That's the type she was.

He had been lucky to marry her and foolish to lose a partner of such value. The loss hurt him and the only consolation was that he realised she deserved better than a quitter like himself. He just didn't have the mettle to cope with a girl who actually loved him. Nor to find another job after the factory closed.

The police interviewed him at his hospital bed. He told them what had happened, leaving out the reasons and the names.

They knew the names anyway and put them to him.

"Dunno. Never even saw the bastards," he said feigning anger. They were uniformed polis. They wouldnae bother with CID for a bum like him.

The leg would never be the same again. He limped from the previous doing. Now he would limp differently. His face healed up but remained distorted. From now on he would be a limping warning to those in the scheme who did not pay on time.

His mother came to visit and was treated like the Queen Mum. The nurses made a point of talking to her. "Don't know how you put up with him." That sort of thing.

Johnny was warm, happy and enjoying himself. The physiotherapy was a bind.

Soon he would be back on the street. His debt was escalating by the week. Jimmy would be looking for his money.

7 Check yourself out

HE COULD hold his head up in pride. He wasn't a grass.

He could walk back into the pub, talk about his beloved Celtic. Even better, he could talk to Jimmy. The fuckin bastard. The cunt wouldn't do it himself.

Johnny liked a swallie, which was part of his undoing. He was far from stupid. He had been married to a pretty girl who lost interest because he didn't care and couldn't get angry about anything. Before his brief but doomed marriage Johnny was an engineer in the Merchant Navy. Seven O-level passes at school were followed by night school at Stow College for a basic engineering certificate.

Five years in the Merchant Navy gave him the carefree confidence of a man who had seen the seamy side of life in many downtown drinking haunts where sailors sought sex and solace from the loneliness of the sea. He had done something few from Garthill had ever attempted – he had sailed the seven seas seeing different sides of life.

That was all behind him.

He'd settled for booze and the pleasure of a rare Celtic game. He was alone now, relying on his ageing but fearful mother for the basics of life – a bed, bathroom and some food in the two bedroomed flat where she huddled out life up a dirty smelly close in a backcorner of the scheme.

Her knowledge of life outside the scheme was based on TV images. It wasn't her fault that her immediate surroundings were repulsive. She closed her eyes to the antagonistic graffiti – Fuck the Pope or Fuck King Billy. Tam's a shitebag. Jessie's a ride. The endless scribbling of tormented idle youths. The nearest they ever came to a political statement was to scrawl an obscenity about the IRA or the UVF and those were only expressions of their birthright. Tims or Proddies.

Mrs McPherson wasn't responsible for the crude vandalising of the walls outside her front door. Nor for the odour of urine that hung in the close. She only lived there, closing her mind to the filth outside, shutting out the fear and the rat-infested backyard jungle.

A decent woman, she had surrendered to the siege mentality of the middle aged. They bore the brunt of the enterprise years. A few of them managed to bridge the gap between the fifties and sixties of their childhoods to wear a uniform and serve in supermarkets for a paltry wage. The rest sat on the sidelines commentating on the state of the nation under the dreaded Tories. Eventually they gave up complaining to watch soap operas dramatise what they already knew. The nightly dramas reflecting exactly what was happening in the streets outside. Familiarity bred high viewing figures.

Her son had a few friends. Fellow boozers. Quitters who had succumbed rapidly to the opt-out life of the next can, or better still, bottle, as they huddled together in a park or wasteland.

Social workers liked him as did the people in the 'social'. He never tried to con anybody. Never begged. Johnny just asked and received because he was likeable. He was unthreatening, non-violent, and he smiled constantly. The perfect poor man.

Johnny made sure he was liked by everyone including the bastards who controlled his life. The same men who sometimes threatened his mother in her ground floor flat up the dark, sour smelling close.

"Tell Johnny we called." Like something out of a gangster movie.

"Tell him that he pays up or we'll be back tae see yi." She didn't cower. She held their eyes, closed the door and cried, recovering after a few minutes to escape into the telly, passing the message on when Johnny finally showed up, drunk but always kindly and talkative. He wanted most to tell her how good he had been at the karaoke that night. They just loved his Noo York effort . . . Start spreading the noos. And he'd been a wow with his Elvis bit . . . Ah'm all shook up.

His mother still kept a picture of the King in her bedroom.

Life for Johnny was a succession of crises. Nevertheless he coped and contributed his friendly apologetic personality to Garthill.

Johnny McPherson knew he was a good singer. He was willing to get up if they liked it that much. He wanted to keep the party going. They liked him for that. Without Johnny the karaoke wouldn't be the same. He was guaranteed to make it a cracking night. Just what they needed.

He didn't sober up when told that Jimmy's thugs had paid a visit. He made another worthless promise to the only woman left in his life – there was nothing to worry about and he would be able to pay. Johnny knew the game inside out.

His mother was safe for Jimmy knew that there were real dangers in having her attacked. None of those young bastards that leeched off him dare strike her. Any violence in or at her home and she would talk. The neighbours would talk. To the police.

So there was little danger for his mother, although she was unable to understand her insurance against a blow to the face or kicks to her body. She was in much greater danger from the uncontrollable drug addicts in the street. The teenagers who, only yesterday it seemed, were being pushed past her home in prams.

The harsh-voiced threats reduced her to tears. He returned home to face her useless advice without resentment. A gnawing fear dogged both their lives, that she would suffer when he suffered.

Anger and fear had merged into self-survival in Johnny's one-way street. He was lost in his own space. He actually looked forward to his next meeting with Jimmy. Laughter, a wee swallie and the love of his fellow strugglers. He'd be back soon. Johnny would be up there karaokeing with the best of them. Sure it would take a long time to get out of debt. He'd have some laughs along the road.

Soon he was back, the crutches gone, and laughing his way through each fear-ridden day.

Outside the butcher's he met up with his sister Jan. She lived close to his maw. He saw her in the street almost daily. Emotionally they were strangers. He'd had a doing. She knew and was not going to explore the details.

"Keep away from them," she said, slipping him two pounds. He pushed the notes into his pocket, looked deeply into her eyes with all the sincerity he could muster and responded.

"Thanks pet. Ah'm gettin a hoose transfer anyway. Ah told the housing that Ah need a move or Ah'm deid. Ah could back that up wi ma injuries. And the polis report helped."

Her voice lacked sincerity. "That's good, if you get the move. The sooner the better, eh?"

She didn't believe him and he didn't try to press the truth on her. Why try to convince her that he was going away to a safer corner of the city?

It was true. The housing were giving him a key for a flat in Nitshill. Across the river. Four miles away. New safe territory. If he came intae toon he'd keep an eye open for Jimmy and his mates.

There would be no dialogue. Just a quick about-turn and off down the nearest exit. You don't try to talk your way out of a debt that totalled one thousand two hundred and forty eight pounds.

He hadn't argued at their last meeting when handing over twenty notes. Just hinted. "It cannae be that much now, Jimmy. Under a thousand. Eh?"

The loan shark's brown eyes flashed with anger at Johnny's effrontery in questioning the size of the debt. "Whit the fuck dae yi mean?"

Johnny regretted his question and made no reply. Jimmy's hand moved toward his jacket pocket and he yanked out the evidence. His anger dropped, the voice was friendly. "It's in the fuckin book. There mate. In black and white. See fur yersel."

Jimmy opened the tatty notebook. Held it out for Johnny to take. "Yir tally's in there."

Johnny looked down the list . . . Wee Jeannie, Plummie, Tam, Big Tam, Irene, Shuggie, the O'Brien sisters, Joanie and Betty, Bent Willie.

Bent Willie!

In that brief moment, in Jimmy's menacing presence, Johnny as always had time for an inward chuckle.

A crook, a poof, or a guy with a bent cock. His mind clicked onto the name. That would be Willie from the high rise block. That boy with the earring. Him with the job in the shop.

Before he could stop himself he blurted out, "Christ, is Willie Edward intae yi too?" Mistake.

Jimmy's voice carried venom. "Jist check yirsel oot. Naebody else, yi nosey bastard."

Johnny's eyes moved quickly down the list searching for his own name. He turned two pages before spotting it. In the left hand column, he was marked up as paying the previous week.

In the right hand column he saw the total debt recorded against his name in Jimmy's handwriting. £1,248. He closed the notebook and handed it back, blanking his mind to the figure. Jimmy folded the book and stuffed it back in his leather jacket. This was not the time to react to the crazy bastard's figure. Johnny knew that the total with accrued interest was correct.

Unfair, but nevertheless correct to the last pound.

"Ay. Ah saw it. Ah've paid yi a score this week. That's it."

Jimmy turned away, moving to the nearby bookies. Johnny watched him go. The loan shark's powerful shoulders blocked the betting shop entrance as a small woman came out. She squeezed past his ample muscled body. Jimmy turned round in the sure knowledge that Johnny would not have moved an inch.

Pulling a wad of notes from his jeans he asked, "Need anythin?"

Johnny smiled back. They both knew he had nothing left. The loan shark pulled a tenner out of the crumpled wad as Johnny held his hand out saying, "Ay. Thank fuck fur that. Ah'll square yi fur that next week, Jimmy."

"Will yi? Same time same place. Now fuck off."

They turned away from each other. The two-minute ritual was over. They had played this fear match hundreds of times during the past five years. Today Jimmy was ten pounds better off. There was plenty more to come from dozens more like Johnny who now had enough for a wee swallie and the chance to pretend he was Frank Sinatra. By nine o'clock the karaoke would be in full swing.

Tomorrow never crossed his mind. He had long since given up on the reality of his one thousand two hundred and forty eight pound debt. It was fucking meaningless anyway. He'd only borrowed twenty pounds for a Celtic game, the bus fare, a ticket into Parkhead, food and booze.

Christ, Mo Johnston was going to sign for Billy McNeill when he'd asked Jimmy for that first score. History now. And Mo fucked off to Rangers for mair money.

He was hungry. Mince and tatties tickled with tomato sauce, washed down with a cup of tea at his maw's.

A shave, a shit and a shampoo, as the smart set say. Eh? And then a good few wee swallies. He was feeling OK again. He limped down past the social work department, nodding to the girl who'd help him apply for a Crisis Loan from the DSS. A wee con to pay Jimmy. It failed. She slowed her Fiesta right down. Threw him a big pleasing smile. It said all he wanted to know. "Great to see you. I like you."

She shared an intimate knowledge of his childhood. Of his drink problem. Of his swift exit from marriage. She even knew that he was into the money lenders. She liked him.

On the way to his mother's he bought twenty Embassy Regal and paused outside the shop to open the packet. The car drew up quietly and he glanced at it. The passenger door was opening and he looked into the face of another bastard. Tommy McFadzen.

Johnny spoke first. "Hi Tommy. Ah tried to get yi last week. But yi wirnae at the usual place. Ah telt Dezzie tae tell yi Ah wiz in. Check it wi him."

Johnny was lying. McFadzen moved across the pavement, grabbed Johnny's arms and spat the words out. "Don't gie us yir shite. Yi hivnae shown fur weeks."

McFadzen was out of his Maryhill territory. For that reason he was exceptionally dangerous. Nobody in Garthill would turn against McFadzen because he had beaten up Johnny . . . the wee man who was too ready with a joke and a song.

Johnny knew the score. So did McFadzen.

"Who the fuck are yi payin these days?"

Johnny was frightened. He relied on his survival instinct, blurting out the truth. The truth would be recognised as such and might save him. He knew that his body wasn't strong enough to take the punishment that McFadzen was capable of inflicting. McFadzen was brutal.

"Ah'm payin Jimmy. Jimmy Tollan."

McFadzen's grip slackened but he didn't release Johnny. He leered, "Yi stupid fucker."

McFadzen stepped back slightly, saying nothing more.

The driver's door clicked open, then slammed shut. A young man in a dark brown leather jacket walked slowly across the pavement. He looked carefully up and down the street which was empty except for an approaching car.

He waited until the car had passed. The truth wasn't going to save Johnny this time.

"Sorry, son," said the young man as McFadzen let Johnny go. The youth's right hand rose above Johnny's face and swiftly swept down his left cheek. He felt the sharp nip of pain as the blade pierced the skin. Fear surged through his mind and body. Into his eyes.

McFadzen saw the terror and was satisfied.

He spoke quietly, almost in a whisper. "Next week pay me. Yi know where tae find me. Ah don't like daein this."

He continued, "Yir in ma book for two hunner and

forty. That's aw that fuckin matters. Get a fuckin grip. Get yir heid in gear and see me regular, startin next week."

That was it. They didn't even ask him for money there and then. He totally forgot that he could have offered seven pounds.

Johnny watched them drive away. He was too nervous to touch the wound on his face. The oozing blood warmed his cheek. He walked down the hill to his mother's home checking the wound in the bathroom mirror. The fresh wound ran between the cheekbone scar and the jaw mess. It looked surprisingly small. Not too deep either. He dabbed some hot water on the cheek.

There was no Dettol so he clumsily poured some Old Spice onto the wound. That decision pleased him. Now it was time to face his mother. He took a quick nervous piss before going into the living room.

She was curled up in the big armchair with a cup of tea watching the news and didn't look up. "There's a pot of good soup. Get yourself some. See the Tories, they are unbelievable. That Mellor. He gets caught, all over the papers, with that woman. Now they're standing in their garden . . ."

She looked up.

"Oh my God."

She stood up, knocking the teacup over.

Johnny was quick to get in first. "Ah'm OK. Ah'm OK." His voice quivered.

He realised from her tone that the wound on his cheek was beginning to ooze blood again.

His effort to control the situation and staunch her fear failed as he finally dropped his guard. "Ah thought ah was gonnae get worse. Ah'm hame. Ah'm no in the hospital. It's OK. Jist a wee warning."

The stupid words told all.

"Which one of those bastards did this to you son?" she cried. He made no reply.

Her hands held his jaw firmly as she scrutinised the wound. In a crisis she was good. "You might need stitches

49

this time. I'm phoning for a taxi. You're going to the hospital now."

The confrontation he feared most was coming. After that he expected her tears. Humour, his brand which inclined more toward fun, was his best defence.

"Listen maw, Ah'm no oil paintin. Ma face has been kicked that many times that a wee scar won't make any difference. That's all it is. Yi won't see it in the folds."

She moved back to the chair picked up the channel-changer and switched the TV volume down. The room would not be right if she switched if off completly, even in this crisis. At the back of her mind was the thought that Take the High Road could start and she would miss it. Picking up the phone she began to dial for a taxi saying. "We'll get you up to Casualty. Who did it son?"

He chose to fight the taxi move first. The priority here was to hold onto the fiver on fares to and from hospital. The tenner was down to seven quid after buying the fags. Hospital would leave him only three pounds. Not enough for a full night at the Black Inn.

What he wanted most was a couple of beers and a right good sing-song. The karaoke night was a much better bet than sitting in a cubicle waiting while a nurse said nice things to him. The doctor would patronise him kindly, using his first name and telling him what he already knew. That the wound was skin deep and would heal up nicely.

He might have to talk to the polis too. The wound probably was not worth a criminal damages claim either.

Mrs McPherson was through. "Can you send a taxi to . . ."

He interrupted, "Forget the taxi maw. Look at me. Ah'm OK."

"Forget it just now. Sorry," she said putting the phone down and launched an attack, while picking up the fallen teacup.

"I asked you who did it son. Who did it?"

"OK. Ah'll tell yi. But it disnae matter now. They've made their point. That's the way it is. They'll leave me alain fur a while. Their method is tae gie yi the message and then let yi get the money. The danger's ower," he said, trying to set up a debate.

That route was not on. Mrs McPherson rarely swore. She took pride in speaking the English language properly, retaining a grip on her own integrity.

This time she let go. "Fucking shut up and tell me who fucking done it!" she cried out.

He told her, softening the full impact of his long term situation by saying that he owed Tommy McFadzen forty four pounds. All he did was knock two hundred pounds off the debt. After all he had only borrowed twenty from McFadzen to pay Jimmy. The lie pleased him.

"What about that other bastard from up the scheme. Him that your father knew. How much are you intae him for? How much?"

His mother was setting the agenda now. She was even using the language of his daily dealings . . . "intae him".

Time to get out.

"Listen maw. There's nae problems there. Jimmy treats me OK noo."

But there was no stopping her. "He almost killed you that last time. So don't give me that shite." His mother's fear had driven her into the language of desperation.

Funny. The very words fired at him by Tommy McFadzen only ten minutes earlier. Johnny didn't recognise that as an irony. Nevertheless the thought flashed through his mind.

Her voice was venomous. "That bastard had wee Mary's boy stabbed in the stomach. The boy was nearly deid. You're goin to get yourself killed."

The fear in her eyes had catalysed into anger and back into fear. He was too weak to take control and stem the horrors she was suffering.

He remembered his ace card. He played it.

"It'll no happen tae me maw. Ah get the keys tae a flat in Nitshill next week. Ah'm no telling anyone where Ah'm goin. So they'll no be able tae find me."

That slowed her down. And after a moment she sat down in the armchair.

"You never told me you were going to get a transfer. That's a good move son. Away from here." Her voice was back to normal.

They were communicating now. He sat on the settee, looking into her tired watery grey eyes. At the edge of her vision she noticed that Take the High Road was starting.

"My programme's coming on," she said as an aside, before getting back to the crisis. "I can't help you son. I just don't have any money. It's as simple as that. You're not asking, I know. But this can't go on and on and on. I can't stand it. It'll kill me."

He leant forward. "Ah'm gettin oot. Ah'll definitely be safe."

He explained what the move would mean to their daily routines. "Once Ah've gone they'll soon know Ah've done a runner. So Ah'll no be able tae come here tae see yi. You'll have tae come tae see me. A wee visit now and then."

The love game was on. A solution was at hand. They could relax. They talked more while Johnny enjoyed a bowl of her home made soup with bread and butter. She switched the TV volume back up and talked over the noise.

Was it a nice flat? Not too far from a pub, eh?

He spruced himself up for the karaoke and chipped in with his humorous parting shot. "Mellor. We saw it in the Sun last week. See if she'd had any decency, that Sanchez woman. She'd no have worn a Chelsea strip. She'd have worn a Celtic wan."

Johnny paused for effect.

"They're gettin screwed every week."

She ignored the joke and had the last word. "The two-faced bastard is back with his wife. They were standing holding hands. Holding a press conference for the TV. You wonder what's going on in the world."

They loved him that night.

Noo York, Noo York,
Start spreading the noos,
I'm leaving today.

That pleased him. The childish thought that he was leaving Garthill.

8 Spreading the news

THE EARLY evening sun picked out the smart-set cars parked along the double yellow lines encircling the smart Holiday Inn in the city centre.

Time and money were more important to the executives wheeling and dealing inside, than the inconvenience of finding a legal parking place, or of paying the sixteen pounds fine.

The secretary could sort it out later.

Two tall gents dressed in dark wool coats, carrying briefcases, alighted from an airport taxi. The more observant took time out to comment. "They must be turning this into a bed and breakfast place."

His companion quipped, "Not likely, John. The great unwashed couldn't cope with the service here."

They turned towards the hotel entrance and the observant one nodded toward two large Transit vans. "One wonders what they are doing here." It was an idle aside.

Sandwiched amongst the Mercedes, BMWs, and Jaguars like uninvited guests in lounge suits at a formal dance their identities weren't even hidden. Strathclyde Social Work Department in bold white letters.

Inside the pianist was settling in. The waiters were busy tickling the open plan restaurant into perfection.

Eddie Anderson, seated amongst the gin and tonic brigade, dressed to his job, was wrestling with a handful of problems. The faded pink pullover sporting the logo of the 1984 Open at St Andrews, the Armani jeans and Adidas training shoes stamped him. He was comfortable in the gear, stylish enough to catch the eye of the right woman. Relaxation was the game.

Yet the TV researcher was tense. He felt insecure, surrounded by enemies who would blame him if the programme failed. He was the cornerstone to a big budget documentary.

They'd sent him on ahead to find the people, the victims, the exploiters – all the key players in the exposé that was already scheduled. They were all here now simply because Eddie had found enough players to stage the documentary drama. They had been painstakingly plucked from any corner of the city. No expense was spared in putting together a gripping investigation of loan sharking in the dark recesses of Glasgow, the city whose image had so recently been polished up considerably with a series of high profile gimmicks.

Sixty eight thousand pounds. To expose. To frighten. To surprise. To bring the dirty back street deals into Mr and Mrs Average's cosy living room. Entertainment. Preferably round about eight. After dinner. After Coronation Street, Eastenders, Brookside, and Take the High Road. And before the big movie.

Eddie had found the bricks with which to build the programme. Victims. Targets to expose. Loan sharks. Social workers. Prostitutes. People running from violence. Frightened children.

Thanks to Eddie's efforts they now had the lot. The tools, the putty, the drills, the skills, to create a war zone, to get out in the front line. Give them what they want. The viewers and the bosses.

He had set up the game with all the players and the locations. The smart-ass producer and the star TV personality, with his rehearsed questions to the evil greedy bastards preying on the poor, were now here to cash in on his ground work.

Eddie seemed the most relaxed person in the lounge. The clothes helped. The easy smile, the wad of notes in his pocket. Reassuring. His mind was racing.

"The girl from Govan. Upstairs in room five four seven. Watching the TV and eating chicken sandwiches. She looked as though she'd do a turn too. Tight little arse in that leather gear. Don't be fucking daft. Aids man? We'll need to record her first. She has a child."

He was concerned about another good talker.

"That sad guy in room six hundred and seven, from Garthill. He's trying to be happy all the bloody time. I shouldn't have shown him where the miniatures are kept. He'd had drink when we picked him up this afternoon."

It had taken three long weeks to find three who would go on camera. Wheeling and dealing through the social work, the local reporter, the single parents' group. And that bunch of alcoholics, peeling them off one at a time until a suitable and willing candidate emerged.

Dropping a tenner here. Twenty there. Promising five hundred pounds for interview on film. Going back to that girl with the expensive clothes and agreeing one thousand pounds for full co-operation.

The promises would be kept. Money was almost no object. There was the sixty eight thousand budget to play with, to keep the programme high in the ratings. The deadline was fast approaching. His contract was up for renewal.

"What the fuck am I doing here?" he heard himself say aloud. The others ignored his spoken thought. Mary's face flashed into his mind. She was holding their son. She was crying. Their marriage was over.

Mary was standing in the back garden. The babygro on the washing line, stretched between the spruce tree and the creosoted wooden fence. The blurred pain of his messy marriage tugged at his thoughts.

A girl in a green uniform leant over and smiled warmly. "Can I help you sir? Would you like to order?" The cocktail waitress. Oh yes. He should get the drinks in. "Nigel, you'll want the usual?" he asked the producer.

Nigel took his time answering. He was irritated. He didn't like the cigarette smoke or the noise from the piano. He loathed the place. The burning steaks. The whiff of perfume colliding with cigar smoke.

"Yes, I'll have a Perrier water please. Thanks Eddie."

Eddie disliked Nigel intensely. Always proper. Always polite. Never under pressure. A bore. His marriage was safe and cosy. He sometimes worried. About the two ponies he'd bought for his daughters.

Eddie moved his question to the laid-back soundman, lounging deeply in the armchair, feet outstretched. Mr Relaxation enjoying a few nights in Glasgow at the current rates. The technician's eyes moved round the bar greedily sucking in the movement of beautifully dressed women. Nipple searching.

"Yea, I'll have a drink now. And later, what about one of these incredible Glasgow curries you're always on about. Let's hit the nearest Indian," he laughed coarsely.

A curry was not on Eddie's pressing schedule. Certainly not in the company of a distasteful stupid English fascist. "Tomorrow Bob. Tonight's a working night. Have dinner in the hotel."

Eddie glanced back at the waitress. "He'll have a pint of heavy. That's bitter to you Bob. And a gin and tonic for him," he added nodding toward the star of the show.

Adrian Russell. Public hero number one. The investigator. The 'righter of wrongs'. Mr Courage. The Award Winner. The moralising man of the people. Famous.

Eddie gave him a reassuring smile. "We're OK for tonight Adrian. There's a guy upstairs waiting to be interviewed. Make-up are working on him."

Adrian responded. "Yes, one of the victims. The best victim?"

"Not half. He's exactly what we want. Owes two loan sharks. He's a wreck too. Broken legs. Smashed face. Perfect. Baseball bat victim."

"I'm ready when he's ready," Adrian snapped back. "I'll do him first. The girl later. I've talked to her already. She understands what we want. That would be two in the can. I'll get them done tonight and I'll take the first flight in the morning. Bob can stay here. I'll get a crew from Viewfield for the oil story."

He was looking directly at Nigel. "Those Viewfield guys are good to work with. We did the landlord stuff with them. They're sharp. They know what they're doing. Pity they weren't available for this one."

He let the barb sink in.

The lounge chatter had ceased. They were all listening. The pianist smiled at the TV star. Adrian Russell felt good. They had known he was here, half hiding behind the paper. Now that he was talking, they were listening.

Eddie had heard it all before. He stood up and went to room six hundred and seven to see Johnny. Tight-fisted Nigel could pay for the drinks. Fewer bags of oats for his fucking ponies.

Johnny McPherson was sitting on the bed. "Ah'm just huvin a wee brek," he apologised, for Johnny was conscious of the money he was being paid.

"She's tryin tae make me intae Robert Redford. By Christ she's strugglin." His humour was his communication.

June, the make-up artist laughed with pleasure. Thanks to this disgusting little blob of humanity, the job had turned out to be more enjoyable than she had expected.

It was a good freelance job. Extra money. A challenge. Change his face so that nobody will recognise him, not even his mother.

"Make him unrecognisable. He will be killed if he's recognised," they told her, adding glibly, "but that's not your responsibility. So don't worry."

The man was a mess. How he must have suffered.

Johnny knew that going on TV to talk about the realities of illegal money lending was one step removed from being a grass. But it wasn't actually grassing. TV wisnae the polis. He could justify his TV role.

In fact he liked the job. There was more to it than the money offered. He had information they wanted. He could talk with knowledge. He was an authority on the subject.

There was the bonus of two hundred pounds. The money goes around and around and around. Eh? Some to Jimmy. Some to McFadzen. The rest for a wee swallie and Parkheid on Saturday. This make-up gemme wisnae too bad either.

His distant education, buried by years of low life, emerged as June caressed his face and indirectly his confidence. "Every man is famous fur ten minutes o' his life. Andy Warhol. Ma turn noo, eh?" was his nervous opener to June. The quotation was five minutes short of being accurate. To Johnny it was the thought that counted. He was reaching out to her so that she would realise he wasn't as stupid as he looked.

He was frightened that he could be recognised. "Naebody must know it's me, except you and me. Eh? So don't fuck up, or Ah'm deid."

He took his eyes off the mirror and looked up at her. "Sorry hen. Ah shouldnae swear. But this is fuckin serious."

He was so genuine. Trying to bridge the gap in behaviour patterns. She was class. As always Johnny remained true to himself. Even in the awe-inspiring surroundings of this classy hotel room. Her warm fingers built the putty across his forehead, changed his jaw line, and filled out his sunken cheeks. Her breasts caressed his back. Unintentionally. He could feel their giving form.

She pencilled his dark eyebrows blond. Gave him longer eye lashes. She rarely got the chance to change a man's face so that it was unrecognisable. She was used to dealing with temperamental actors, professional newscasters and chat show hosts, taking the glisten off their foreheads, shortening their nose shadows.

Johnny was something else. He was ugly. His conversation was uninspired but infectious. "This is a Lon Chaney shot. Eh? Man of a Thousand Faces. James Cagney. Did yi iver see it, hen?"

"Yes, I did," she replied in a crystal clear voice. "In fact it was on the telly four months ago. I taped it. Chaney did the make-up himself. His father was deaf and dumb and was treated like a monster because of others' ignorance. He suffered personal humiliation because of his inability to speak or to hear."

Johnny remained silent allowing his new friend to talk freely. He enjoyed her voice, so clear, caressing and deep. Like warm sunshine in the sharp Spring. Sexy. Full of promise.

59

She purred more. "Chaney wanted the world to see that people with a disability were no different inside themselves than normal complete human beings. So he created a series of monsters to let the cinema audiences see the kind heart and decent human beings behind the grotesque masks."

June stopped talking. She wasn't quite sure where this conversation was leading. Was she inadvertedly insulting this ugly beaten man as she changed his face?

Johnny took up the slack. "Right hen. Ah understaun whit yir sayin. The Hunchback of Notre Dame. Eh? Let's hiv a wee drink."

He didn't know what the point of it all was. So he opened the fridge and selected two miniatures of whisky. "Wan fur you, hen. And wan fur me. Eh?"

"No thank you," she purred. "You go ahead. Put the other one in your pocket. Stop calling me hen. My name's June."

By the time the researcher arrived there was only Johnny's hair to do. Eddie studied his star victim, reassuring him. "I wouldn't recognise you. I'm pretty sure I wouldn't. Bigger nose. Rounder face. Let's see you with a wig."

June pulled a grey wig over his thinning dark strands, and tugged it down neatly.

Johnny made his own assessment in his own inimitable way. "Pretty good, hen. Sorry, Ah mean June. If Ah didnae know that wis me, Ah wid think it wiz somebody else. Ay. But no Robert Redford." He said, gazing into the mirror, "maybe a bit mair Richard Gere. Eh?"

He was quite struck by the change in his face. "June, yiv done a wee miracle here, hen. Eddie, got a number fur Julia Roberts? Eh? Pretty Woman, walking down the street . . ." They could smell the day's drink.

Eddie and June ignored his fun. They glanced at each other. This was serious. They weren't sure that he was unrecognisable. They felt he was recognisable. Eddie didn't want Johnny's death on his conscience. Eddie feared for him. Beaten up without the constitution to survive. Stabbed through the stomach. Left to bleed to death in some Garthill back court, with the resulting murder investigation in which the police would quickly establish that the stupid loan shark victim had appeared on television with tragic consequences. The public interest didn't extend to causing a murder.

Were two hours work not enough to ensure that Johnny would remain unknown when the glare of the TV lights made him a star witness? June added a beard to his face change. The beard, all fuzzy and curly, covered up most of his face.

The crew arrived ten minutes later. They carried the lights into the bedroom, set up the sound recording equipment. The furry microphone. The works.

The pink room was packed. Producer, sound man, camera man, June, the interviewer and Eddie – all gathered to make the most of their star. Johnny was squeezed back into a corner, next to the fitted wardrobe. His hand searched inside his trouser pocket for the miniature. No, he'd have that later.

Eddie rehearsed his man.

"Adrian will ask you about the worst beating you ever took. Just tell him the way you told me in the pub last week. He will then ask you why you needed the money. For the electricity bill. Tell him about the loan shark. About Jimmy Tollan and the violence. Remember, don't mention Tollan by name, just repeat what has happened to you. Adrian will ask you how much you borrowed and how much you have paid back – how much you owe because of the interest the bastard charges. Tell him that you borrowed from another loan shark to pay back the first one. Don't mention the name of the other loan shark either. You went to him because you were afraid of another beating. Don't mention the name of the hospital you were in. Just tell him in the same words you told me in the pub. Try not to swear too much."

Eddie liked Johnny. They were almost pals. He leant forward. "No fucking swearing."

He added, "Relax. We can always do it again. And

we'll cut out any mistakes, anything that might point the finger at you."

"Ay. OK mate. Ah'll no let yi doon."

He was getting hot. Very hot. The wig. The beard. The stuff on his face. The arc lights. The hotel heating. The windows were sealed shut. The air seemed bone dry. There was nothing to smell. Johnny looked decidedly uncomfortable and therefore appeared tense.

Adrian Russell tried a little reassurance. "I have been talking on camera for fifteen years and I still can't get it right. I was in France once, doing an investigation into sheep smuggling, and I had to do fifteen takes."

"Don't tell me, yi didnae know how tae say Ba Ba Black sheep in French?"

Nigel was impatient. "Stand over there. At the window." Johnny did as he was told and the cameraman said, "Come forward a bit. That's it."

Nigel fired in the next one. "If you just look out through the window toward the cranes on the Clyde there. Look back when Adrian starts to interview you."

Johnny practised this while the sound man moved in a boom.

He was beginning to feel like a fuckin prick. He could cope with a physical beating on a rainy night in the scheme. But all this crap?

They were ready. He was on. He couldn't resist fuckin them up a bit and was ready when Adrian asked the first question. "What is the worst beating inflicted on you Willie?"

They had chosen to call him Willie.

"Ma leg wiz broken. And ma face smashed. A baseball bat wiz used on me. It wiz a serious hospital job."

The room relaxed. There were off and running. They would need a bit more detail but the guy was talking violence. Good. The second question was, "Who did this to you?"

Johnny was laughing within himself. "Three Gers fans. Celtic had beat the Gers in the Cup. Ah wiz havin a piss in a lane aff . . ."

He was interrupted angrily.

"Christ almighty! That's not funny. Not funny at all." Nigel was seething. He turned on Eddie. "Speak to him. Get it sorted now."

He turned back to Johnny. "Nice one Johnny. Don't have any more to drink."

Johnny looked him straight in the eye. "Listen mate. Yir daeing ma fuckin heid in. Why don't yi get a wee drink yersel? Eh?"

The crew were smiling. June could no longer control her laughter. It bubbled out.

They had watched Johnny make a small statement about himself. They loved that. Even Nigel was forced to smile at himself.

Then Johnny told them about borrowing from loan sharks. The way it was. This time they gave him his space. Moving back in the jammed room they allowed him the time to make his mistakes. There was no laughter. No smiles. No smirks. No interruptions. Only a stifling silence you could touch as they absorbed his sad words.

There was one problem. The accent. The vernacular. Would the southern viewers understand his words? They concluded that even if some viewers failed to pick up on the exact words they would all understand the fear, the exploitation and the violence. His face would have told the story if it wasn't hidden behind a beard.

Later they would relish his words as they ran through the film in the editing room. "That's fine, there. He is talking about the baseball attack. You can hear the fear in his voice. We'll use that as a voice-over in the opening shot. Then cut to a close-up of the loan shark's tally book. Turning the pages, but holding on each page for ten seconds to show names."

"Wait a minute. We don't have a loan shark's tally book!"

Nigel looked at Eddie. "I thought you were getting one? Never mind. That won't be a problem, will it Eddie?

You could get hold of one from the courts, from the productions in an old case?"

Eddie covered his back. "That is a problem Nigel. It's a long time since any loan sharks have actually appeared in a Glasgow court. The productions from the last case have disappeared. You can't expect the courts or the police to hold onto evidence forever."

Time to compromise again.

"We'll write one up ourselves. Get a hold of Johnny. He knows exactly what is recorded in the tally books. He's seen Tollan's book. Send a taxi up to his house and get him now," said Nigel seeking an instant solution.

"Wait a minute. We can't just send a taxi up there," said Eddie angrily. "For fucks sake. You'll get him killed. I'll get in touch with him through a third party and get the tally book details off him. OK?"

Johnny was delighted to give them the extra inside info for it earned him another tenner.

The programme was going to make it. They agreed with Nigel. "It is all good stuff. We're getting there, slowly."

Johnny had given them what they wanted. He had told them of his five years' financial deals with Jimmy Tollan and the consequences. One-sided deals. He was two hundred and ten pounds better off, with more to come when he fingered Tollan.

Plus several more miniatures.

9 Spreading some fear

KENNY WATSON was pissed off being nice and nasty to order. Jimmy's orders.

His role in the sad money grabbing marathon had palled. Five years as the collector had earned him little except the fearful respect of the weakest members of the community.

No pay rises. No holidays. He saw the cash almost every day, yet he tamely handed it over to Tollan. His years of loyal service went without recognition, without even a rise to counter inflation.

No car. Nothing. He was, he realised a "fuckin idiot." A gopher. Go for the money or go for their throats.

A mere thirty pounds a week to top up his dole money, giving that wee bit extra needed to keep Mary and the boys above the desperation line. Thirty notes. To keep busy, buzzing about in Tollan's Audi, up the scheme. Round the post offices. Into the pubs. On the move every day. Thanking. Asking. Telling. Threatening. Seeking.

Regularly thanking. "That's smashin son. Gie us a score next week. Fine. That's good pet. Zat man o' yours keepin out of trouble?"

Always asking. "Where the fuck is he? Are yi goin' tae pay? Will yi definitely be here next week?"

And telling. "No good enough. Nae excuses. You'll need tae pay us. He'll no be happy."

Often threatening. "Yir wasting ma time. Yi didnae show. Wan mair chance and that's it. Ah've nae alternative if yi dinnae pay. Get a fuckin grip."

Sometimes seeking. "Do yi know where they've moved tae? When will he be back? Where's he drinkin noo?"

They were the dead words of a despairing daily routine. There was no love or genuine affection in the poverty business. Just units to be contacted in the crazy pound notes lottery. Once a month there might be fifty notes up front for a baseball job. A hundred notes for a life-threatening job to those who did a runner.

Kenny was well built, five feet eight inches tall, strong and good looking in a raw, powerful dark way. He did not carry any macho-man fantasy. Nor was he psychopathic. He did the job and that was that. The work could at times be boring, parked outside a pub, at a close, or beside the high rise blocks for hours waiting on Tollan's recalcitrant clients. No messing. In and out. Get the job done. Drive the baseball bat into the legs and ribs. Break bones. The knife was used on their faces. Draw blood where the damage could be seen rather than inflict any life-threatening stabs to the body.

Sadly there were occasions when more than the message had to be passed on from Jimmy. The families who did a runner by securing a house transfer and moving permanently to another corner of the city, were sought out and savagely dealt with. The men in those families were taught a cruel lesson. To keep paying when they were released from hospital! The severity of the lessons depended solely on the audacity of the client.

The punters avoided Kenny's eyes. They made friendly overtures and desperate promises. Kenny vaguely understood their problems. He had no friends, not even Jimmy Tollan, for theirs was a working relationship and nothing else.

Kenny had been a good footballer at school. In fact he was an all round sportsman who never looked back on his wasted potential. He rarely thought about his lost chance. The subject came up often enough though. "Kenny, you should have signed for Chelsea, then yi'd no be hassling us fur payments. See if yi hid signed fur Chelsea when all they scouts were efter yi, yi could huv been runnin yir ain book."

The banter included pathetic ingratiating jokes. "It's no the scouts that are efter you now Kenny. It's the polis."

He took the gentle ribbing in his stride. The punters had nothing else they could talk to him about except the money they owed Tollan. That was not a suitable subject for the endless idle chat that dragged out the long days stretching into years on the dole.

Poverty did not preclude humour, though the middle class rarely reflected this truth. The punters were poor therefore they must be miserable. Their homes belonged to the state in an era when ownership spelt success. The so-called winners had seen their investments rocket in value, while those with real money watched their shares double. A ticket for the match was now a seat price. Soon there would be nothing but seats. God it must be terrible to be poor.

There were plenty of people around to remind them of their plight. Politicians, sociologists, ministers, priests and media pundits, queuing up to plead the case for the poor, pointing out that they were suffering in the extreme.

No money for a power card. Nothing for food. Or cigarettes. The communion dress. The football match. A drink. A pair of trainers for the wean. A suit for the wedding. Cash for the catalogue payments. Christmas. The poor were ping pong balls.

There were endless reasons for their debt. Nobody stops smoking because they have lost their job, or cannot get one. Nor did they become vegetarians because they were living on supplementary benefit.

Stuck on the dole quickly translated into long term unemployment, with long term solutions. Long term. Chop carrots, turnips, onions and leeks. Buy a bone and make soup like your granny did.

Income support surely did not exclude them from a video recorder. Or for that matter from hiring tapes. After all the video shop was next to the chippie.

Market forces and new technology targeted them too. There was no health warning on the endless hype of monetarism. All they could do was blame that bitch Thatcher, and wriggle like fuck. Kirby grips in the electric meter. Plastic cards to stop the gas bills clicking up. Poll tax cop outs. Black market jobs. False housing benefit claims. Survival jobs. Fake perfume selling, buy cheap suits and sell them as stolen. Clock cars and electricity or gas meters. Services. Enterprise yourself.

The more the government squeezed, the more the poor twisted and turned. The game went on and on and on. A marathon of monetarism, in which unemployed families became profitable units. They quickly grasped that six months stacked in an employment training scheme meant ten pounds a week to them. Less their fare. With fifty pounds per unit, them, going to the boss.

Kenny vaguely understood the business he was in. The daily runs. The night time violence. The rewards weren't enough to keep Kenny going. Five years in his dual role of credit controller and enforcement officer had not improved his lifestyle. Tollan was the one with the bank accounts. A caravan. A car and the best of gear. Holidays in Spain.

The repetition was boring Kenny Watson. He was barely coping with his worthless lifestyle when Tollan gave him explicit instructions to make Jessica pay.

His instructions in the corner of the Black Inn were implicit. "Ah'm fucked aff wi her. She hisnae shown fur five weeks. She's no answering at her hoose. Ah want sixty aff her next week. Ah need it fuckin regular. Go an' see her."

Tollan quickly dropped the subject. Kenny had his instructions, however brief. They both understood. Jessica would be dealt with seriously and soon. She should start paying.

Tollan changed the subject introducing the latest imminent signing at Ibrox.

"Souness is goin tae sign on at Ibrox on a long term contract. That's the best news of the week. The guy's tough. He manages the way he played. He knows exactly whit he's daein. Championships, league cups and we're eight points clear at the top o the table. He knows exactly what he's fuckin daein. Souness has nae intention of goin tae Liverpool tae replace Dalglish. There's nae chance of him leavin. No according tae the Rangers News. He says he intends bein the boss at Ibrox fur years. He sees his short term future at

Ibrox and he sees his long term future at Ibrox."

The hangers-on had listened patiently to Jimmy's long speech on the subject of his hero. Tollan liked aggressive, uncompromising winners, judging them on their uncompromising power. He looked no further than results. That was good enough for him.

As always Kenny agreed with his boss. "He knows exactly whit he's daein. There's nae doubt about it – he's turned the club roon."

The enforcer's opinion counted for he had played the game very well but was not interested in merely watching. He tried a spot of fun. "Soonness, Sooness. Sooness, Sooness." It dropped like a lead balloon.

Tollan took the conversation back to reality. "Jessica needs tae be dealt wi. Fur serious. Right Kenny?"

"Ay, right Jimmy. Yi telt me awready."

They were both trapped in their own cage, unable to see beyond the bars. To see the realities of terrifying a twenty year old slip of a girl. The impact was not considered. Only the intended result – that she start paying.

Kenny did exactly what was expected of him, taking a getaway driver in the Audi. They parked at the foot of the high rise block at dusk. Kenny finished a cigarette. Before he could take the lift to the seventh floor and the cowardly job, a bonus emerged from the concrete pillars supporting the massive Legoland construction.

He would not need to terrify the woman. Here was a real target.

"That's Jessica's man. Jack wiz the wan that knew Jimmy and got her the money in the first place. Ah'll gie him the message," said Kenny getting out of the car swiftly to lift a baseball bat from the boot. He walked quickly round to the driver's door to tell the youth at the wheel, "Keep the motor runnin."

The air was damp. All that could be heard was the noise of a TV from above. Jack stopped under the massive concrete stanchions waiting on Jessica who was behind with the pushpram. He had left her to make her own way from the lift and through the awkward security swing doors. Jack was incapable of making the effort to help anybody, which was why he spent most of his time back at home with his mother.

He never saw Kenny until the last moment, when it was too late. He had glanced back at the heavy security doors to see Jessica and the baby struggling through and sensed that somebody was approaching.

Turning, he faced Kenny who was carrying the bat in his right hand holding it behind his right leg.

"Hi Kenny, how's it goin?"

"Fuckin badly, yi stupid cunt. Get her tae pay," said Kenny swinging the bat at his prey's legs. Jack felt the blow on the side of the knee but did not fall to the ground. He stumbled against the concrete pillar. Jessica screamed, "Leave him alain. It's no his fault."

Kenny ignored her plea and one-handed swung the bat down on Jack's upturned arm. The blows were, by Kenny Watson's standards, fairly soft. In the few moments it took to complete the attack, Kenny subconsciously realised this was not for him. His heart was not in the job anymore. It had never given him any satisfaction or, for that matter, pleasure. He had only been doing it for the money.

Kenny walked quickly to the car and was driven back to the Black Inn reporting a successful visit to Jessica.

"We got her man instead. Really fuckin got him. She was there. She'll start payin."

Jimmy called to the barman. "Tommy, gie Kenny a pint."

Jimmy never saw Jessica again.

70

10 Value for Money

THEY FACED each other across the kitchen table at tea time. Jessica had changed the baby's nappy.

They were set for another serious talk. They had no telly to switch off. Just a space where its reassuring presence had been until five weeks ago when she sold it for next to nothing.

Jack started. "Ah love you. Ah know, you know that. So anything Ah say is because Ah love you. What Ah'm telling you is fuckin important."

Her mind was numb. Frozen in fear for two days. She hardly heard his words. The rain hammered on the window. The smell of yesterday's bacon hung through the flat.

Jack sensed that Jessica wasn't absorbing his words. Or the truth in those weak words. Her head was down. She was staring at the flattened carpet, unable to escape the image of her man being beaten. She was hypnotised in fear.

"Listen to me. Please," he implored. Her eyes lifted to his. "Ah know what Ah'm talkin about. Ah know the score. Ah know the way it is. They'll huv me. They're daft enough for anythin."

She dropped her eyes.

He waited while she took a sip of tea. Then he tried again, stretching his hand across the table to hold hers. He took his time with every word.

"We've got to stick together on this. Don't go to the cops. Please. We'll get out of it. Please. Believe me."

Finally she uttered some words. "Jack. We've got to do something."

The rain hammered on the window. The baby let out a soft cry.

Jack looked down at the carpet. Then stared bleakly at the window. She filled his cup, poured the last of the milk, and waited.

They were in slow motion.

"What can we do?" he asked weakly.

Jessica said nothing.

Jack stood up and walked round the table, putting his arm round her chest from behind. Jessica looked up. He kissed her softly on the mouth. There was no response in her lips.

He moved back round the table but didn't sit down. "We can't go to the cops. That's definite."

They tried to think their way out of the debt to Jimmy Tollan. Not the way to do it. The telly was sold. Her engagement ring had gone. Jessica broached the subject of prostitution. She didn't mean it, but used the idea as a catalyst to make him think of some way out.

"You're no going doon the toon. No fuckin way!" he cried in anger.

Jessica's voice wavered. "Roberta done it and got her and Eddie off the hook."

He stood up. "Eddie's left her."

He stormed to the door. "Ah'm gettin out the house before Ah kill you."

He was quitting for Jack had no solution. He never had. There was nothing to talk about. He opted out. Jack went for a long walk to his brother's house in the maisonettes at Anderston.

For five minutes Jessica sobbed uncontrollably. She gathered herself, took an old jotter out of the sideboard and wrote a letter. She was not yet sure to whom it would be sent.

The Chief Constable? The Social Work? The Papers?

Dear Sir,
I know you want to crack down on money lenders. I've got some big information on big money lenders. I think they deal in drugs too. They are the Tollan gang from Garthill. They run the loan sharking from three pubs, the Black Inn, The Wee Hauf along the same road, The Rhum Do. And they take in the money every day. This lot are real bad people. They hit my boyfriend with a baseball bat. For not paying

£210 on a £30 loan from Tollan. I saw them doing it and I was going to phone the police. But my man stopped me. He is terrified of them. He says they are killers.

The flat was cold and dormant except for the occasional movement of the baby sleeping in the pram. Jessica put on her coat for warmth and tried to inject some of the realities of the violence into the letter.

She justified the letter which defied her husband's fear of grassing.

What Ah'm telling them is the truth. How will they realise it is the truth? It's happening to us. We have paid back four times the amount he borrowed. It took him too long. He missed so many payments over the first three months that the debt is up at two hundred and ten pounds. We'll never get out. The whole thing's too dangerous.

With the Biro poised in her hand she murmured aloud. "They must get it into their heads that this could end in murder. Then they will do something."

Jessica had already made the decision to withhold her name. So the letter had to carry enough conviction to instigate action.

She wrote more.

My Jack says that they have already put other people in the intensive care unit. I was at the park with the baby. They pulled up at the park gate. One of them got out of the motor and punched me in the face giving me a big black eye. Another one pulled a knife out and pointed it at the baby. I was told that if my man did not pay she'd get it. I am at my wits end I am shaking like a leaf writing this. I can't tell my man because he is scared. God knows what is going to happen. I am taking nerve tablets. I'm terrified. Jack is terrified. Please, please get these monsters away from us. I am too scared to go over the door. I have even wrote this letter left handed. Just in case it gets into the wrong hands.

The second attack in the park was pure invention, designed to alarm the authorities, whoever she chose to tell, into taking some action. Her fear created a pathetic animal cunning as she tried to impart the truth to anybody who might help.

The page tore slightly as she pulled it from the jotter. Jessica kept the letter hidden, as a token of her despair. Like women who keep a diary chronicling their unhappy marriages. The act of writing the words was a cry for help.

Jessica waited, sleeping with the help of tablets and zombying through the bleak days. Sad. Troubled in her sleep. A beautiful girl. Slender legged, long necked with a round face and dark hair long enough to plait.

Her bright diamond blue eyes in the patchy white face were beginning to dull. The sparkle was disappearing. On Monday she collected her income support cash at the post office. Kenny Watson was waiting.

For a few minutes Jessica chatted to the other women standing outside the butcher's. She tried to smile, tried to be warm, tried to sound interested, then made her way across to the collector, pushing the baby in the pram, a barrier to his anticipated aggression.

"Kenny, Ah need tae talk tae you."

He was listening. Carefully. Giving her time to make her excuses.

"Ah'm sorry Ah didnae make it last week. Ah was sick and ma granny got ma money for me."

Kenny nodded down the street. "Let's take a wee walk, hen. We'll talk in private ower there."

There was no need to move from where they were already standing because nobody came within listening distance. The women all gave him a wide berth. The walk away to another place simply stamped the air of severity on the talk. He made his way to the doorway of an empty shop. She caught up and stood with her back to the street.

He opened firmly. "First things first Jessica. Ah need sixty from yi." She gave him the cash.

That left her eleven pounds. For a week. For food.

For nappies. For two power cards to keep the lights on and give them some heating. The next demand had to be resisted.

"Now gie me yir book."

Her face fell. She crumbled. "Kenny. Ah cannae . . ."

He grasped her firmly by the forearm. "Nae fuckin hysterics. Don't argue Jessica. He wants yir book and that's it. Gie me it."

Jessica was sinking fast. Her resistance collapsed. Lifting the benefit book out of her handbag she said lamely. "Just for one week. That's all."

"Ay. Ah'll tell Jimmy that yir hoping tae get it back next week."

"What about next Monday?" she inquired hopelessly.

"Ah'll be doon here at ten o'clock. Ah'll see yi then. Don't worry."

He was off. Back up the street for more collections.

In her cold flat Jessica realised that they had no bread, no food and she had forgotten to buy a power card. The fourteen pound emergency supply was almost finished. The electricity would soon be off. After lifting the baby out of the pram and carefully tucking him into the cot, she made a pot of tea. There was no milk.

There was nobody to talk to. The crisis could not be shared. Jack might turn up sometime. He often stayed away for days. The relationship was crumbling. He often said he loved her. When he was around.

He seemed to spend more time with his own family these days.

She heard the lift clunk to a stop and the clatter of the doors opening. The letter box rattled. Jessica moved the cot into the kitchen and closed the door quietly, then tiptoed down the hall to stand in silence behind the door. Her ears strained for a clue as to who it was. The letter box rattled again. "Jessica."

It was a woman's voice. Roberta.

"That you Roberta?"

"Let me in. Whit are yi playin at?"

There was no reason for Jessica to hide in her own home. By now Tollan had her sixty pounds and was holding her benefit book. She was shaken by the loss of the book. Her lifeline had gone. She was drowning.

Hiding from anything. Frightened of the power that Tollan now wielded. The loan shark had total control and therefore took on a greater evil role in her mangled mind. Her thoughts moved constantly, chaotically, in a downward spiral.

Jessica had somebody to talk to and for an hour she poured her heart out. Roberta knew what the score was. She too was into Jimmy Tollan for a lot of money. She had gone down the same one-way financial street. Borrowed forty pounds, she missed a few payments and saw the debt rocket to over two hundred pounds. Unable to meet the weekly payments out of her Monday book she faced the threats. In uncontrollable fear she turned to prostitution.

Roberta saw the work as the answer to Jessica's problem. "Come doon the toon wi me. Ah'll show yi the ropes. Nae problem."

"Ah couldnae do that. Ah'm no married, but Ah couldnae do it," she said.

In an instant she realised that she might have offended her friend and added sincerely, "There's nothing wrang with going on the game Roberta. Ah jist couldnae do it. Ah wish Ah could. Ah just cannae. That probably sounds daft to you."

The words were burlesque. For the first time they both smiled.

Jessica stood up and put the kettle on for tea. "There's sugar but no milk."

Over the tea they talked. Jessica tried to heal the hurt she thought Roberta might have been suffered at her rejection of prostitution. Roberta wasn't hurt. In her mind the moral question was just not in it.

She was on the game now. The loan shark held no fears for her. The money was good. The payments were easily met each week, with plenty left over. The benefits far outweighed the risks of violence. She hadn't yet summoned the courage to have a blood test. That was for another day.

Roberta was doing very nicely. A steady cash flow. A big TV. A warm furnished home. Smart clothes.

"You shouldnae take life so seriously Jessica," was her parting advice.

Jessica did.

The following day she left the baby at her mother's and walked into the park. Two girls and a boy, all aged about six, were tearing up a loaf of bread and throwing pieces into the pond. The ducks had a feast. The kids were enjoying themselves. When the bread was finished they looked round for any crumbs to continue the game.

The happy carefree scene drove her deeper into sadness. In the lift to her home she remembered that the emergency electricity was almost finished. Maybe Jack would be in.

The house was empty.

So was Jessica. Cold and empty and alone. The sleeping tablets were in the bedroom on the chair. Without knowing why she lay on the bed sobbing uncontrollably. The sobs died away.

Jessica wanted a rest. A long deep rest. Trembling in fearful confusion she went to the kitchen, filling a glass of water. It spilled on the way back to the bedroom. She placed it on the chair, opened the bottle of tablets and stuffed a handful in her mouth. In almost the same movement she grasped the glass, gulping down the water in two full swallows.

Jessica lay back and died in her sleep.

Her death was put down to emotional stress at the break-up of her relationship with Jack. There was no evidence of violence. Nothing suspicious. The death was recorded as suicide. An overdose of sleeping tablets.

Her letter begging for help was found four days after the funeral by Jack. It was under the settee.

He read the desperate words, tore the letter into many pieces and flushed it down the toilet. He was without guilt.

He felt no anger for Tollan. Just fear. Jessica was gone. The baby would be brought up by her mother. There was no percentage in being a grass. Whether Jessica was alive or not.

Jimmy Tollan learnt of her death from Kenny outside the bookies. He was sympathetic. "Christ, that's a shame. Her marriage wiz breakin' up."

Kenny put him right. "They wirnae married."

That night Jimmy phoned Kenny to ask how much money Jessica owed. The debt against her name stood at three hundred and five pounds. It was recorded half way down the page between Wee Tam, who owed one hundred and forty five pounds and Squinty Gibbs owing forty pounds.

Jimmy pulled on his leather jacket and called to Rita. "Ah'm away oot. Ah'll be back later."

The Audi crept across to Kenny Watson's home. Kenny was surprised by the visit. "Come in Jimmy. Whit dae yi want at this time o' night?"

"Get the books oot fur me."

"Are the polis ontae us."

"Naw."

Jimmy sat in the front room while Kenny lifted the carpet at the bottom of the stairs, rolled it up three steps and prised up a square of wood to lift out a small plastic bag. He handed Tollan the bag. "Want a drink Jimmy?"

"Naw."

Jimmy first checked the tally book scoring Jessica Thompson's name off the extensive list. He went through the Monday books like a pack of cards, turning each onto the coffee table, until he found Jessica's.

"Burn that wan," he told Kenny, who was beginning to tire of the whole scum business. The weight of Jessica's suicide hung so heavy in his mind that after Jimmy left, he unburdened himself.

"You'll have tae decide what you're gonnae dae. Ah cannae decide fur yi," was his wife's response.

He made no firm decision about quitting on Tollan.

For several days he saw Jessica's sad face, the bright blue eyes, pale cheeks and her long dark hair. Her voice echoed in his head – "Leave him alain. It's no his fault." The echoing words were the forerunner to the images that began to haunt him. Jessica with the pram at the foot of the high rise block as he hit Jack. Jessica in the street, unable to hold onto her Monday book.

Jessica swallowing the pills.

Kenny Watson had most certainly contributed to her death. He didn't even try to move the guilt to Jimmy. After a few weeks as Kenny continued the daily routines, Jessica's death blurred. But a deep-set hatred of Tollan crept into his psyche. At first Kenny was unaware that he could no longer stomach his boss's presence.

In the Black Inn where they had shared a few plots and many pints Kenny began to reject his running mate of five years. It started with the little things, Jimmy asking him if he wanted another pint and Kenny replying, "Naw. Ah'm away up the road."

"Are yi comin' to the gemme wi me on Saturday?"

"No. We're goin over to her maw's."

"Ah'll gie yi a lift over then. Before the gemme."

"No thanks Jimmy."

The loan shark put the change in attitude down to greed, telling Rita, "Kenny's gettin' right mumpy. He's gonnae start asking fur mair money."

Kenny Watson hardly recognised the change in himself, sticking with the daily routines, round the post offices and in and out of the pubs, being nice and nasty to suit the varying financial situations.

Tollan should have thought more carefully about the behaviour patterns displayed by his cohort before ordering him to frighten the shit out of Jenny Mullen. "God knows whit she's playin at. She hisnae paid fur three weeks."

The death of Jessica was too fresh in Kenny's mind. It was an order too far. He resented the order. He feared it. It triggered a reaction to the years of exploitation by Tollan. For thirty pounds a week Kenny had terrorised the weakest without any decent rewards. That was the surface issue.

The real issue for Kenny was eating away at his soul. He couldn't cope with another suicide. Jimmy was pushing him toward the edge. Kenny Watson turned devious.

He was alone in the car with four hundred and eighty five pounds in one pocket and twenty two DSS books in another. He pulled up in Maryhill Road to consider a plan that had come at him in a blinding flash. The thought simply emerged from the back of his mind.

At twenty nine years of age he had a fair knowledge of where to get anything he wanted, cheaply. He knew the sources of TVs, videos, clothes, forgeries, tapes, porn, cannabis, and if the worst came to the worst, guns. He was no stranger to the cheap corners of the underworld. He turned the car onto the M80 and headed for Falkirk, skirting the town to wriggle into a squalid little industrial estate.

The yard was black hardened earth, impregnated with engine oil. The office, an upstairs room in a narrow building jammed between a car spraying garage and a locked builder's yard.

The men he wanted to meet watched him arrive from behind the dirty window of the grimy first floor office. The receptionist downstairs was worse then the Berlin Wall. "Who are you? I don't know if they are in. I don't work for them. They just rent an office here. Did they know you were coming? Why don't you make an appointment?"

Anger was mounting in Kenny when a voice rasped out from above, "It's OK. Ah ken him fine. Sen' him up."

The carpet on the stairs and in the office was dirty. John Forsyth had his feet on a coffee-stained metal desk. His brother Tam was drinking lemonade from the bottle. Kenny's eyes moved past his fat weak face to two half-empty lemonade bottles on the filing cabinet. The bottles obscured a colour picture of a nude girl bent over touching her toes. Picture taken from behind.

"Good to see you son," said John, who considered himself as the brains and therefore boss of the operation.

"What the fuck are you doin in Falkirk?" he asked

moving to the door and calling down the stairway. "Betty. Get us three coffees."

Kenny had the set-up sussed in seconds. They were deluding themselves. Kidding themselves that they ran a business. Playing the current game. He answered the overly familiar question. "Ah wouldnae come to Falkirk unless Ah wanted something, mate. Yi still dealin in duddies?"

John dropped his feet off the desk and shook his head in disbelief. "That's no fur you. Small beer that. Fuckin hard work, ye ken."

They had first met in Shotts Prison. Kenny was doing time for serious assault, John for a fraud using stolen cheque cards to buy clothes.

You do what you are good at. Kenny had no objection to inflicting serious damage on human flesh.

John was a big man. Tall and on the fat side. Liked to wear a track suit and trainers. Bragged that he was a black belt in judo. In truth he was a coward. He made money with his mind, hooked on the thrill of the con. The brothers dealt in stolen cars. They bought stolen cheque books and cards. And they sold forgeries. Criminals, working out of an office.

Kenny, not adverse to frightening old men, young mothers and alcoholics, despised them for their trickery.

"Hard work or no Ah'm here fur duddies. If yi hiv any, Ah'm in the market," said Kenny. He wasn't going to get into a discussion with this fat Falkirk asshole about the merits of one crime as opposed to another.

Betty arrived with the coffees on a dirty tray. She left quickly, knowing that the business was not for her ears. Kenny chose the cleanest looking mug.

Tam had not spoken a word and Kenny was aware that the younger brother was watching him intently. He resented the impolite attention but chose to ignore the stupid bastard. He was here for the duddies and knew how to get them.

He pulled out the readies. Four hundred and eighty five pounds belonging to Jimmy Tollan.

Tollan's money? The taxpayer's money. The women's money. Those poor frightened crawlers back in Glasgow. He had some of their cheque books in his pocket. Their DSS books. Monday books. Invalidity books. Pension books. Collateral.

Tam, Mr Staring Eyes, couldn't keep his mouth shut at the sight of the cash. "We can definitely do some business here. We got a delivery from Manchester two days ago. Good quality stuff, son."

Kenny noticed the 'son'.

His brother wasn't pleased. "Get a fuckin grip, Tam. The man disnae want to know where they came fae."

The older brother was on the hook too. Like a whiz kid broker in the City offering shares in gas, electricity, and telephones, John Forsyth saw the chance of a quick profit. Easy money. Champagne later. Something for nothing. A guaranteed profit. Nothing earned. No risk. They were all in the monopoly game.

Another dealer's day in downtown Falkirk.

Kenny knew the sale was now on. He didn't have to wait on their agreement. "Ah'm a busy man. Ah huv a few turns back in Glesga. Ah need tae get back."

He rapped out his order. "Ah want a hunner pounds worth. That's one thousand. Right."

There was no bartering. They all knew the going rate for the worthless currency. Tam was dispatched to bring in the cash. Kenny studied a few notes agreeing with John that they were "fuckin good."

The speedometer needle stayed below seventy on the return trip to Glasgow. His greatest fear was that the police might pull him up.

He was, after all, driving Jimmy's Audi.

11 The full price

JENNY MULLEN heard the car slow down from fifty yards away. It was behind her. Yet she knew that it would stop exactly five yards in front of her.

Sure enough it did. The passenger window was down. Jenny's blue eyes brightened. She tightened her buttocks, pulled her stomach in and made her way casually to the open window.

She was in mode. Feel attractive and you'll look attractive. She backed it with the slow 'come on'. Jenny leant down at the open passenger window. Not too close, allowing the street lights to highlight her firm breasts.

There was nobody in the passenger seat, which was no surprise to Jenny. The driver, who looked like a well-off gent, stretched his left arm along the back. The watch and the cufflinks were gold. On the surface a successful man. He was businesslike. "Are you working tonight my dear?" he asked pleasantly.

"Yes. I am," she replied, matching his confident friendly approach.

"That's good. Can we go to your place?" There was a hint of a smile. More in his voice than on his face.

It was her turn to be businesslike. "Of course. But that'll cost you," she replied inferring that there would be an extra charge for the comfort of her bed. No figure was mentioned. Each liked what they saw in the other and were confident that the price of sex would not be in dispute. The exact terms would of course have to be formalised at some stage before they went to the bedroom.

At thirty-five years of age, Jenny was no mug. She was easy on both the mind and the body. Prostitution was a relatively new experience for her. She did not consider herself to be a failure, to be in the gutter, although she was far from being a happy hooker. Circumstances had ruled it had to be done to solve this year's problems.

Last year her divorce came through. The year before Bert left her for that woman at his work. He had fallen in love with the woman. Jenny conceded that. It wasn't just a bit on the side. Jenny could see that.

He disappeared from her life. A Christmas card for herself and the child was all the contact that remained, apart from the occasional calls from his mother who was deeply distressed at the marriage failure. She kept in close contact and was never off the telephone, regularly offering to babysit. "If you want to get out and make a life for yourself, remember I am not far away."

Granny might as well have shouted down the phone. "Get yourself another husband, to share your bed and your life and help bring up Christine."

Jenny's mum was dead.

After the separation Jenny dyed her dark hair a subtle red, glamourised up with dark stockings and smarter clothes. She was much more comfortable with herself than she had been in her unfulfilling marriage. A few weeks of loneliness quickly passed. New men crept into her life briefly. They didn't stay long. It was not that she made them unwelcome. She simply did not want a man in her life.

"They're more trouble than they're worth," her mother-in-law would say with a weak smile. Jenny was in total agreement with the cliché.

She was quite tall, five foot six, walking erect and square shouldered. Eye catching and almost elegant. She enjoyed the occasional romantic interlude based on physical attraction leading to a rare exciting sexual romp. Anything more than that was on her rejection slip.

The reason for her fall from single mum status to whore was, in her view, quite simple. Jenny had been stupid. She borrowed one hundred pounds from Jimmy Tollan and missed a few weekly payments. That was more than a year ago. Today she owed him six hundred and eighty pounds. The loan had been for a holiday at Colwyn Bay in a caravan. Something she felt was imperative for her daughter's standing at school.

Last year they stayed at home throughout the long summer. Christine had been bored playing in the street, going to her granny's and generally idling her way through the two months' school break. Her friends went off on their holidays, to Spain, camping in France, Scarborough, and the North of Scotland. Jenny couldn't stand the idea of Christine listening to her pals relate their holiday yarns while her daughter could only say, "We don't go holidays anymore."

It was a costly bid to beat the shame of going without a holiday for another year. Like all the other women who borrowed from Tollan, Jenny had a reason. A justification for the sheer stupidity. The cash was for unpaid bills, Christmas, to avoid furniture repossession, a wedding, a carpet, or to replace the washing machine.

Jenny rationalised the foolhardy loan from her own perspective – "You can't keep your guard up all the time." She took the risk for the sake of her daughter and was trapped. She took the blow squarely, stood up and took the course of action needed to solve any problem.

Her parents were good Highland people. Dad came south to work in the shipyards. Mum was a cook in a primary school. It never crossed her mind that her parents would turn in their grave if they knew of her services.

Money is money. Jenny stood firm on that. Her man had gone and she was in serious financial trouble. Money was the key to her escape. So she made the most of her tall obvious beauty and her situation and became a part-time prostitute. If a client was willing to pay more for sex in the comfort of her bedroom and Christine was away at her Granny's then the service was supplied at her home.

Mostly it was routine straightforward sex, with a condom, with men who simply wanted physical relief. Many were sexually inexperienced.

Jenny absorbed her clients' needs like ink on blotting paper. The men who wanted to talk about their wives. Talk about their businesses. The regulars who brought her presents. There were some surprises. She expected men to ask for a 'blow job'. But not to urinate on her. Or to tie her to the bed. Profiting from sex proved at times to be a funny old business. She kept her nerve when first asked, "Could you give me a good spanking." She thrust her mind into neutral and kept it there while spanking his big white bum as he knelt on the bed.

For the client a fantasy fulfilled. For Jenny it was a farce, which she soon accepted as part of being on the game. Her innate courage was no match for the vicious streak that emerged in some. She learnt to cope as best she could with the odd man who thought that paying up front for the service included violence.

These men approached her in the street with the minimum of words. The sight of her undressing inside her bedroom seemed to unlock their tormented personalities. The violence started with gentle questions. "Have you been busy tonight?" and progressed past, "Do you have any kids?" to "Do you take drugs?"

Jenny was careful when answering those troubled questions with a casual smile. "No. It's been quiet. I went out late tonight."

No, she didn't have any children she lied, knowing that a mother on the streets was sometimes an unpleasant image for the odd man to deal with.

And no, she was not a junkie.

The businesslike man with gold cufflinks and good manners was one who turned into a monster in the space of a few seconds. He started by asking her if she had been forced into prostitution.

"No."

"So why the fuck are you on the game?" he inquired with a twisted mouth.

She trembled in anxiety. Another nasty one. This was almost as frightening as anything Jimmy Tollan and his thugs might do if she failed to keep paying.

Jenny kept her eyes off his. She tried to prevent the onslaught of his attack.

"We're going to have a good time. I know we will." It

was the wrong thing to say and she knew it. Her fear forced the foolish words out.

A waste of breath. He despised her for her profession. She had failed to meet the standards he expected of a woman. The cancer was in his subconscious. He thought he'd come into town for sex. He had in fact driven into the city centre to beat up a fallen woman. Jenny should have known better than to bring men to her own home where the dangers were even greater.

He was standing above her, his face contorted. "Listen you stupid whore. I wouldn't fuck you if you paid me."

His right hand smashed against her cheek. He grabbed her red hair and dragged her off the bed. Her buttocks bumped to the floor and he kicked out connecting with her thigh.

Jenny was powerless, clinging to anything that might stem his brutality. She begged.

"Don't kill me," she screamed. "Please? Please? Please? No more. Please, stop."

The client felt an extra surge of power. He felt the roles were reversed. He had control now. He unleashed more of his troubled punishment, dragging her back onto the bed. He raped her, dressed quickly and left.

Jenny lay for minutes before limping to the door, locking it and checking out the damage to her face in the bathroom mirror.

She phoned her mother in law, who was unaware of Jenny's new life style and asked, "Could you keep Christine tonight?"

The understanding granny was delighted. "Yes I will. I'll take her to school in the morning and you can pick her up from my place tomorrow night."

Granny enjoyed having the little girl's company. She felt that her son had let Jenny down by walking out. Anything she could do to help Jenny recover from the broken marriage was a salve to her conscience. She felt strangely responsible for Bert's failure to stick by the lass. Her fervent hope was that Jenny might fall in love with a better man.

So she inquired hopefully about the reason for Jenny's request that Christine stay overnight. The question was clumsy if indirect. "Some romance in your life Jenny?"

Jenny almost smiled as her face began to stiffen and blacken. Her emotional recovery from the ordeal was rapid. She had a black eye, a bruised cheekbone and a sore thigh. She was alive.

Her biggest problem was the shattering impact of the rape. The sheer intrusion into her spirit was already beginning to drag at her thoughts. She could sense the consequences. The brutality of the rape would scar her for life.

"No. There's no man staying here tonight. I just have some serious thinking to do and it would suit if Christine stays with you. Don't ask me anything. Good night. Kiss Christine good night for me." She hung up, sat down and sobbed uncontrollably. Then she turned the bath on and made a cup of tea.

In the deep hot bath Jenny cried as delayed shock set in. She made some decisions. It was time to get out of this mess. She would ask Jimmy Tollan to freeze her debt. He would not want to but might consider it if she approached him the right way.

The introduction to Tollan had been made through a friend she'd met at Christine's school. Another single mum. In the corner of the pub Tollan had assessed Jenny carefully as she stood at his table. Smartly dressed. Well spoken. A solid looking lass. She was asking for a lot of money. One hundred pounds.

"I can pay you back the lot in five weeks. I know I can." She was eager to get the money to pay for the holiday. Too eager as it turned out. Tollan liked what he saw, enjoying the power of his situation even more than usual because of her quality. He could afford to be friendly and businesslike. A nice warm attitude. And Jenny was a good looking woman.

Better than some of those pale faced slags dragging their weans around all the time. There was no end of fucking hassle trying tae get money out of them. Stupid ungrateful bastards!

"Sit doon. Want a drink Jenny? "

"Whisky and lemonade, please."

She sat down with her friend and Jimmy told her the deal. Five pounds on every twenty pounds she borrowed. Per week. So for one hundred pounds it would be twenty five pounds interest next week.

Her drink arrived with a vodka and lemonade for her pal. Jimmy knew what her pal drank without asking. They chatted for fifteen minutes, interrupted regularly by people who seemed to have nothing to say to Tollan except, "Hullo Jimmy. How's it goin'? "

They hung about the table for a few seconds as he gave them his boring reply. "OK, how are yi goin yersel son?" That was it. They drifted off.

Sometimes the conversation extended a little. "See the Gers got screwed?"

"Ay, but Aberdeen havnae got the bottle tae take the title. Wan thing's fur sure. Celtic'll no be there at the end o' the season. No if Brady buys any mair arseholes. Six million? For whit?"

The spasmodic interruptions came as Tollan explained the deal she was entering. "Ah want yi tae understaun the score, love," he said firmly.

She was 'love' while the other women who approached the table were 'hen'.

"Ah need tae know a few facts. Whit's yir address?"

She told him.

"Got anythin on yi tae prove that?"

She showed him a letter from the school.

"Have yi got yir Monday book?"

No, not with her, but she could show him it tomorrow.

"Nae need fur that, love."

The friendly businesslike atmosphere began to disintegrate as he explained the repayment arrangements. No hiding from the criminal side of it all. He tried to make it seem all friendly and above board. "Ah don't want to send anybody to yir hoose. See efter yi'v been to the post office on Monday, come doon here tae the pub. But don't come in here."

He called up to the bar. "Kenny?"

The powerfully built Kenny put his pint down on the bar and came over to the table.

Jimmy introduced him. "Kenny. This is Jenny."

It was unintentional. Tollan made the most of it. "Ah'm a poet and Ah don't know it," he growled.

Jenny smiled. Kenny didn't bother.

"Whit is it, Jimmy?" he inquired.

Jimmy ignored the question, telling Jenny, "He'll collect yir money on Monday. He'll be here, in the close next door tae here, between eleven and eleven thirty on Monday mornin. That OK?"

Before Jenny could reply Kenny spoke. "Ah'll see yi on Monday. Don't be late Jenny. Ah hate hivin' tae wait on people." He went back to the bar.

"Wait here, love," said Tollan standing up. "Ah'm goin tae the toilet. Ah'll be back in a sec."

In the toilet he peeled one hundred pounds in fivers off a wad of notes. He rolled up the wad and put it back in his pocket. He rolled up the one hundred pounds carrying them back to the table inside his clenched hand. He sat down then moved his hand across the table saying, "There yi are love. Put it away noo."

As she carefully placed it in her handbag Tollan asked. "Want anither drink love?"

"No thanks Jimmy. But thanks a lot for the help."

The bath was getting cold. Jenny leant forward and turned the hot water tap on. The soreness in her thigh had eased in the bath. Her face was sore. She could feel her eye beginning to close up from the crazy psycho's blows. Her leg and hip were bruised where the client had kicked her.

The next day she sought out Jimmy Tollan.

He was immediately sympathetic, taking one look at her face and asking, "Whit bastard did that tae yi hen?"

He didn't ask what had happened. He simply assumed

that some man had beaten her up. Jenny switched his attention from her injuries to her long term finances. "Never mind about my face Jimmy. I need to talk to you about my loan."

They were in his Audi at the Cross.

He switched off the radio. "Ah'm listenin hen."

She started her plea the wrong way. "Jimmy it's a year since I borrowed that hundred pounds from you. I've missed paying you many times. Too many times. I know."

Jimmy had heard this line before. He was bored with punters preparing their plea to be let off the hook. He didn't want to hear. Yet like a bank or building society manager he was more than willing to listen.

Jenny continued, "I have paid you a lot of money. I know exactly how much because I marked each payment up in a book I keep. I made thirty payments. Seventeen of them were twenty five pounds. Nine were twenty pound. The rest were fifteen pounds each time."

Jimmy twisted round in the driver's seat to face her. "Gonnie cut the crap, hen. Get tae the fuckin point." He already knew what the point was.

"Jimmy, please hear me out. The point I'm trying to make is that I borrowed one hundred from you and I've paid you back six hundred and sixty five pounds in one year. I wanted to ask you something."

He was silent, staring impassively ahead.

"If I gave you another hundred pounds could I get out of the debt. Please?" she said trying to find his eyes.

Tollan switched on the car engine and placed both hands on the steering wheel. That seemed to be his answer to the question. Starting the car was code for end of conversation. Time to leave. Jenny put her hand on the door handle and clicked it open.

He revved the engine. The power of the car transferred to his mind. He had control of something. He spoke gently. "Listen hen, when yi wanted somethin yi came tae me. Ah helped yi oot. Ah'm no runnin a fuckin charity. Yir in ma book for eight hundred and eighty. That's the fuckin truth."

91

Jenny saw a chink in the armour. He was talking. She took her hand of the door handle. She could now strike for her real target. To get the debt frozen.

"I'm not denying that I owe you eight hundred and eighty pounds. The interest has mounted up. I'm not arguing on that. I will pay it all off. What I'm hoping is that you'll freeze the debt. Give me a chance to get out. Just keep it at eight hundred and eighty and I will pay it all off."

Suddenly, imperceptibly, sexual attraction invaded the discussion. Tollan had always felt that Jenny found him attractive. There was something in there which he had never explored.

He closed the discussion. "Whit Ah will dae, is this. Ah'll tell Kenny yir aff the book. Ah'll collect yir money masel. Ah don't want Kenny or anybody else knowin that Ah done yi a fuckin favour. That's no a bad deal, is it? Ah'll come up to yir place to collect on Tuesday mornin. Nae hassle."

Jenny liked the sound of this. She uncrossed her legs and straightened up in the seat. Jimmy saw what he was meant to see – the inside of her strong thighs and the curve of her breasts.

"Thanks. I'll see on Tuesday mornin. About ten thirty. I'll be ready."

And she was.

So much so that Jimmy Tollan fell in love with her. She had looked appealing in the car that afternoon, gently teasing out his dormant interest with the movement of her long legs in the restricted space. In the warmth of her home, with Christine at school, Jenny turned up the animal attraction.

Ten thirty is not best of time to seduce a man who knows you are a prostitute and has you in his financial pocket. A subtle perfume, a loose black cotton dress, no stockings and no bra, and a little rich red lipstick, but no make-up. Her nipples, almost upward on firm breasts caught the dress material. His eyes followed her shapely ankles above the pink slippers and long legs down the hallway as she took him to the neat living room in the small two-bedroom flat.

He wasn't too sure of himself. "Ah didnae think yi'd be in, love. Thought yi'd body swerve me," he said with a laugh.

She ignored the opportunity to respond to the friendly comment with any innuendo about body swerving. "Not at all Jimmy. It's nice to have you come up to see me. Would you like a cup of tea? Milk and sugar?"

The kettle had been boiled in preparation. She'd overlooked getting in some booze. Lack of money. He followed her into the tiny kitchen as she pressed the kettle back on and turned brushing past him to open the fridge door and lift out a small jug of milk. There were two delicate china mugs and a bowl of sugar on the worktop next to the sink.

Jimmy tried to move out of Jenny's way as she straightened up from the fridge turning to place the milk jug next to the mugs.

"There's no much space in here," he said, observing the curve of her cleavage. Jenny looked into his dark brown eyes and smiled. "You can say that again. You get to know people intimately in my kitchen."

"Let's no bother wi the tea just now," he said as she placed the milk jug beside the sugar bowl. Jenny turned her body back to his. They were facing each other, almost touching.

"We'll get the tea later. Follow me," she said warmly.

"Wait a minute Jenny. Whit aboot a wee kiss?"

"OK."

He gave her a restrained but firm and open kiss, and felt the thrust of her tongue exploring his mouth gently. Their mouths parted in unison. Jimmy looked into her blue eyes as his cock grew to erection. "Wait a minute Jenny. Yir tryin a bit too much."

"I'm not."

"Yes you fuckin are."

"Don't mention fucking. Just follow me."

She squeezed past and he asked, "Where's the toilet?"

"On the left hand side in the hall."

He came out and went into the wrong bedroom. A cuddly toy on the pillow. Wet Wet Wet on the walls. Family pictures. A kid's two wheeler bike.

"Where are you?"

From another room he heard her tease. "I've changed my mind. I'm going for the messages."

"Oh no you're fuckin not," he said walking into her bedroom, his erection enclosed in a condom.

Jenny was lying, not in the bed but on it, naked, long legged and relaxed in the knowledge that the seduction had gone better than planned. Jimmy Tollan had come to the flat for sex without realising that Jenny had enticed him, with the intention of getting his body and then some control of his mind. So far so good.

"Take your socks and shoes off."

He sat on the bed to take them off while she pulled his T shirt up.

"Fur fucks sake, wait a minute Jenny." She was kneeling behind him, rolling the shirt up. She lay back allowing him to undress completely before turning to lean down and kiss her upturned face.

He placed his hand on her breast feeling the nipple in the palm of his hand.

"Do you want to take the condom off?"

"Naw. Ah'll keep it on."

"You can if you want but there is no need of it," she said confidently, "I'm on the pill and nobody since my husband has screwed me without one on."

He sensed that the morning's sex would be particularly enjoyable. He was excited anticipating a varied exploration of a new woman and wanted the condom off.

"Are yi sure?"

"I'm sure but it's up to you."

The only sound in the nicely furnished warm flat was the occasional passing car. The atmosphere was of a friendly conspiracy.

"I'll take it off for you, if you want Jimmy?"

He said nothing. She slipped her hand across to draw the condom off, dropping it onto the floor. Her long thighs, firm flesh, blue eyes merged into a sexual concoction which totally satisfied his appetite. They had sex twice. Jenny faked an orgasm the second time.

Jimmy came as close to falling in love as was possible for him. He was getting something more than physical satisfaction – he was hooked on a sexual performance that inflamed his passion awakening thoughts of a long term relationship. Christ she was a good looking woman. They chatted over tea.

"Ah didnae know yi wir married Jenny?"

"I never told you. Why should I? He left me for another woman."

"He must be fuckin daft," said Jimmy with cheap flattery. Jenny took the words at face value.

"No. He was far from daft. It was never really going to last. We weren't compatible."

"Yi mean he wisnae any good in bed."

"He wasn't bad. Sometimes. But he wasn't that interested. That's the way it goes I suppose."

The morning could not have gone more perfectly for Jenny who felt that the worst scenario would be for Tollan to get a free fuck to his satisfaction and agree to freeze her debt.

The ideal outcome was that he liked her so much that he would either wipe the debt off if she was very lucky, or more likely freeze the amount. One or other was now looking like a decided possibility, for she knew that Jimmy Tollan was a happy man. Jenny believed that she had wrested some of his power off him. That they now had a relationship based on mutual attraction forged in passionate sex that gave her a better status than the other women trapped in his financial web.

She broached the subject of freezing the debt, going directly to the heart of the matter. "Jimmy I think you and I are compatible. I feel that . . ."

He anticipated her every thought and outfoxed her easily turning the conversation into a sad joke. "Ah'm spoken fur already love. Rita and me are a fixture. That's a fuckin fact o' life."

"No. That's not what I was going to say. I'm happy with this arrangement. Just as long as I know when you are coming up so that, if Christine is off school I can take her round to her gran's."

She paused. He knew what was coming and said nothing allowing her to introduce her plea for financial mercy.

"What I mean is that it's obvious you like me. I feel the same way. So why don't we come to an arrangement about the money I owe you?"

"We've got an arrangement already hen. Ah come doon here every Tuesday tae save yi goin up tae pay Kenny," he said with a glow of satisfaction.

He was again exercising his power. They were in another game now. Their relaxed sexual pleasures a few minutes earlier forgotten as Jenny failed abysmally to manipulate the loan shark entrenched in his monetary fixation.

Jenny was in deeper now. The bastard was immoveable. The fear that drove her into this farce, the terrible beating from a client who might have murdered her, had dulled into just another bad experience. Now she was trapped in a sexual relationship with Tollan, instigated by herself without his knowledge and worthless on all fronts.

There was no love in it for her. Nor money. There was an understanding that she fancied him. She couldn't charge him for sex. And she would have to make sure that Christine was never around when he arrived.

The stress factors in Jenny Mullen's life were extending remorselessly. Ahead lay a minefield of consequences to herself, her daughter, her mother-in-law. Her chaotic life would be invaded by social workers. Her ex-husband would re-appear to pick up the pieces of his daughter's dismal childhood.

She was out of control.

Easy pickings for the TV researcher Eddie Anderson who offered her two hundred to tell the nation about her poverty, the violence, the prostitution and her fear of an unnamed loan shark. The social workers acted as a go-between telling her that it was entirely up to her whether or not she helped them. She would not have to give her name. The cash was handy. Her motives were understandable. Jimmy Tollan the lover she seduced but failed to manipulate might be arrested as a result of the programme.

For the present however, Jenny faked her orgasms every Tuesday morning after collecting her cash from the post office. Tuesday was the highlight of Jimmy's busy week for this was power beyond his wildest dreams.

Jimmy continued to collect his cash and enjoy his Tuesday morning sex.

12 Fleece and flies

THE INJUSTICE of it all was too much for Margaret Hazlewood.

Her heart bled for them. The poor struggling families who turned to loan sharks. The whole mess angered Margaret. She hated the government rather than the loan sharks.

The Tories were the enemy. When given the chance to help spread the news about poverty levels leading to entrapment by loan sharks she jumped in at the deep end. Money was not her motive. Hatred drove her into danger. Hatred of the money-grabbing spivs she watched nightly discussing the state of the nation. TV talking heads trying to win power and influence people.

Margaret, a tiny slip of a girl with glowing cheeks, was immensely beautiful, yet millions saw her on TV and none of them noticed her. They didn't realise that they had seen her. They weren't looking for her.

In the safety of their homes they gazed at the glittering TV screens and they saw what they were meant to see. The images designed to entertain, shock, and hold their attention until the tea break.

They saw the evil loan shark. They heard him growling instructions at a poverty stricken mother begging for a loan. The TV tube took them inside a Glasgow pub. They saw the power of the loan shark, his weighty shoulders hunched inside a black leather jacket and they sensed his authority within the dingy establishment.

Twelve million viewers heard Jimmy pulling the financial strings. The instructions fired out at Kenny Watson had the authority of the boss – "Send her across tae me."

The voices were as rough as steel rasps. Grating on the ear. Designed to command. Developed to spread fear. The viewers were caught, mesmerised by the raw action unfolding in their front rooms. They didn't notice the five feet one inch tall girl leaning at the bar only three feet from Tollan. She was no eye catcher. Her beauty was only seen by those who looked more closely. By those who met the girl, who understood the humanity in her deep blue eyes. The viewers never saw her face, nor did they hear the loan shark instruct the barman. "Tam. Serve this wee lassie."

That was edited out. The name of the game was to present a rounded package. To inform, to expose, and to present the evidence. And in the classic completion of investigative TV reporting, present documented proof to win a court conviction.

Margaret was in there, in the heat of the action carrying the microphone that picked up the very voices of the participants in the filthy financial deals.

Yet Margaret Hazlewood was far from streetwise. She found the colourless scheme streets offensive and was therefore unable to settle within the street environment. In fact she was repelled by the poverty of spirit, the lack of hope, that hit her with repeated sledgehammer blows.

She was sick to her stomach of seeing so much human wastage. She was full of simmering resentment. Her participation in a loan shark hunt began with a phone call from above.

"Hello. Margaret here. Can I help you?" she said on autopilot, expecting it to be one of the social workers from Garthill. They had a report to do on a child abuse case and would be seeking guidance on this highly sensitive matter. There was also an application being prepared for European funding.

"Hello, Margaret. John Campbell speaking, would you come up and see me please?"

The Depute Director no less. On her way in his secretary asked, "Tea or coffee?" Tea was her choice, milk, no sugar, and she chose an upright seat at the end of his conference table. Stay upright. Stay alert. Pay attention.

He smiled warmly. "Margaret I have a job for you that is a bit different from the usual. Are you interested?" he teased.

"What is it? Why the mystery Mr Campbell?"

"I want you to be a minder. Look after some people for us." The voice was friendly. His eyes twinkled.

There weren't going to be any problems here. The boss was in fine fettle and obviously expected her agreement. He let her into the secret. An independent TV company were in Glasgow to film a documentary on illegal money lending. The department were keen to co-operate. He didn't have to explain why they were committed to supporting the programme. Socialism was an unspoken pact these days. They both believed that any exposure of the plight suffered by the poor would damage the Tories. Eventually the country would realise the folly of policies driving broken unemployed families into the gutter.

Her role was to support the researcher and producer. At the same time she would attempt to shield the loan shark victims from too much exposure on TV. First stop was the Holiday Inn where she met the front runners in the programme preparation. Eddie the researcher, Nigel the producer and Walter a hardened hack ex-tabloid newspaper man, who seemed to be relishing the food more than the conversation. He devoured a T-bone steak, followed by apple pie and cream. He washed it down with several brandies, at lunch time, and he didn't slur his words, of which there were many.

His contribution was an endless stream of odd-sounding clichés. "We'll hit these loan sharks with the facts. These guys won't know what hit them. I'll check the voters' roll for addresses. We've got the names and three of the streets. The problem might be ID'ing them in the pub. We'll stake it out first with one of the victims."

The more he drank, the more bizarre was his input. "A baseball bat. That's what we'll need. I'll get one at the Sportsman's Emporium."

Walter was right. They would need a baseball bat and they would need to buy it. The chances of catching a loan shark baseball batting a victim were a million to one. He was right about everything. It was the way he talked. Was she in the right movie?

She tried to change gear, to tune in to this amazing world of news and make-do. Facts and fantasy. All in the name of truth. They talked about finding a professional to sing a song about loan sharking. A sad ballad about a girl who turned to crime to pay off the loan sharks. They played around with some lyrics.

Margaret wondered. What was she getting herself into? Was this all a mistake? Her perspective of illegal money lending and its consequences was somewhat removed from a satirical song! Should she report back to the Depute Director on the direction in which the programme appeared to moving?

Nigel, sensitive to the mood changes in those he led and those he manipulated, picked up on her unvoiced doubts.

He looked her in the eye. "I can see what you're thinking and I don't blame you Margaret. But don't worry. Television has its own problems. We have to think in picture terms. And if that means buying a bat to use a stunted sequence on the legs of our own researcher then so be it. We know that these things happen Margaret. We have to depict them happening. Would you like another lemonade?"

Her abundant red hair bounced as she laughed freely at his efforts to retain her confidence in their professionalism.

"Don't worry Nigel. I'm not worried. I am sure the end product will be fine. Anyway it's not for me to make any judgements on how you put your programme together. I wouldn't expect you to be able to make decisions on which children are taken from their families for their own safety. Each to his own."

Nigel's response was half serious. "That would make a good programme."

She gave him a knowing look. "Leave that one until next year Nigel. We've got enough on our plate with loan sharks."

The 'we' reassured him that Margaret was still

101

committed to making it all happen. She had reservations though. They wanted too much. The names of families who had begged for financial help after being trapped in loan shark deals. The children taken into care when their parents lost control. Women who had turned to prostitution to make the payments.

She listened patiently as they sold the idea of telling it like it is. Then she got down to brass tacks. What did they want first from the department?

"Two social work vans please. We need them for surveillance at the post offices in Garthill, Ruchazie, Drumchapel, and Royston. And at two or three addresses in Garthill and Maryhill. We would like to change the side and back windows in each of the vans. Make them one-way so that we can watch them and they can't see us."

She smiled at that one. "Yes that's the way to do it. Watch the poor going about their daily business, borrowing and paying. Watch their paymasters at work."

He understood her wry reaction. "Yes. It does reek of big brother at work. Maybe of voyeurism. That can't be helped however, because we need to show how the poor have to pay more for what they need. Credit costs them a fortune, and so does a can of beans. They pay more for beans in the schemes than at the large supermarkets. Of course they can't afford cars. Not many of them."

Margaret responded with a wry smile and a bad Cockney accent. "Not a lot of people know that."

Nigel smiled back patiently and tried to pull her away from cynicism back onto socialism. He needed her wholehearted support.

She didn't let him off the hook easily. "Yes, Nigel. And the poor buy mince that is pink not red like the good steak mince in your local butchers. They eat more fat in a week than you do in a year. Why don't you expose the butchers who are ripping them off with fatty mince? Or the local shops charging them three and four pence more for all essential items? Not sexy enough?"

They were sparring with each other with the ethics of

102

the day. He defended himself. There was a lift in his voice as he answered that one with confidence.

"I'll have you know that before producing these investigations I worked on a series of health programmes for afternoon TV. We had two chefs preparing good healthy meals. How to eat well on twenty pounds per week. What to eat to avoid heart complaints. We costed out each meal. Most informative it was too. I'm following some of the advice myself."

The conversation was turning into a discussion. It was in serious danger of becoming a nasty little argument as they sparred over the delicate matter of motivation.

Margaret stood her ground. "No doubt it was a most responsible programme Nigel. Millions of poor people started eating vegetables, Weetabix, and low fat milk. They stopped buying meat. Started eating fish and fruit. Maybe they even stopped smoking."

Then she got serious. "You don't change a nation's eating habits overnight by a TV programme."

"That's right. You don't. Still, every little helps."

She wouldn't let go. "Every little helps fill up the day time schedules. You don't get people to exercise by having a man prance about on the TV every morning either. That's when people have a cup of tea. Or read the paper. Get shaved."

"Not if they are unemployed."

"Nigel," she paused for impact. "If they are unemployed the chances are they are still in bed."

"I give in."

"No. Don't give in, or you'll never get the programme in the can. That's the expression, isn't it? In the can?"

"Not these days it isn't. It's video film now. And we need to get at least one loan shark on tape, plus, if possible, interviews with a few more victims."

Margaret went home carrying another load of soiled social baggage. She ducked the hardest job, leaving her husband to check their son's homework.

Margaret Hazlewood had grown up in the country,

on a small sheep farm in the gentle Argyll hills behind Oban. She rose in a loving world where mother nature ruled in the wetness of mild winters and the soft warmth of spring bringing dark green gorse, light green bracken and the haze of heather. Argyllshire was in her soul.

Her memories were precious. They cost nothing. No trips to Florida, or Spain, or even a caravan. Her parents had never been abroad. They were too busy on their rented hill farm to worry about a suntan or the price of a package holiday. A day out was to the annual Oban Highland Games. The skirl of pipers in competition, the little girls dancing their flings on drizzle covered platforms, the caber tossers. A day of muscle and music, jammed car parks ending in a ceilidh and staggering harmless drunks.

She remembered her father losing his temper very rarely. Over a lost lamb or a tractor breakdown. His edginess when a summer storm ruined the one hay field they relied on for the two milking cows' winter feed.

He was an active man. Doing, rather than watching. Doing, rather than buying.

He included her in everything. She went along when he took her young brother fly-fishing from a rowing boat on a deep brown loch not far from home. They stayed out until after dusk. Sometimes she got to hold the rod while he changed the trout flies. They rowed back and tied the boat up to the old tree next to the gravel inlet at the burn. The long walk up the hill. She was always last going up that hill, but made sure that she caught up with them before they entered the house.

She didn't want to miss the fun. Margaret delighted in the game he always played, giving the brown trout they had caught to her young brother who dropped the bag of fish outside the door. Her father bent into the low roofed farmhouse. They followed him in. Her mother had heard their muffled voices carrying in the dank midge-filled air. There was always a pot of tea on the table, some scones, and her mother's question. "Did you get any tonight, Angus?"

He lifted the teapot to pour himself a cup and sighed. "A bad night. They were jumping earlier. We lost four flies."

William joined in the game. "My line got snagged twice on the weeds near the entrance to the burn. I lost one fly."

The fishing flies would be replaced by her father's patient application. The image would never leave her. He would take a size fourteen hook out of his little box, cut the edge of a pheasant feather, take some brown wool and another piece of feather, then meticulously bind them onto the hook. Home-made trout flies that more often than not fooled the trout.

Mother fell for the failed fishing trip story every time. "You would all have been better staying here. John McKay and his wife dropped in on the way to the whist drive. They wanted us to go with them."

As she talked William would nip out and return with the bag of fish, to state happily. "You can give them one of these tomorrow. I got two of them. Dad got the other three."

He took hold of the largest sea trout at its back tail fin, holding it up for his mother to view. The little game never palled. Mum was pleased and five fish caught in the darkening light on the loch produced dinner for the following evening.

A myriad of such memories glittered in her subconcious, never to be erased. They would still be there the day she died. When the games she played for this TV documentary had faded into a blur of nameless people and unidentified locations.

Margaret might have got the etchings in her mind from books. She might have received her insight from music. She never rationalised her childhood, which left her ill-prepared for her job in the big city. She was shocked by the the barren lives of dole families, trapped in soulless schemes with little hope and less money.

Too many years of Toryism. Her mind screamed in rage. Benefit cuts at every turn. Grants for bedding and cookers turned into loans overnight. Crisis loans that dried up within months of being on offer. Kids joining the adult

105

game without any money after the Tories cut their benefit to nothing.

Nobody seemed to respond to the government's message. Stand on your own two feet. Be enterprising. The gap was too wide between the rich and the poor. It was a chasm. Too wide to cross. It wasn't so much money, although that was a major problem. Or feelings. Lifestyle. Conviction. Confidence. Communication. It was everything. The gap was enormous.

Several rungs of the ladder were missing. In her heart she knew that the ideal of glorious or even comfortable yesterdays just wouldn't come back.

She would work hard to catch Tollan, the product of Tory policies.

At least that was how she saw it.

13 Parole of inconvenience

JIMMY TOLLAN was nervous and it showed. He was chewing gum ferociously. Tapping the grey desk with his fingers. His dark brown eyes flitted round the office.

"How long is this gonnie take. He's gonnie take his fuckin time today," he mused.

Outwardly Jimmy was trying to create a different impression. "Yea Paul. Things are goin awright. Ah thought it would be more difficult. Rita's made it easy fur me. She's pleased Ah'm hame. Genuinely pleased. She's OK."

He convinced himself and in so doing almost convinced the parole officer.

"And what about the little boy? How is he managing with you back in the house? Even more important, how are you coping with him?"

Jimmy could field this one easily. The boy would never deny that the relationship was good. He simply was not old enough to comprehend and Jimmy never put any pressure on him directly. Sure he had a good relationship with the boy. He bought him the new trainers and took him to the caravan.

"Ah love wee Matt. Ah do. We'll always get on fine."

'Love' was not a word that crossed his lips very often.

This was his seventh fortnightly visit since being released. The parole game he knew inside out. At the beginning this guy had been a bit heavy with the advice though. Don't get into any more trouble. Slow down. Take it easy.

The usual stuff. "Any problems come and see me. This is an introduction to me. We won't make it too long. Come back and see me in a fortnight's time."

Now, seven visits on, the conversations were more intimate. The social worker had more knowledge of Jimmy's domestic situation, his lifestyle and his thought process. He knew the man's demeanour. Knew where he could plug in to start a dialogue.

"I see Rangers have sold Steven for a lot of money. They made a profit on him."

Jimmy didn't see it that way. "They'll regret sellin him. He makes it all happen. You don't sell quality players if yi want tae win the European Cup. They'll pay fur that sale."

Mr Anderson introduced the domestic scene neatly. "Does Matt go to Ibrox with you?"

"Naw, he's too wee. He's no interested anyway."

"How's he doing at school?"

"Awright."

The conversation was drying up to the point of no return.

Mr Anderson dropped the subtle line, using his official position to ask some direct questions.

"How are you getting on in the job hunting field? Any interviews yet?"

"Yes," he lied. "Ah hiv a good chance of a job as a roofer with a wee firm aff Duke Street. The guy knows ma past but he's no bothered because he's no that clean himsel."

Mr Anderson saw the danger signs there and advised Jimmy. "Don't get yourself into something that could lead to more trouble. A job is important, but not that important."

Jimmy had him on the run and pressed on with a little more deceit.

"Ah know whit you're saying. The guy's dodgy. Ah'm taking that intae consideration before Ah decide tae take it or no."

He added more to the nonsense. "Ah've been goin doon tae the Job Club at the Cross. No much daein there."

The farce of deceit and self-deceit was endless as they acted out the ritual that earned Mr Anderson eighteen thousand pounds a year and wasted Jimmy's valuable collection time.

The session ended on a sympathetic note from Mr Anderson. "You seem to be doing allright. I'll be on holiday for a fortnight, so I'll see you in three weeks."

Jimmy walked from the building slowly, turned the

corner, crossed over the street and jumped into the Audi with Kenny already at the wheel.

"Up tae Johnny McPherson's hoose. Fast. Before the wee cunt disappears fur the day."

He made no reference whatsoever to the parole visit. Kenny didn't want to know and he understood that Jimmy would not want to talk. It was, in both their books, wasted time.

Kenny swung the Audi round, taking the shortest route to Johnny's home. He wasn't in.

"We cannae waste time on him. He'll show up eventually. Did yi get all of them at the post offices this mornin?"

"Most of them. Jenny Mullen didnae show. Ah thought we could rely on her. She's intae yi fur over eight hunner Jimmy."

Jimmy retorted. "That fuckin bitch is provin mair trouble than Ah thought. She's fuckin us about."

Kenny rarely indulged in a joke. This one was too good to resist.

"She's no just fuckin us about. She's fuckin half o' Glasgow. She's on the gemme."

Jimmy laughed grotesquely. "That's good news for us pal. It means she's got the money tae pay me. Leave her tae me. Ah'll sort her oot."

Jimmy hadn't told Kenny that he was now sleeping with and collecting from Jenny Mullen.

There was nothing personal about his day to day relationship with Kenny. It was 'us' when there was a problem of payments and 'me' when talking money.

They were as deeply trapped in the sad game as the people they hounded daily for payments. Not that Tollan and Watson considered it for a moment but in the loan sharking game there were similarities with the financial dealers in the city. Hard work. Concentration. A ruthless streak. The difference was that Jimmy and Kenny, operated outside the law. They understood the consequences of crime. The ups and the downs. Coming out of jail was an up that required careful attention. Fuck up parole and Jimmy could be back inside.

He was four hours late for the next meeting with Paul Anderson. He should have clocked in with the bastard at ten. He made it at two. The parole officer was mildly irritated but relieved to see his client turning up on the required day. There would be no need to file a report to the board that Tollan had broken his parole terms.

The loan shark compensated for being so late by indulging himself in his own brand of honesty coupled with sincere declarations of intent. "Sorry Ah'm late Paul. Ah've nae excuse. Ah'll make sure it disnae happen again." He spoke like an innocent little schoolboy. It had to be said and it had to be heard.

"Jimmy. This is your eighth appointment and you are four hours late. You're beginning to slip. Not good Jimmy. We need a commitment here. The reports from jail were very positive. In fairness to you Jimmy, you didn't come up with any crap about a job interview. Or trouble at home. But you should be here on time." That was supposed to be said.

He stood up. "Tea or coffee?"

"Coffee, milk and sugar please," he replied standing up to put his hand into his pocket. "Ah'll get them."

The social worker waved aside the change proffered. "Don't be daft. Save your money. I'll get them."

Jimmy started with the honesty stuff. The truth. "Rita and me urnae gettin on so well. Ah'm moving oot the hoose. That's the way it is. Ah feel that's best fur all of us. Wee Matt too. Ah'm hopin tae get a place up the flats at Carnwadric."

He paused, leant back in the chair, looked into Anderson's eyes and waited for a response. He got what he wanted. Sympathy and understanding.

"That's a setback for you, I know. Give her time. She made the visits when you were in prison. There were factors for her to come to terms with when you came out."

He took a sip of tea and resumed. "Bear in mind that

Rita has been living alone for nearly three years now. Give her time. Give yourself time."

The only other reference to the split was about Matt. Jimmy made sure there was no problem on that front. "Ah can see Matt regular like. That's nae problem."

Jimmy Tollan had slipped into the role that would satisfy the social worker. The harsh truth was that he had told Rita he was not putting up with any more interference. She had asked him to let a client, one of her acquaintances, out of the trap.

"Take her out your book. She cannae manage. Her sister asked me tae ask you."

This was a challenge to his authority. To his control. Rita saw his eyes glint. She heard the words before he spat them out.

"Fuck aff and mind yir ain business."

The request escalated into a nasty row with Rita telling Jimmy to, "get out of my fuckin house."

He was so angry at the loss of control that he walked out telling her he would get his own place. He would go back for sex when he felt like it. When he wanted back in on a permanent basis he would buy a few presents or take them up to the caravan for a weekend break. That would sweeten her.

Mr Anderson began to doubt his client. He never learnt the details of the couple's fall out. It was not his job to spy on nor investigate Tollan and his girlfriend. Just to act as a link between prison and a normal life and to see that Tollan obeyed the rules of his parole. But the social worker sensed that Tollan was beginning to break loose.

Jimmy pressed his sincerity bit. "There's nae danger of me haunin out any mair cash. Ah'll no dae it. They huv been at me and Ah'm turnin them aw doon."

"That's good," said Mr Anderson. What else could he say? It did cross his mind to enquire as to how Tollan could make loans when he was unemployed and drawing dole money. He decided that raising it would only irritate Tollan. Keep the pressure off him.

They talked for a while, about life as single man, about living alone. About the pressures of life without a job. Too easy to drift into drink. To lose the will to get out of bed. They were filling in time. That was all.

Jimmy, believing that he had set the right tone with Anderson, decided to assert himself a little. He stood abruptly up.

"Ah've got a bus tae catch. Ah'm goin doon tae the housin to try fur a flat."

"I won't keep you any longer. A decent flat is what you need more than a talk with me. I'll expect you back in two weeks time."

The following day Mr Anderson received a minor jolt. He saw Jimmy Tollan coming out of a restaurant in the city centre. Dressed to the nines. The loan shark crossed the street and climbed into a brand new Audi.

At the next meeting the parole officer inquired about his client's car. He phrased his inquiry gently. "Jimmy, I have seen you several times in a smart car. What's the score?"

Tollan shrugged. His right shoulder actually moved. He said. "The fact is Ah'm OK financially. Ah hud money put away before Ah went tae the jail."

The visit was desultory. Neither talked with enthusiasm. They were uneasy. The truth lay before them. That Jimmy was doing well financially and that the social worker was merely fulfilling a role to earn enough for the mortgage and a four year old car.

Jimmy Tollan had ceased trying to ingratiate himself. He could buy and sell the bastard with the cash he was raking in every week. Anyway he was only doing the punters a service. The punters were his people. The impact of prison was receding fast. The parole was almost played out.

Yes, he had found a flat. He had 'nae problems.' No, there was 'nae danger' of slipping back into crime. That was the brief and he stuck to it for the duration.

The worst crisis occurred when some youths broke into Rita's, stealing the TV, video recorder, music centre and ninety six pounds from the drawer in the rosewood wall unit.

Jimmy told Mr Anderson of the break-in. "Ah don't know who they are yet. They must be fuckin mad. Breaking intae ma Rita's place."

Mr Anderson saw, what he perceived to be the danger, pointing out that whether on parole or not Jimmy should not exact retribution.

"Retri-fuckin-bution! They won't know what's fuckin hit them. And it'll no be down tae me."

He paused to let that piece of street-cunning sink in, then explained the pain and suffering inflicted on himself by the break-in at Rita's home. "Dae yi know how much it cost me tae replace the fuckin stuff? A TV? A video? And a fuckin music centre?"

The social worker was lost for words.

Where was the deferential ex-prisoner, intent on become a caring family man? The man seeking a crime-free life and a job?

Tollan couldn't drop the subject. "Ah don't live with Rita any mair. So why the fuck did Ah pay oot tae replace the stuff?"

The answer as he well knew was that he had the money to spare. That his son lived with Rita. That he was the man. With the money. Tax free money on tap.

Tollan had ceased any pretence of seeking a job. He no longer spouted platitudes about becoming an honest citizen intending to settle down in the community.

He was what he was. A convicted loan shark. A hard man with a record as long as his arm. What was he supposed to do? Take a job on the buses. Fuck aff. His business was expanding. The book was bigger now than before the jail sentence. He was helping more punters than ever.

Remorse? That was for fuckin mugs.

Parole was part of the business. The easiest part.

When asked about his free spending lifestyle, petrol for the new car, smart new clothes, and the cost of replacing items stolen from Rita, he admitted that he had cash in several building society accounts. Only from his previous dealings, he assured him.

Jimmy maintained there were 'nae problems.'

Not to Kenny though. The problems were numerous. Old Dennie wasn't coming up with the cash regular. Johnny McPherson had done a runner.

Kenny Watson was another problem. Tollan couldn't quite figure him out. He was keeping something to himself.

Jimmy kept everything back from the social worker who closed his Continuation Sheet without much conviction that Jimmy would stay on the straight and narrow. As the parole time drew to an end Jimmy dropped his carefully developed image of the contrite remorseful criminal, while maintaining that he had not returned to illegal money lending.

Anderson's written words reflected his serious doubts. And at the end of six months parole the social worker was in little doubt that his client would return to crime. The final entry read,

Client now admitting that he has plenty of money.
Client has money in three building society accounts. Says the money is from the money lending case for which he was jailed. Considering his attitude to that crime, that he was providing a service, it seems likely that Mr Tollan will again offend.
Case closed.

The parole of inconvenience was over. He had told them what they wanted to hear. He fooled no one and he didn't care.

14 It's how you tell them

WALTER HARVEY almost quit the job on the first day. The sight of the pub shook his resolve. The taxi that carried him from the Holiday Inn to this eyesore was disappearing in the drizzle behind the towering concrete flats. His lifeline to safety had gone. He turned round to take a good look at his destination.

The Black Inn, haunt of the hardest loan shark in the scheme, where Jimmy Tollan clinched his miserable one-sided deals.

A more uninviting hostelry he had never seen. "A fuckin pillbox!" – this from a man who had supped in the best and worst, from Plymouth to Wick.

His eyes drifted across the squat square building. A miniature prison. Dirty graffiti-smeared concrete; iron bars guarded the windows; the roof was encircled with razor wire. The message was simple. Keep out. You are not welcome.

If a building could be evil, this was it. Though it was hardly a building. More a statement. "Fuck you lot. You've no money. There's no profit in you. It is this or nothing."

The pub extended its business into money lending, fencing of stolen goods, drug dealing. The sort of business that would attract local custom. The poor needed money, or goods at knockdown prices. Their children, shaken by the instability of their home lives, wanted drugs.

Supply and demand. The market ruled.

The Black Inn often changed hands from one criminal to another. They ducked and weaved changing locations when circumstances ruled. They used the till to launder the profits of crime.

Walter recoiled from its violent exterior. He was frightened. The harsh realities of this particular job were piercing his mind. He wasn't even inside the pillbox yet. If the taxi had turned in the street he would have hailed it and headed back to the hotel for a quick drink.

The gleaming red Audi parked outside the door amongst the broken bottle debris was the only clean thing in sight. Everything was dirty and ugly. Even the children and the dogs. They looked lost and manky. He went ahead, ducking under the half opened shutter door into the dark hole. There was some light spreading inward from three small windows set high on the walls. The gantry was lit. He walked straight to the bar. Natural like.

The barman was in conversation with a heavily built man in a black leather jacket. They both ignored him. Almost a minute had passed when Walter made the conscious decision to make his presence felt. Only because he was there to find Tollan. To observe the man at work. It had to be done.

Walter established himself as a punter in for a pint. "You serving here mate?" he asked the barman, who glanced up and asked, "Whit dae yi want?"

The question was so general in both words and tone, that Walter considered replying. "Could you help me please. I am looking for Jimmy Tollan, the ruthless loan shark. Is he here and if he is, what is he doing in this shitty pub?"

The crazy questions zipped across his mind. Internal tension.

What he actually said was – "A pint of heavy, mate." He sat down at one of four tables in the half light and realised that he had come without a prop. He had taken the precaution of removing his tie. Nobody wearing a tie had ever been in here. Maybe somebody from the brewery on the day the concrete shit hole opened.

He had forgotten to bring a newspaper. He was sitting in splendid isolation. Alone. With a pint and nothing with which to lower his profile, a stranger in the pub without a newspaper. Nowhere to point his eyes.

He shook himself. Get a grip. Nobody in the pub knows you are a spy. You are just a middle-aged stranger drinking a pint. Sure they wanted to know who he was. They wouldn't ask though.

He was halfway through the pint when he decided to take a minor step into the investigation. He went to the bar and asked, "Have you got a paper mate? For the racing?"

"Naw, Ah hivnae. Jimmy hiv yi got a paper?" the barman called over to the man wearing the black leather jacket who had moved to a table and was chatting to a square set, well-built young man.

"Ay. There yi are, pal. Gie us it back when yir finished wi it. See if yi see a cert, tell us aboot it," he said. There was no threat in the voice. He was as friendly as anybody could be in such a den.

Jimmy Tollan's street wisdom was switched on. He wanted to know what the stranger was about. The game was on. And it was being played at home, on his dirty park.

Jimmy punted regularly. He had the money. Almost two hundred thousand pounds a year in takings. Plenty for Rita and Matt, when it suited him to push them a bit extra. Plenty for petrol, a car, a caravan, clothes, holidays. There was plenty left to gamble.

Walter was gaining confidence. The very act of talking to the black leather jacket had helped. This, he felt sure was his target. Jimmy Tollan. All he had to do was read the man's paper slowly, order another drink, wait, listen and watch surreptitiously.

Tollan had other ideas. He called over to Walter. "Goose Pimps looks a cert in the two thirty. It's no carrying the weight it had at Plumpton."

He might as well have hit Walter with a baseball bat, or a stun gun. For he never bet the horses or dogs. The hack preferred to spend his money on quality whisky and good wine while talking newspaper politics and big stories.

"Ay, right," he said.

Jimmy came back with a direct question. "Whit dae yi fancy yersel?"

"I'm not sure," said Walter trying to sustain some credibility. He was holding the paper open at the TV page! Shit.

Tollan turned away. The communication ceased for

a moment. Walter quickly moved to the racing pages and selected a horse running at Hamilton. "I like the look of Warts Blimp at Hamilton. It's due a win."

Tollan looked across and asked. "Are yi goin doon tae Hamilton?"

Walter was floundering. It had been too easy for Tollan who didn't even know that Walter wasn't a betting man.

Walter fell at the first.

"No. It's too late. I'll just put it on at the bookies."

Tollan hit back casually. "It's no too late. Yi could fuckin walk there in time. Warts Blimp's in the seven thirty."

Walter's heart missed a beat. He looked more carefully at the Hamilton race card. Evening racing. Jesus!

He looked across at Tollan who had turned away to face the hard looking young man who shared his table. He was talking quietly to the guy, who was concentrating on the loan shark's every word.

Walter measured the distance to the door, making a mental note that he would need to duck slightly to avoid the three quarters open shutter.

Walter couldn't hear the words between Tollan and his drinking companion. He imagined them to be, "We will need to find out who the fuck he is."

He was almost right.

Jimmy had muttered, "Ah want tae know who the fuck he is. He's no a cop. They wouldnae come in here. They're no that fuckin stupid. No wan at a time."

Bravado.

Walter was suffering the opposite of bravado. His stomach was churning. He knew that the stakes were high. That Tollan would act there and then to prevent any danger of exposure. Nobody in this pub would help. None of them would see anything. He could be dragged to the toilet. Knifed.

His saviour was a tall good-looking woman. She straightened up after dipping under the shutter to enter the pub. Tollan had his back to her. She paused for a second, brushed her dark red hair back off her eyes, pushed her leather skirt down her long thighs so that it fitted snugly and walked across to Tollan.

"Hi Jimmy. I was up seeing a friend so I dropped in to see you. I've got it with me," she said placing her handbag on the table and starting to unclip it. The words were spoken softly but carried in the dead of the empty pub.

Walter heard every word.

Tollan's voice was sharp. "No here hen. Sit doon and fuckin shut up."

There was a pronouced pause between each of his next words. "Keep your fuckin mouth shut. Say fuck all."

The loan shark was the one fighting to control the situation now. Being out of control made Jimmy Tollan dangerous. He didn't want to lose control of himself because he did not know the strength of the stranger. A cop? No. But who was he?

Walter grabbed his chance. He moved his chair back slightly so that he had the space to make a smooth exit. In one direct movement he stood up and stepped away from the table walking directly to the door ducking under and out of the menacing concrete trap. He kept moving at speed without actually running. The paper he borrowed was abandoned. The pint unfinished.

Forty yards along the pavement he paused to cross the main road. It was an excuse to glance to the right. Back toward the pub. Tollan and his companion were standing outside in the drizzle, eyeballing him.

They had sussed him. Who he was they did not know. Or why he had been there. He was well and truly marked in Tollan's mind.

Walter grabbed a taxi back to the hotel. Deeply disappointed that he had failed at the first hurdle. Strictly speaking he should now declare himself out of the race.

But nobody had seen him fall. So he stayed in the race. That was all he had to do for a £2,000 payment. Two weeks work. Guaranteed money. The wages of fear were not going to be earned easily now. His reward for dipping into deprivation would have to be worked at.

Walter Harvey managed to get his slice of the poverty pie without much effort. The gravy train had come in at eleven thirty after a late breakfast last Monday.

He hated Mondays because he was out of regular work. Ahead was a week of hunting for the offbeat story that he could talk up and sell to some Sunday paper. To any news editor with a thin schedule line who had learnt that his splash story was falling down. There were plenty of them around these days. Struggling news editors and falling down stories.

Walter liked spreading the news. With a bit of jam on it!

"I have a goodie for you. A landowner up here is evicting a whole village. He bought the place for a song, four years ago. He has upped the rents. The village hate him. Most of them are talking to me. Good quotes. And he's Dutch!"

That was his last one. Two hundred pounds including expenses. On top of that he snapped the guy getting out of his Range Rover at the gates to his estate. Good pic. Another fifty notes. There was nothing on the horizon. Just sparse trees and peaty heather in the foreground and sea in the distance. A few financial clouds too. Jean was tired. The wheel had turned full circle.

They married in Oban in nineteen seventy four. Moved to Glasgow. Two babies. Promotion to Manchester where the kids grew up in Cheadle Hulme amongst the well-to-do in detached suburbia. And on to London. Walter enjoyed the power and the glory on the front line. Fleet Street. The wine bars. The glory days. His teuchter accent wore down.

Jean coped as best she could with the strange English tribe in the quaint Essex village. He commuted to the excitement of Fleet Street. She soldiered on, rearing the kids whose accents were a weird mixture of Lancashire and Essex, tinged with odd Scots jargon they picked up from their parents. As teenagers they were strangers to Walter. Jim and Sally. They both made it OK. No thanks to him.

Fleet Street eventually turned its back on Walter. They

packed their bags and headed north to a house in Bishopbriggs on the outskirts of Glasgow, while he made one last effort to stay on the payroll of a national paper by covering the big Scottish stories for the Mail. That was short-lived. The money men moved in cutting staff levels to the bone.

They packed again and ended up where they began. In Oban. A nice little house overlooking the Ganavan sands. Seaweed. Mackerel. A view. The smell of the sea. The good life. A real life. Tainted with a scarcity of money.

Needs must and Walter kept pushing the boat out with any yarn he could embellish to sell at a premium price. Not for him the drag of filing a small local story each day at twenty quid a time. Walter wanted at least two hundred for 'a belter.'

That was the only way to retain his self image. To remain in the big time he had to find or fabricate big stories. Not as easy as it sounds. The People had knocked him back on the feature about cannabis coves – the remote highland coastline where cannabis was smuggled to meet the huge demand. The local Customs and Excise boys were only too keen to see their profile raised giving them a chance to moan about cutbacks costing jobs.

"Been done before. Not new," was the knockback. So he tried it on the Sunday Mail and got the same response.

There was nothing on the financial horizon that Monday. Jean was washing up the breakfast dishes when the phone on the kitchen wall rang.

"I'll get it Jean. It'll be the boy wanting to know when we're going down for the wedding." Their son's wedding in Essex was the next uplifting event for Jean.

It wasn't Jim. It was a blast from the past. "Nigel here. Atco to you. Remember me on The People?"

Nigel Atkinson.

Walter clicked into the good old days. Generous expenses, big enough for the average family to live off. The best hotels on 'Out of Towners.' Animal cruelty stories.

121

Runaway teenagers marrying middle-aged ministers. Pop stars and pot. Car chases. Beating the News of the Screws. Passport in the pocket.

The big time.

"Christ, yeah. Nigel. Good to hear from you," he said, visualising that creepy clinical young reporter who never smoked and always brought a fresh-faced girl to the pub. She was all perfume, golden hair, red lipstick, white teeth and firm biggish breasts. An English fucking rose.

The rest of the team got pissed. All Nigel ever had was a couple of drinks. Disappeared into the night, saving his slim body for hillwalking in Derby peaks or a walking weekend in the Lakes.

A right killjoy. And none too hot a reporter either. Steady, reliable, efficient. That was all. No real drive and lacking the magic quality that secured the big stories.

"Yes, Nigel. I remember you. How are you?" Walter dropped the words down the phone.

"Fine. I'm working for Northern Insight TV now. An independent mob. Producer with the documentary department," he said.

The documentary department! Fuckin hell. This definitely was Nigel Atkinson.

Walter let two more words drop down the line. "Very interesting."

"We're up in Glasgow. I was wondering if we might meet for lunch and a beer. I'm looking for somebody to help us investigate illegal money lending in Glasgow. A reporter who knows the score. You fit the bill."

Walter slammed his brain into gear.

Nigel continued, "Maybe you could help us. Would you be available?"

The hack was ready. "I still have some good contacts in Glasgow. I will need to rekindle them you might say. They'll know about illegal money lending. I did a piece on loan sharks a couple of years ago. Certainly I'm interested."

Interested? He was desperate.

"Could we meet in Glasgow for a chat? There just

could be a contract in it for you."

A contract! Walter could see the money piled on the kitchen table. A contract!

"I'm going down to Glasgow tomorrow to talk to the Sunday Mail editor about a feature. I could meet you for lunch."

"That's fine. We're in the Holiday Inn. See you in the lounge about eleven thirty."

The Holiday Inn! He could smell more money and feel smooth booze.

"See you tomorrow Nigel."

He was in Glasgow before eleven. A couple of whiskies, two Benson and Hedges and most of the Record read in a pub in Hope Street. He tried to kill time and to control his excitement. This was worse than his interview for the Express back in '76. He walked to the hotel, ordered a Glenmorangie and chose a deep comfortable seat. Atkinson arrived on the dot.

"I'll get the drinks." He said glancing down at Walter's glass. "Another whisky, and a Perrier for me, please."

They should have known to quit when they were ahead. When they were still friendly. Half an hour later Nigel knew he still disliked Walter intensely. The hack drank too fast and too much. He talked too loudly. He was almost fat. Walter was experiencing the same revulsion of the man sitting opposite. He never liked him in '79. He liked him less now. Too poised, clean, controlled and polite.

They signed a deal for two thousand pounds – a TV contract giving Walter two weeks work, overnight accommodation in the hotel and travelling expenses."

"That's your copy, Walter," said Nigel, handing him the carbon.

"Thanks," he replied casually.

The relationship was downhill from that moment. Walter phoned home with the good news of contracted cash. He was staying in Glasgow but might get home at the weekend, depending on how well it went. He booked into his room, spruced up with a shower and helped himself to a miniature whisky from the ice box, before phoning Nigel to suggest a meet in the restaurant for lunch and a detailed update on the operation to find loan sharks.

Nigel had a plate of carrot soup, a brown roll and a cup of tea. Walter tucked into breaded mushrooms, steak and kidney pie, apple pie with cream, washed down with coffee, allowing himself the thought that dinner would be even better. And two grand in the not too distant future. He leant back lighting another Benson and Hedges. The good times were back. He listened to Nigel spouting enthusiasm and commitment.

"We envisage the programme as being two-edged. An exposé of illegal money lenders and a social documentary highlighting the consequences of poverty. First the loan sharks.

"That's where you come in. We need to get them on film. We need to get them on sound. We've had a researcher in Glasgow for six weeks. He's done well. You'll meet him later. We already have the names of three loan sharks. We know where they operate. We need somebody right in there, wired, to get the deals. We need somebody capable of being accepted in their scene."

Walter got the picture. "Me. Muggins here. I'm your man."

Nigel moved swiftly on with the briefing. "Our main target is a man called Jimmy Tollan. He's heavy. No doubt about that. He has a record as long as your arm for assault, robbery, extortion."

Walter interrupted to state the obvious. "Sounds like a nasty bastard." He threw it in to indicate that nasty bastards came ten a penny in his business and that he was following the briefing enthusiastically. He was actually considering which of his old journalistic sparring partners he should contact for a chinwag that night.

Nigel had laid the foundations. Now he was setting the standards. He was aiming at the moon.

"We need to secure evidence against Tollan that will result in arrest by the police, a trial and imprisonment." He was dreaming. He threw in some flattery. "That's why I brought you in."

Walter nodded. "Yea. Good move, pal. I get my head kicked in for two grand and you get the glory."

It was the following day that the hack had jumped in at the deep end at the Black Inn. Sussed at his first attempt.

Walter knew that he was now of little use to the TV team. There was no way he could carry a hidden microphone to pick up the Tollan conversations. The hack's contribution to the daring documentary would be virtually nil.

He would not however, throw away the cash. There was a contract, signed sealed and delivered. All he had to do was keep the TV mob sweet and his share of the sixty eight thousand was on the way. No point in too much honesty at this roulette wheel.

The stakes were too high. He was averaging two hundred a week selling 'belters' to the Sundays. Two grand was three months income.

Christ Almighty he was on the poverty level himself. The punters who borrowed from Tollan and his like weren't much worse off than him. Housing benefit paid their rents. They got income support, invalidity allowances, family credit etc, etc. Walter was thinking like he was supposed to. The pressure of circumstances had him rationalising the right wing theories.

The mortgage and the car they needed to get into Oban for shopping. The good times when big bucks flowed into their bank account from Fleet street excesses had gone. He should have saved for a rainy day. Christ they had cashed every insurance policy he ever took out. Deposits on all those houses in Glasgow, Manchester, Essex. Lawyers' fees. Surveys. Removals. Carpets. Furniture. Fuckin roses for the quaint little gardens. The money game.

This time he was on a wee winner. Back at the Holiday Inn after his exit from the Black Inn he phoned Nigel arranging a meeting at the bar around four. Dead time of the day.

Walter opened his report enthusiastically. Nigel listened eagerly. He needed to know that progress was being made.

"I made contact with Tollan. Talked to him."

Elation rose within Nigel.

"He was in the Black Inn, standing at the bar when I walked in."

"Are you sure it was him?"

Walter helped himself to some cashew nuts from the bowl the barman had filled. He looked at the nuts in his hand and threw some into his mouth. He chewed them leisurely.

Nigel couldn't wait for the answer. "What made you think it was him? We've got to be certain it was him before we show our hand."

They were like little boys playing games with each other. Walter made him wait even longer, chewing the nuts thoroughly before swallowing.

"I think it was him. He fitted the description you gave me. He was about five feet seven or eight inches tall. Brown hair. A scar on his chin. Round face. Tough looking wee bastard. He was wearing a black leather jacket and jeans."

Nigel had been given the description by Jenny Mullen and Johnny McPherson. It seemed to fit.

Walter helped himself to more cashew nuts, studied them in the cup of his hand, and without looking at Nigel added, "He was doing a deal with a girl. Maybe not a deal. Difficult to tell. She was paying him."

Nigel was mystified but willing to be convinced. How could Walter, a stranger, possibly have witnessed a deal? Tollan wouldn't do that in front of a stranger.

"What do you mean. A deal?"

"A girl came into the pub. She discussed making payments to him. She took thirty pounds out of her purse and paid him."

Walter had almost seen that happen. He simply added in what would have happened if he had remained in the

Black Inn.

That was exactly what had happened a few minutes after he escaped. Jenny Mullen made a payment in the hope that Tollan would not turn up later in the week for his sex and cash.

Nigel Atkinson was still unbelieving. "She made a payment in front of you?"

Walter leant forward. "Yes. Now listen Nigel. I will tell you exactly what happened. A blow by blow account."

Walter described the pub interior. The position of Jimmy and Kenny. The arrival of the girl. "She was a good looking woman in her thirties, wearing a black leather skirt. Dark red hair. She said she was sorry she had missed him, offered to pay him there and then. She paid him and he said, 'Thanks Jenny.' That was it. Dead simple. I was sitting only a few feet away."

"Jenny!" Nigel dropped his cool exterior. "What did Jenny look like?"

"I just told you. Tall. Red-hair. About thirty-five. Don't tell me she's working for us!"

The machinations of the media. Everybody was in the game in preparation for the amazing exposé designed to shock the nation.

Nigel laughed. "Sort of. Jenny's helping us. We met her last week. Eddie found her through the Drop In Centre for prostitutes. She's going on camera. She's on the game to pay off Tollan. She gave us a description of Tollan and told us he would be in the Black Inn."

Walter was pleased that his story had been accepted. He knew that fifty per cent of it was true. The rest probably was correct. It's how you tell them that counts.

He wasn't too worried that Jenny might, at a later stage, reveal that he had left the pub before she paid Tollan the money. He hoped that it would be in the region of thirty pounds.

Jenny turned up at the hotel that night when the TV mob was sitting in the lounge bar discussing the following day's work. Walter confirmed with Nigel that she was the woman who had paid Tollan the cash.

Jenny was there to pass on more info on the lure of more cash. They gave her forty pounds to replace the forty she said she gave Tollan that day. Tollan, she told them would be operating in the Wee Hauf the following day.

Introduced to Walter she said, "They're onto you. You're the one they followed out into the street. He's more than curious about you."

Walter grimaced, "Fuck it."

After she'd gone he brushed off the tenner difference between the thirty pounds he said he had seen her pay Tollan and the forty she did pay him.

"She's a whore, Nigel. She's conned you out of a tenner."

Walter didn't even have to seek a way of avoiding Tollan at the Wee Hauf. Nigel did it for him. "No point in you checking him out tomorrow. He would wonder why you were following him from pub to pub."

All in all, a smashing day for everybody. Walter was another step closer to his two grand. Jenny had paid Tollan forty pounds recouping it from the TV big spenders. She had been paid fifty for describing Tollan and telling them that he could probably be found in the Black Inn that day. She got more for telling them that the operation was moving to the Wee Hauf.

So Jenny Mullen was ahead of the game. Ninety pounds better off. It all helped. With any luck the TV programme would result in his arrest.

In room five one nine at the hotel Walter helped himself to a miniature whisky from the ice box, ordered a round of chicken sandwiches, lay back on the bed and phoned Jean.

"A good day darling. Knocked it off with a bit of old-fashioned investigating. There won't be any problems. I should be back in time to go down to the wedding. Love you, very much. Goodnight pet."

He was getting old.

He switched on the telly. The sandwiches arrived and

he tipped the waiter a pound.

He awoke at six to an incessant bleeping noise. The TV. The sandwiches were curling on the plate.

15 A stupid question

JIMMY TOLLAN could delude himself with ease. Nobody told him to his face that he was a greedy bastard.

Interest rates at ten million per cent APR were not the issue for him. Just the next handful of pound notes. Readies. And the niggling irritation that somebody might rip him off.

Interest rates weren't the issue for his clients either. Interest rates were for banks and building societies. For financiers. For the Money Programme and the Financial Times.

Jimmy loaned them the money for essentials. He was the man good enough to save them from the dark. A saviour. What power he wielded!

The women offered him smiles of gratitude while the men treated him with the respect afforded a bank manager by desperate businessmen begging for survival.

Moneymen were magnanimous. They helped their clients and when things went wrong they kept their cool, offering sound advice in a caring understanding fashion.

Beyond a certain crisis point they quietly moved the problem on to the lawyers who moved debtors quickly through the courts to sheriff officers and repossession teams.

Jimmy thought of himself as a decent bank manager. Nothing less. A local man, who knew his clients well having been to school with some, met others in the pub or the bookies. He was on more than nodding terms with them. They were people he could help. Friends who were grateful, becoming clients who became creditors and finally useless bastards. The dark-eyed tallyman rarely revealed his anger at failure by a client to pay. Nor did he have to dirty his hands with threats. Tollan left the Mr Angry stuff to Kenny Watson, the credit controller who would, if necessary, use the baseball bat or the knife to order.

All Jimmy did was take the heavy decisions. To inflict

pain or even serious injury on those who had ignored a warning or failed to grasp the seriousness of the situation.

So most days were quite enjoyable. He wandered round the scheme, in and out of the bookies, across to the pub, and sometimes into town for a decent meal at an Italian restaurant. Saturdays were particularly good for he had a season ticket to Ibrox and could enjoy the Rangers success.

Jimmy Tollan was, in his own terms, at peace with the world and on his own territory. Everything seemed as normal that Tuesday afternoon. He was in the heart of his kingdom, outside the bookies.

The smell of frying fat, tinged with a suspicion of vinegar hung in the street air. A group of kids dogging it from school were guzzling hot chips.

Johnny McPherson lurched across the street.

"Hi Jimmy. Ah missed yi this week. Ah've got it fur yi," he said pushing six fivers into the outstretched hand.

That set the seal on their relationship for the moment. Johnny had paid without having to be hunted down. So they were both instantly in good spirits. Jimmy because he was richer by thirty notes and Johnny as he now had no reason to fear any violence. He was paid up for another week. So they chatted about football.

"The Celts hiv a history of real fitba," said Johnny. "That's whit'll make them great again."

Jimmy was practically benign in his reaction. So friendly for a man who had, in the past, arranged to have Johnny's legs broken. "They'll never make it back tae their former glories. They're history noo. That lot don't understaun the real value of money. Rangers dae."

They laughed at the joke and Johnny launched into his theme. "Rangers know the value of money. Ay. But dae they know the value of real fitba? Be fair Jimmy. Are this team as good as the Celtic side of the sixties? In fact they're no even as good as the Quality Street kids, Dalglish, McGrain, Macari and co?"

Jimmy Tollan allowed the runt to have his words. The loan shark was comforted by any friendship offered by his clients for it reinforced his delusion that he was their benefactor.

Johnny fired on. "Ah'll tell yi somethin. This lot urnae even as good as the Baxter, McMillan, and Henderson wan. They hardly won anythin, but they were worth payin tae watch."

"How dae yi know that? Yi never saw them play!"

"No. But Ah've seen the videos. Money's no everythin. The Lisbon Lions cost next tae nuthin. Stein made a team. He only bought three of them, Auld, Simpson and Wallace and he got them fur peanuts. Souness just spends mair money. That's all he's daein."

The amiable discussion was interrupted when Kenny Watson came out of the bookies to give Tollan the good news that French Willow had won the three-thirty at odds of five to one.

"Good. That's me right oot the shit. Ah hud twenty notes on it. Good price at the weight," said Tollan, with the air of a man who knew the horse was going to win.

Johnny saw that Jimmy was in benevolent mood. To hold Jimmy's attention he re-introduced the debate on Rangers, Celtic and money. There was a good chance of getting a tenner out of Tollan while he was flush with the winnings and still talkative. Keep the patter going and wait for Tollan to make the offer. It would come with the usual question – "Need a wee help fur the weekend."

This time the offer never came.

Jimmy had warmed to the subject of finance and the power of money. "Rangers hiv bought a few good players, but they've bought some bummers too. The thing that matters Johnny is that they can afford tae make some bad buys. Celtic cannae because . . ."

He ceased in mid sentence.

The stranger came at Tollan with a microphone in his right hand. He was backed up by another man carrying a massive TV camera. There was somebody else lurking in the background.

Jimmy could have coped better if these strangers had

been armed with a baseball bat or a knife. Christ, they were recording him.

Fuck me. A microphone. In front of his face. A camera. Shite. Stop the bastards.

He heard the sharp Scots voice – "Jimmy Tollan. Why are you charging such massive interest rates on illegal loans to the poor?"

What the fuck. Run. No. That will look worse. Turn away. Run. No, don't run.

He made two responses – "Fuck off!" and "Yiv got the wrong guy."

Jimmy covered his face with his right hand but couldn't bring himself to turn away, walking straight at the camera and then veering past it, to dive into the bookies. The women in the street saw the desperate scene unfold.

What the fuck were these bastards doing in his patch? What right had they to be here in heart of his kingdom? What the fuck?

He hadn't seen them coming. He was angry with himself for being so naive as to get caught. The TV mob had emerged at speed from a social work van parked between the bookies and the chippie. He had been too intent on giving Johnny McPherson a lesson in football finance. Idle chat.

The question was so hollow. Adrian Russell's clearly enunciated words were reverberating round Tollan's mind.

"Jimmy Tollan. Why are you charging such massive interest rates on illegal loans to the poor?"

The man with the microphone sounded most unconvincing. What did they know?

The sentence was bizarre. But then everything in Jimmy's crazy monetarist world was off the wall. Cloaked in authenticity yet totally bogus.

The sentence was deliberately overloaded because the TV star was hedging his bets. If Tollan turned and ran they would at least have something to edit into the programme – proof that they had confronted the evil, greedy loan shark. Tollan was an essential ingredient in the recipe for a night's serious hard-nosed investigative TV reporting.

If Tollan faced up to both the camera and the questions it would make good TV. If he ran then at least Russell had fired in his question branding him a loan shark and asking about the massive interest rates. The sentence even included a reference to the poor.

The very same poor who were forming groups on the pavement for a front row seat to a crucial section of the forthcoming TV documentary being made in their very own street. They would have five weeks to wait for the TV showing, when they would be able to claim proudly, "I was there. I was were there when Tollan got his fuckin comeuppance. I saw it happen. Tollan shit himself. I'm telling you, he bottled it."

Others were able to claim, "That's nothing. I was in the bookies when Tollan rushed in. The bastard ended up in the pisshouse."

Jimmy Tollan was crucified that afternoon.

Johnny McPherson was one of the poor who actually appeared twice in the film. Once as himself talking to Jimmy about Rangers and Celtic, and secondly as an unrecognisable victim. A sample. A unit. He was perfect. A member of the underclass. The poorest of poor who borrowed twenty pounds and paid the price, owing more than a thousand. Yet he had paid back more than a thousand. The mind boggled.

Those were the facts. The truth was that the TV mob lifted Johnny above the poverty line for a few weeks. He was doing very nicely these days. A regular drink and a good few free meals from the TV mob plus between ten and fifty pounds every time he talked about the loan sharks in the comfort of the hotel.

Now his benefactors were here in the street. Jesus! Johnny realised that it was a farce, no matter how real it was.

He was as shaken by the unannounced arrival of the TV circus as was Jimmy. He was scared. What the hell were they doing here?

A week previously Johnny had enjoyed a meal, a few drinks and Russell's company after the interview at the Holiday Inn. Christ they might have told him they were going to turn up at the bookies. What the fuck was going on?

Johnny kept his mouth shut and sidled across the street. Inside the busy bookies Jimmy attempted to use his right hand man to solve the crisis drawing Kenny into the corner to tell the enforcer, "We're in the shit. There are some TV bastards ootside wi a camera and a smart-arsed cunt asking questions aboot money fucking lending. Get out there and check it oot."

The tannoy drowned Tollan's instructions with a hectic description of the three forty-five at Wincanton . . . "Bonny Boy leads from Harping Glory going into the final jump, with Pink Man closing fast." The voice rose. "Bonny Boy is a faller and on the long run in . . ."

The commentator was whipping excitement into the final furlong as the punters anticipated a cash victory or financial ruin.

Another financial farce, fraught with tension, was emerging in the bookies. The TV guys outside. The loan shark inside. Johnny the Karaoke kid was now standing in a close entrance, watching developments from a safe distance.

Kenny Watson was reluctant to become involved for he sensed that the camera would be pointed at the entrance to the bookies. They weren't going to shoot him. He made a quick assessment of the situation realising that if he did as he was told by Tollan he would end up as a TV star!

"Jimmy. We're no in the shit. You are. Ah'm no fuckin daft, and Ah'm no goin out there tae get ma face on TV."

A punter walked in from the street, taking centre spot in the busy premises to announce the news. "We're gonnae be famous," he told the assembled punters. "There's a TV crew filmin ootside here."

The punters rushed outside. Some sought the chance

to be filmed, while others hung back. The more gallous thrust themselves forward and the air was filled with Glasgow banter.

"Want tae interview me?"

"No he disnae want tae film uglies."

"Tell him aboot all yir women, luvver boy."

"Any fee fur an interview?"

The word was spreading fast that Tollan had been asked about illegal money lending.

One wag called out. "Ah can tell yi all aboot loan sharking. Pay me and ah'll gie yi the inside story mate."

Another voice interjected. "On location filmin, is that yir gemme?"

Nigel was decidedly unhappy. Crowds were allright if they were under his control. But when they were laughing that was awkward. The mob was building up and his sixty eight thousand pound programme had turned into a circus.

Inside the bookies Jimmy Tollan retired to the toilet fearing that the TV mob might invade the premises.

Outside Nigel took the decision to cancel filming for the day telling Russell and the cameraman that there was little point in continuing. They retired sheepishly to the social work van and drove back to the Holiday Inn.

The day's effort was summed up as, "a right fuck up."

Nigel took control of the disappointed crew with a positive attitude – "Not as bad as you think. We have him on film, and Adrian asked him the key question."

The lounge was empty in the late afternoon. Nigel, Eddie and Adrian rested in the soft armchairs sipping soda water and beers, while the cameraman took the equipment to his room.

Nigel repeated the point with satisfaction. "We have him on film."

The excited street slowly calmed down. Kenny informed Tollan in the toilet that the loan shark hunters had gone. The angry duo made their way sheepishly through the bookies and along the street to Jimmy's Audi, passing Johnny on the way.

Jimmy paused to tell him. "Ah want tae know who the fuck grassed me tae they TV bastards. There's a score in it fur yi."

Twenty notes. Only ten minutes before Johnny had paid Tollan thirty pounds, out of the cash Eddie Anderson had quietly slipped him as they left the Holiday Inn the previous night.

Money was made to go round. Especially when there was so little of it.

Jimmy decided to throw some friendship Johnny's way. After all the wee bastard was about to do him a turn by finding out who might have grassed him. So he returned very briefly to the subject of Celtic and Rangers. To the chat that had been so dramatically interrupted.

The friendly return to the subject was brief and rhetorical.

"Celtic cannae win the league. They'll only get it if Rangers lose it. And there's nae chance of that," he said, walking away to his car.

Beneath the calm exterior Tollan was wrestling to control himself. He and Kenny held a two hour discussion into who could have helped the TV crew pinpoint him as a loan shark. They carefully studied the names in the tally book coming up with twenty one out of two hundred and eighty four possible grasses.

The last people he considered were Johnny and Jenny. One lurched about on two broken legs. He was terrified. And Jimmy was sleeping with Jenny so she wouldn't grass. She fuckin loved it.

Jimmy doubted that any of the suspects would have the bottle to talk.

A bit of lateral thinking might have helped for he was considering each in terms of the fear. He forgot about the power of money. It never occurred to him that the TV mob could be dishing out cash too . . . in handouts. Free, gratis and no need to pay it back.

Jimmy stayed away from his regular haunts for a couple of days before venturing forth amongst his fearful clients.

Nobody made any reference to the afternoon he ran away to the toilet. For the moment the TV circus was an occasion to be talked about behind closed doors.

16 The baker's dough

JOHNNY McPHERSON knew all about the power of money. The more he could get, the less chance he would be hospitalised. So he made the most of his injuries.

The nurse gently squeezed the syringe of steroids into Johnny's jaw next to the jagged wound and pulled the needle out. She rubbed the pin prick with gauze soaked in cleansing alcohol.

"How's it looking doctor?" Johnny asked. "Ah think it's getting a bit better. No much though. Ah still hiv trouble shavin."

"It is showing considerable improvement," said the consultant, taking hold of Johnny's jaw and studying the healing flesh pulped by the smooth hard wooden baseball bat.

Johnny could smell the garlic as the consultant added, "The steroid treatment is now completed. You have had five injections and the wound has responded well."

Johnny interjected, "Is ma jaw gonnae be muscle bound?"

The surgeon smiled. Nevertheless Johnny explained his quip. "The steroid treatment. That's whit thae Olympic athletes use tae build muscles tae win the medals. They end up heroes, wi medals and money, and muscle bound. Eh?"

He glanced at the nurse who had dropped the gauze in a waste bin and was preparing for the next patient. He looked back to the consultant offering another half joke. "Whit aboot ma sex life? They steroids can turn that aff faster than five pints."

His infectious fun was escalating. They both understood that this shell of a man was trying to impart something of himself. Indirectly he was telling them not to judge him on his appearance. He could enjoy life despite being an obvious loser and he had some general knowledge.

The nurse responded. "You better check that out with your girlfriend tonight."

"Ah think Ah'll settle fur five pints," he said with an enormous wide open smile, his blue eyes lighting up with pleasure as he sustained his joke.

The consultant gave his speil. "The raw red appearance has declined and has returned as close to a natural colour as we can hope for. It's healing well. I don't think we can take it any further, so this is your last visit. We will give this, your last injection, time to work. If you are not satisfied please arrange another appointment through your own doctor John. I don't think that will be necessary for the wound has healed surprisingly nicely."

The surgeon's words disappointed Johnny who was far from pleased at improvement. The last thing he wanted was the wound to heal well. For that would mean less money in Criminal Injuries Compensation.

He attempted another piece of homespun philosophy.

"Did youse ever see The Magnificent Seven with Steve McQueen and Yul Brynner? That wiz a great Western, in the same league as High Noon and Shane."

The nurse and the surgeon exchanged knowing looks. Much as they liked him it was time to send him away. They both admitted to having seen the film.

"McQueen and Brynner wir tryin tae recruit a team tae sort oot bandits who regularly raided a poor peasant village. Every year the bandits led by Eli Wallach took the peasants' earnings fae the corn and maize crops."

The nurse lifted a card from a table and raised her voice. "The next one is Louise Allan. She was referred from the burns unit. This is her second time here. Dr McAllister saw her the first time."

Johnny knew he was overstepping his time. "Gie me a second. This is important. It's about ma scarred face." They had to listen.

"McQueen and Brynner were sittin in a bar wi the leader o' the peasants who wis paying them tae get the bandit aff thir backs. A guy walked intae the bar wi a badly scarred

140

face. Like mine. The guy wis bigger than me and meaner lookin. The peasant told Brynner . . . 'That man looks tough enough tae recruit'."

Johnny paused. At last he had reached the punchline. The surgeon and nurse gave him their attention for they knew that he deserved the chance to complete the story. They liked him. He had a strange courage. The beatings had not extinguished his spirit.

"Brynner telt the peasant . . . 'The man we want is the man who gave him that face'. Eh?"

Neither of them seemed impressed by his little anecdote.

The nurse asked Johnny a straight question. "So who inflicted the damage to your face Johnny?"

The punchline had been turned back on Johnny. He ducked the question while trying to hold their sympathy.

"Ah know who done it. Whit Ah mean is Ah know who ordered it. Ah'm no saying. Ah want tae stay alive."

They understood. They shared the same unspoken thought – the drink will kill him before any baseball bat. They were ignorant of his circumstances.

The nurse gave Johnny directions to the orthopaedic department where his leg was to be examined. He decided to have a smoke before the check-up and went to the WRVS canteen, for a cup of tea. Two nurses at the next table watched him out of the corner of their eyes. He ignored the No Smoking signs on every wall, rolled, and lit up. Nobody advised him that he was in a no-smoking area for they feared approaching him. His carved up face, broken walk and cheap clothes marked him as a person to be avoided like the plague. He looked decidedly unpleasant.

There was no sugar on his table and he turned to ask some nurses, "Can Ah borrow yir sugar, please?"

He helped himself to two spoonfuls before handing the bowl back and in his own inimitable fashion started the conversation. "Ah know Ah shouldnae be smoking but Ah've been in the hospital fur an hour and Ah've got tae go tae the orthopaedic department next. How do smokers manage, working here?"

The nurses had reassessed his human value. They were reassured by his polite request for the sugar, followed by his explanation of why he was ignoring the No Smoking signs. He had even offered sympathy for the hospital smokers.

Johnny was off and running again. Chatting naturally to the two young women who had been wary of him when he lurched into the canteen.

The younger pointed out of the window and replied. "The smokers are round the back of that building across there. Follow the trail of fag ends," she said with a wry smile. "It leads round the back and from there to the cancer ward. After that the cemetery."

The conversation expanded from smoking, to the orthopaedic department, to Ward Ten where Johnny had once spent three weeks after a beating. He even mentioned loan sharks. The nurses, experienced in life's turmoil, were surprised yet entertained by his yarns. All he kept back were the names.

They showed him the way to Orthopaedics where the consultant opened, "We'll have a look at your leg, Mr McPherson."

Johnny started to take his trousers off. The surgeon, drawing three X-ray photographs from a large envelope told him to keep his trousers on, and placed the first X-ray photograph in a viewing box on the wall.

"These are the X-rays from last week."

They both looked at the image. "You won't be playing any more football. And I think your dancing days are over too," he said with a comforting smile. He was one of them. Make the jokes gentle folks.

The healing joins were visible in the cloudy bone images. It wasn't a pretty sight. Even Johnny, with his limited knowledge of X-ray pics could see that his left leg was a mess. He was having some difficulty walking without limping. Now he would limp like a cripple.

"That looks a right mess doctor, eh?" he said without

any concern in his voice. Johnny was again counting the cash he might receive on appeal to the Criminal Injuries Board.

His claim had been submitted months before. The board had notified him that he had been granted one thousand six hundred pounds. The cheque would be sent to him and, pending further treatment to the face and leg he could be awarded more if the treatment failed to improve the scar or if the leg did not improve.

Johnny hoped for more cash. A lot more. After all, his leg was badly damaged. His face was further scarred. Unfortunately it was beginning to respond to the treatment.

The doctor's report might be unfavourable in that he would write that the scar was returning to a natural skin colour. They might not increase the sum.

On the claim form he had written a lengthy discourse on the consequences of the face scar.

"I will now find it very hard to get employment. Potential employers will be put off by my face. They will assume that I am a troublemaker. Any chance of a job will be gone," he had written.

Johnny McPherson had not worked a single day since the factory closure and his marriage breakdown. Just those three years after leaving the merchant navy to marry the lovely Marie. The leg injury was serious. He made the very most of that.

"I can no longer drive a vehicle, although I do have a driving licence and had hoped to get a job as a van driver. Labouring jobs are also out because my balance has gone in both legs."

Returning to the driving subject he extended the theme. "I was hoping to get a bus driver's job because I have a friend who is leaving the buses and was going to apply for his job."

There was no question of Johnny trying to pull the wool over their eyes. He simply tried to make the best case for some real cash.

There was a glaring weakness in his application that

143

couldn't be overcome. He had co-operated with the police to a limited extent, giving them a statement about the attack and little else. Where and when and how. But not why or who.

So the police submitted their report to the Board without the full story of the attack. They had repeatedly tried to get names and possible reasons for the brutality.

Johnny's response was a shrug of the shoulders. "A mystery tae me. Ah hivnae any enemies. None at all."

He thought for a moment and added with a cackle of laughter. "Not unless Monica Thomson's husband has found out about us."

The cops were exasperated. They gave him forced smiles. One said, "For a man with no enemies you aren't doing too well. You must know why this happened. There is some reason behind it Johnny."

"Nothin Ah can think o'," he lied.

So there was a lot of negative replies to questions in the claim form for Criminal Injuries Compensation. Names, arrests and convictions would have swelled the pay-off to Johnny by another one thousand. Tempting, but not tempting enough. He would not grass.

A fortnight after his last treatment the cheque for one thousand six hundred pounds dropped through his mother's letterbox. She opened it. Johnny was due to make a flying visit that night from his hideaway home on the southside. She placed the cheque carefully into the top drawer in the bedroom dressing table.

Johnny made his way carefully across the city reaching his mother's home after the pubs closed. Friday night was a good night to make a furtive visit. Tollan and his mob would be out enjoying themselves. On Saturday they would sleep late. The scheme slept late to recover from Friday night's excursions.

Johnny was far from sober. After paying the taxi driver, he was totally skint. His mother took one look at him and decided to leave the good news until the morning.

He slept deeply, the sleep of a drunk without

responsibilities. He was a man with no job, no prospects, a broken body, no love life whatsoever, and no money. Like some of the long term unemployed he sensibly made a virtue out of his hopeless situation, turning the negative lifestyle into an existence verging on the carefree.

The only setback was the daily problem – nae money. Johnny couldn't be bothered attempting to improve his financial circumstances by crime. So he borrowed from Jimmy Tollan, his pal in the corner of the pub, and ended up in hospital. It took no longer to come to terms with the massive debts that accrued in interest rates, than to adjust to life on the dole. Poverty was relative after all.

The morning brought the good news from his mother. She turned the happiness quota up to Christmas level.

"Mornin Johnny." Her voice bubbled as he creaked into the living room at eleven, trying to generate some movement in his stiffened legs and beer-soaked body.

He sat on the settee. Sitting was an effort, so he swung his legs round and stretched out.

"I'll make you a nice breakfast. Bacon and eggs. And potato scones. Through to the kitchen," she called and he obeyed. He was unable to eat the breakfast, even for his beloved mother.

"Ah'm sorry maw. I cannae eat a breakfast. I'm wrecked. Just a cup o' tea. Ah'll take a piece of toast though."

She put marmalade on the toast.

"What are your plans for today, son?"

A ridiculous question. Days weren't planned, they simply happened. She was turning the clock back as though he was about to take his boots and strip for a game, cycle up the Campsie hills, or even join his pals for an hour at the Maryhill swimming baths. Next thing she would be asking him when he'd be in for his tea!

"Ah dunno yet," he replied, smiling at the naiveté of the question. As if he would be doing anything, never mind have planned to do anything.

Another slice of buttered toast and marmalade was placed before him. She refilled his cup and sat down opposite. Her face was alive. The way she was before his father left, when Johnny and his sister enjoyed the good life. Dad was working then, mum had a part time job and he was playing for the local juvenile team.

She looked so much younger this morning. There was almost a physical change in her eyes – the movement of her head, the way she walked. She was his mother again. Husbands leave but sons stay in touch as he had done even when he was married.

The dull companion he took for granted, who shared his fears, had mysteriously disappeared to be replaced by this wonderful woman. The transformation rarely happened. When it did Johnny himself was lifted to forgotten heights. His pride was rekindled. He was lifted out of the gutter. Life was real again.

"I'll tell you what you are doing today. You're going to see that man Tollan."

Johnny put down the cup.

"Am Ah? That's news tae me, maw."

There was absolutely no point in seeing Jimmy that day or any other before Thursday when Johnny would cash his Giro at the post office. Tollan wasn't worth a visit unless you had a handful of notes.

His mother was preparing the ground for the 'Christmas present' that had arrived the previous day. The Criminal Injuries Compensation cheque she intended to cash through her brother's bakery business in Battlefield on the south side of the city. They would do it today, for it would take at least three days to clear in the local bank where her account held the princely sum of twenty two pounds. She was keen to move the cash rapidly to Tollan.

So Mrs McPherson had the day planned for them both.

Not only would she cash the cheque at the only source available, she would escort her son to the loan shark. That way she could be certain that the total debt was paid off.

The gift was to herself as much as to Johnny. A gift to both. Peace of mind.

146

"I'm going with you," she said almost gleefully. "We're going to pay him off today."

The penny dropped. The compensation had arrived in the post. Johnny held his inspirational guess back, allowing her to continue.

"I know exactly how much you owe that bastard. A lot more than you tell me. The figure I got, when they came to the house, was one thousand two hundred and forty eight pounds. We can pay him off today and that is exactly what we are going to do."

They were a bonded mother and son for the day. He demurred to her caring dominance allowing her to take control, for there wasn't an ounce of malice or bully in Johnny McPherson.

"Maw, stop haverin and tell me aboot the big fat cheque that came fae the Criminal Injuries," he said with a wide smile. His twinkling eyes sought hers.

"You've been in my bedroom. You saw it on the dressing table," she said with a laugh.

"No. Ah jist guessed, maw. Let me see it. Ah want a look at it."

She went to the bedroom. He followed her, lifting the cheque out of her hand. "One thousand six hundred. That's the first one. Ah might get mair if the scar stays red. My leg's no gonnae improve, that's fur sure. This wan's an agreed interim payment. Ah think there will be mair tae come. Maybe."

Mrs McPherson took the cheque from him and proceeded to implant some sound commonsense. "Never mind what you might get. Let's deal with what you have got."

She folded the cheque, returned to the kitchen and placed the cheque carefully in the centre pocket of her purse. It was safe there. Johnny knew better than to attempt to take it out. That was hers. She knew that when it came to her purse he was honourable. He might have lifted it off the table or the mantlepiece. It was safe in the purse.

She explained her carefully thought-out and well-intentioned plan to cash the cheque, pay off Tollan and then pay off the lesser debt to McFadzen.

Johnny was flabbergasted. Not by his mother's motives. He expected that sort of sound old-fashioned action from her. She wanted him off the danger list. If he was out of Tollan's tally book then he was out of the firing line. He understood his mother.

He was dumfounded at the thought of transferring one thousand two hundred and forty eight pounds in cash to Jimmy Tollan and tried to imagine the bastard's response.

"Thanks a lot pal."

No.

"No need to gie me it all."

No.

"Hiv yi robbed a fuckin bank?"

No.

The one reaction he fully expected from Tollan was anger born of resentment. "How the fuck did yi get that sort o' money?" would be the words as Tollan tried to come to terms with a client who had found independence.

Johnny's instinct told him to give Jimmy thirty pounds. That way they would both be happy. With the interest at twenty five pence in the pound per week, the debt would not be reduced by a single penny. That was a financial fact.

The truth was that Jimmy Tollan would be delighted to receive a regular payment of thirty pounds a week. He would be pleased enough with thirty pounds a fortnight. Tollan had had his money back a hundredfold already. Missed payments were the reason for the size of the debt.

Johnny could keep Jimmy sweet for at least forty two weeks by paying him thirty pounds a week. He could double the time by paying once a fortnight. That would be in keeping with Johnny's reputation as an unreliable client.

A year and a half without any danger of violence from Tollan. Ya dancer. Unfortunately there was also McFadzen to consider too. Nae luck.

There was the consolation that if he only repaid Tollan the fear factor in his daily life could be halved. Then again he could pay McFadzen who only had him in the book for two hundred and forty.

Tollan might ask why Johnny had not been seen around the scheme for a couple of weeks since he moved to the south side. Unlikely though because here he was . . . paying thirty pounds! The bastard would probably offer him a tenner back.

Johnny was unnerved by his wealth. Fantasy took over as he considered a three-piece suite, a TV, a carpet for his new flat, and trousers, underpants, two shirts and a pair of trainers. And something special for his mother. Maybe a weekend in a Blackpool hotel, with spending money thrown in.

Christ. The possibilities were endless. He could open an account in a bank and buy the three piece suite on no per cent interest! He had the deposit too. He could cash the cheque and stash the money in his Nitshill flat. First he had to get rid of her for the day by insisting that she stay at home while he cashed the cheque and took the taxi to the bookies where Tollan would be most likely to be hanging about.

"Yi kin trust me. Ah know this is oor big chance tae get oot. Gie me the cheque and Ah'll cash it at the pub," he said sincerely.

"Don't be stupid, son. They'll take ten per cent for cashing it for you. You know that," she said. "We'll cash it at my brother's shop. I'll go with you. Then we'll find Jimmy Tollan."

"Ah'm thirty five, no ten. You're no goin with me." The words were lame.

"Oh yes I am. I have the cheque. My brother will cash it for me. He won't cash it for you, unless I'm there. So I will have to go along."

"It's ma cheque."

"I've got it!"

"Ay, but you cannae cash it without ma signature, maw."

Neither was in the slightest bit angry with the other,

for they both felt confident that they would win the argument. Anyway, they loved each other.

They were sparring, each from a position of strength. After all, the money was there in numbers and in words on the cheque. God, it made them feel good, a shot of relaxation, a shot of confidence. He was off the tightrope of financial fear. She could feel the black fear for her son lifting from her worn thoughts.

Johnny was incapable of asserting himself in the face of his old mother's love. They could still share the fun of the money. Johnny had only seen it once. So he asked for another look. "Ah won't take it. Ah jist want tae see it again. You can hold ontae it maw." His voice crackled in mirth, his eyes sparkled in his coarse face.

She placed her thumbs and forefingers round both ends of the cheque and held it firmly in two hands, allowing Johnny another look. "This is the last time you'll see it before we get to the shop. Then you can sign it and give it to my brother. I'm phoning for a taxi."

Johnny quit in the hope that when it was cashed he might be able to change her mind. As always he gave in gracefully lacing his capitulation with humour. "Yir brother won't cash it fur us. He'll take the cheque and pay us in steak pies fur the next ten years. He's a right breidheid."

In her excitement she missed the joke completely. She was enjoying the thought that not only would Colin cash the cheque but he would also give them two loaves of freshly made bread.

"He might give us a couple of pies. He'll definitely give me two loaves, a big white and that fruit one. He always does." Her mouth was watering at the thought and she added, "I'll get fresh unsalted butter after we pay them off."

The taxi took them round the city on a bizzare mission to the bakers, a bookies, and a boozer.

The shop was busy with families stocking up for Saturday night and Sunday morning, with those who couldn't afford a joint of meat or who preferred to spend their cash on booze and bingo. His steak and mince rounds

150

were popular, fired in the ovens only a few steps away from the counter. Housewives liked the smell, the idea of heat raising the dough to a succulent flaky pastry. Much more appetising that the pre-packed frozen offerings in supermarkets. Colin was busy serving.

"I'll be with you in a coupla minutes pet. Go in the back shop. There's some tea left in the pot."

He joined them after five busy minutes. "How're you keeping Jean? You're looking very well," he said with the sad warmth he felt for his sister whose life was far from easy up in the corner of the scheme from which he had so successfully escaped. The shop was small but the profits were good. A bungalow in residential Giffnock, a BMW, a greenhouse, roses and a comfortable trouble-free marriage. Those were the rewards for turning his navy training as a chef into a basic bakery business.

Colin had a soft spot for Johnny. He thought of him as a likeable lad without much drive who had fallen to drink. "Are you going to Parkhead today?" he asked.

"No. Ah cannae really afford tae go," he said glancing with a wry smile at his mother.

"You mean, you cannae suffer any more."

Mrs McPherson took the opening neatly. "No Colin. He means he can't afford to go. But he's never been better off."

That was enough to set the agenda and soon Colin was studying the Criminal Injuries Compensation cheque with his sister's quiet words in mind. "The cheque is genuine. Believe me. Johnny will countersign it and you can cash it in your bank. You'd be doing us a big favour Colin, if you would cash it for us."

Colin placed the cheque on the table and looked across at his sister, waiting for an explanation of some sort. She had not told of why they wanted it cashed quickly or what had happened to Johnny that entitled him to such a massive sum. It was obvious that Johnny had been attacked from the red scar on his face.

"I need to know a little more about . . ."

151

She stopped him. "Don't ask Colin. You don't want to know."

"All right Jean," he said standing up and taking a wad of notes from a deep pocket in his white overalls. There was a lot of cash mostly in one pound and five pound notes. He sat down and began the laborious chore of counting them. He went through to the till and collected more cash, eventually reaching the magic figure of one thousand six hundred pounds. Saturday was his busiest day.

The money was piled in three stacks on the table.

"I think you should look after it Jean," he said handing his sister the wads one after the other. She placed them carefully in her handbag.

Johnny sat and watched. The enormity of the occasion between siblings was not totally lost on him. He saw the weight of feelings in their eyes. The level of emotion didn't dampen his natural inclination to humour. "Thanks a lot Colin. That's a lot more dough than Ah've ever seen. Eh?"

Colin looked him directly in the eyes. "I have a feeling this is no joking matter. So don't waste that money," he said cryptically.

"We won't Colin. I'll see to that," said Jean. "We need to go now. There's a taxi waiting in the street."

The room, laden with the smell of baking, was still charged with love. There was no particular reason for this. Colin had not given them the money, nor had he loaned them it. The cheque was safe. The transaction was based on love. Jean had carried her fears for Johnny into the backroom at the bakery for Colin to share. She stood up, stepped round the table and hugged her understanding brother, before walking out of the shop with Johnny trailing behind.

They were inside the cab when Colin shouted from the shop entrance. "Jean. Jean. Wait a minute."

Johnny's heart sank. "Jesus. He's changed his mind."

"No. I don't think so."

Colin stepped out of the shop entrance carrying a plastic bag that he handed to Johnny, telling his sister,

"Don't say I'm no good to you."

Jean smiled happily. "Thanks a lot, Colin. Is there a fruit loaf there too?"

"I'll see you Jean," he said turning back into the shop.

Johnny realised that he was not to get his hands on the money. His mother was now in charge of the situation. The TV, carpet, and three piece suite were out. As was her trip to Blackpool.

They said little to each other during the taxi trip to Tollan. The amount of money in his mother's old leather handbag was uppermost in their thoughts. A fortune. More than either of them had ever owned. Real money.

Johnny's thoughts were predictable. "If only I had been able to get that cheque before she did. I could have cashed it myself at the pub. That would have cost me ten per cent. That's what they take for cashing Giros or cheques at the pub. Ten per cent of one hundred and sixty off one thousand six hundred? Nothing."

His mind drifted onto the profits the pub was making from cashing DSS cheques for punters with no bank accounts. It had started with Crisis Loans for furniture being cashed for a ten per cent fee. The DSS closed that loophole by insisting that the beds, cookers and baby cots be bought and delivered to the punters' homes. The punters jumped that one easily, taking delivery of the beds in plastic wrapping and the following day flogging the beds unwrapped to the nearest second hand furniture shop.

Johnny's situation was not lost on him. Here he was taking the government's cash to the loan shark who had ordered the beating that led to the Criminal Injuries payment. Jimmy was already raking in government cash every week in his cut from Johnny's DSS payments. Maybe, not every week, but at least every two weeks.

The taxi crossed the Clyde stopping at the Jamaica Street lights. Johnny woke out of his thoughts. "Christ it's a crazy world."

His mother agreed. "It certainly is."

They lapsed back into comfortable silence until the

taxi pulled up at the betting shop in Garthill where Johnny exclaimed, "He's in. There's his motor."

Big city taxi drivers have seen it all before. The driver tried to keep his mouth shut while Mrs McPherson counted out one thousand two hundred and forty eight pounds from the notes in her handbag, handing the money to Johnny who placed it his trouser pocket. The driver's eyes never left the mirror.

"Could you wait a few minutes driver. He won't be long. He's just going into the bookies," said Mrs McPherson.

The driver was unable to control his reaction at the sight of a middle-aged woman handing all that cash to a man who was obviously on the 'low side of life.' He watched Johnny hirple across the pavement into the bookies. He twisted round to tell his passenger, "Listen dear. It's none of ma business. But you've given that man a lot money. I don't know how much. I couldn't help seeing in the mirror. I don't want to know how much. That's your business."

He was struggling to say what he felt had to be said.

Mrs McPherson helped him, "Don't worry, he's my son."

"Oh. Right. That's allright I suppose," he said adding with a nervous laugh, "I hope he backs you a winner."

Johnny found Jimmy listening to the tannoyed commentary. "Can Ah see yi fur a minute ootside?"

"Ay sure, mate," said the loan shark anticipating a tenner or at best a score. "Ah've nothin in this race."

They made their way a few yards up the street. Jimmy streetwise to the point of paranoia since the TV incident, noticed the taxi and the passenger. "That's your maw in the taxi. What the fuck's she daein here?"

"Ay Jimmy. She's waiting on me tae finish ma business wi yi."

"Ah telt yi before. Ah don't like people knowin ma business. No even yir fuckin maw. Whits she daein here?"

"Yea, Ah know. She's the wan that's decided Ah pay yi aff. That's why she's here."

"Whit dae ye mean, pay me aff? How can yi pay me aff?"

"Ah've got it here," said Johnny taking the rolled up notes out of his pocket.

"What the fuck are yi daeing showin cash in the street? Intae the motor."

Johnny sat in the back seat. Jimmy twisted round. "Let's see. How much hiv yi got there?"

Always questions. Jimmy Tollan talked in questions. Five years a loan shark had turned him into an incessant questionmaster.

"Ah hiv exactly one thousand two hundred and forty eight notes. Whit Ah owe yi."

"Gie me it."

Johnny handled over the bundle of rolled notes.

The questions flowed from Tollan as he counted the cash. "Where did yi get this sort o' money? Yir maw? Where would she get it? Whit the fuck's goin on?"

Johnny started to reply. "Remember a year ago Jimmy. Ah got a right doin. It's the Criminal Injuries money. Ah had tae wait . . ."

Jimmy interrupted. "Wait a fuckin minute. There's naebody watching us? Is there?"

"Fuckin hell, Jimmy. Naw."

"OK. Yea, Ah remember yi got a right bad doing. Nuthin tae dae with me."

"Ah'm no saying it wis you Jimmy. Whit Ah'm tryin to tell yi is that Ah got one thousand six hundred fae Criminal Injuries. That's whit Ah'm paying yi aff wi."

Jimmy relaxed.

Johnny relaxed too, repeating his dough joke. "Ah got the dough fae a baker. Ma maw's brother. He cashed the cheque fur us. He runs a bakery on the sooth side."

Jimmy participated in the sad joke. "You're a right fuckin doughball Johnny. Ah never thought Ah'd get this much bread aff yi."

He added, "Yir oot ma book noo."

"Any chance of a receipt to show ma maw Jimmy?"

155

"Fuck off."

"Ah wiz kiddin. Sorry Ah asked. It was jist tae make her happy. Eh?"

"Whit dae you think Ah am? Fuckin stupid? Dae yi no trust me?"

In the context of the crime, money lending without a licence, Johnny did know that he could trust Jimmy. That was the strangest aspect of the transactions. Strictly speaking loan sharking was extortion. Johnny had paid Jimmy thousands of pounds in interest over the previous five years. Their agreement, while not a gentleman's agreement, was never written down. The deals had resulted in several beatings for Johnny. That was all part of the business. Today it was concluded in the luxury of Jimmy's Audi. Jimmy became conversational.

"Are yi goin tae Parkheid.?"

"Ay. Ah might. Ah've a wee bit left. Ah'm going to gie ma maw a wee trip tae Blackpool. That'll use up maist o' it though."

It was the focal point. The money. The windfall. The jackpot. The stuff that would soon be gone.

"If yi need a wee tap later on come and see me," said Jimmy.

"Ay. If Ah need a wee help."

And he did.

For his mother made sure that the rest of the cash was paid to McFadzen that very afternoon. He gave the Maryhill loan shark two hundred and forty pounds clearing that debt. There wasn't enough left to give her a trip to Blackpool. The three piece suite, new trousers, socks, trainers and underpants were yesterday's dream.

He went to the game. Bought his pals a drink, and on the Monday bought his mother a pair of slippers. By Giro day the money was all gone.

Two weeks later he went back to Tollan for another injection of fear. He got a thirty pound loan.

17 A redhead's anger

WITH THE best part of sixty thousand pounds spent or spoken for, their programme was in financial crisis. They were running out of money and time.

Nigel was under pressure. This one was proving a right bastard to complete. The cash had gone on hotel bills, flights from London for researchers, Adrian Russell, Nigel himself, the cameraman, the make-up girl, and wages.

In addition, the best part of five thousand pounds had been paid out to an assortment of contacts and informants, two prostitutes working the streets to pay off two loan sharks, a young mother whose children had been taken into care because she could not afford to look after them, two old age pensioners, and a family who would only speak about their debts if they could be re-housed with enough money for beds and furniture. The council found them a new house and Nigel authorised an eight hundred pound cheque for three beds, two carpets, and redecoration costs.

There were four weeks to the transmission deadline and the team were struggling to meet standards required.

They had three loan sharks in the frame. That was fine, except that proving that any of them was an illegal moneylender was virtually impossible. Yet that was the benchmark of the programme.

Nigel called the team in for a conference in the lounge at ten o'clock giving them the instruction to wrack their brains overnight on a method of proving that Tollan or any of the other loan sharks was actually involved in this sordid illegal business.

They had plenty of film. Victims telling their sad stories. Tollan hiding in a bookies. A Church of Scotland minister reflecting on the failure of society to recognise the depth of poverty afflicting so many families. Unidentified women describing the life on the street to pay for their stupidity. Senior social workers warning that the poor were increasingly becoming victims to loan sharks.

Nigel put it to his team. "We need proof. We have four hours on film, more than we need. It is all good stuff. A lot of very atmospheric stuff. It more than illustrates the depravity of the poor and their fears.

"What we do not have is the cornerstone to the programme in that we cannot prove that one single person is a loan shark. They are loan sharks but we don't have the proof."

He looked round the assembled team and hit them with the tired question. "Anybody got any ideas?"

Eddie Anderson, the researcher who alone had braved the pubs, the schemes and the darkened streets during the winter to trace both victims and sharks, put himself forward as candidate for the most dangerous of jobs.

"I could go in to the Black Inn every day for a week, until I was accepted as part of the scene. Then ask for a loan."

"Where are you going to live?"

"I could ask the Housing Department for a local council house. There are plenty empty ones round the Black Inn. Most of the houses behind the pub are boarded up."

"Rather you than me, Eddie. That might work. Timewise we are struggling. It could mean that we have wasted a full week if it fails."

"Anybody got anything better?"

Walter Harvey, nursing a hangover was still in the game determined to make some contribution to justify the juicy two thousand pound cheque that would soon be landing in the hall at his Ganavan home.

"I could . . ."

Nigel stopped him instantly. "There is nothing that you can do, Walter. Believe me. Nothing. You can't go near Tollan. That's that. I feel that you have made your contribution."

Walter nodded in agreement. He could take the sarcasm from the acidic producer. There were only a few more days to go. He had been involved to the limited extent of sitting in cars outside pubs, relaying information on the movement of the targets, describing their smart cars and noting number plates. There had not been that much he could do since Tollan sussed him in the Black Inn.

The TV mob fell into blank thought.

Margaret Hazlewood strolled into the lounge to check out if they still needed the two social work vans.

With her warm smile beneath the bundle of red hair topping her tiny stature, she was a breath of fresh air to the crestfallen tired team. They all enjoyed the presence of this outspoken little socialist with anger for the system and empathy for the poor. Cynical she was not. Just a pleasing mixture of compassion and education.

They respected her. Eddie was thinking about making a pass at her. Just a passing thought.

"How are you getting on?" she asked, knowing that they were constantly in turmoil. They seemed to be wrestling with one insurmountable problem after another as they tried to tell the public what the public already knew. That people were so poor that they turned to money lenders. That the most vulnerable diced with danger when they failed to meet even the interest payments.

They left Nigel to answer. "We've plenty of good film, much of it thanks in no small way to you arranging interviews and supplying the vans for surveillance work. What we don't have Margaret, is Tollan, on tape, talking about loans."

He smiled weakly. "We've hit a brick wall Margaret. God knows how we are going to catch a loan shark."

The conversation hardly faltered as Margaret instinctively said, "I'll do it. He doesn't know me."

There was a deadly hush as the mighty national TV investigation unit considered her offer. They could all see that she would be ideal. Who would ever guess that she was wired? She was tiny. Not a threat. Inconsequential. Tollan and his cohorts would certainly notice her because she was so small, yet attractive. The bushy red hair and her fresh smile. That was all he would see.

Nigel was the complete gentleman. "Absolutely not

Margaret. Far too dangerous a job for you," he said firmly.

He was a bit late in responding to her brave offer. It was obvious from the his delay in replying that he, and the others, were seriously considering her in the role. So Margaret knew that if those evil loan sharks were to be exposed she could take a bigger part.

She was decidedly unimpressed by their efforts. The honest but tired hack. The polite prissy producer. And Eddie, so earnest and hard working, carrying so much personal grief. They needed a bit of help. This was her chance to expose the consequences of poverty under the Tories.

Her motives were pure. Maggie had consistently rejected money and preferred to go home for dinner with her husband rather than sit about amongst the movers and groovers who simply put dinner on the room number. Her granny would have been proud of her.

"Listen," she said, looking round the faces of the team. "Who'd ever suspect me of working for a TV company? Tollan will be looking for men, who look like detectives, researchers or even worse reporters."

Walter smiled, "I'll drink to that Maggie."

They all knew how badly he felt about his failure on day one. His intention had been to give value for money. It simply hadn't worked out.

Only prissy Nigel blamed him for the cock-up in the Black Inn. Nigel had a low tolerance level. At home in Cheadle Hulme, he was the producer of socially aware TV documentaries who could be relied on to take his daughters and their friends to the gymkahna in the Volvo.

Here in Glasgow the nitty gritty of dealing with what he liked to term 'low life' was only a means to an end. The good life was first on his agenda and after that, promotion to join the decision makers at management level, where he at least would be dealing with a better class of people. He wasn't a snob so much as blind to the qualities of courage and humour in the breadth of humanity that flowed through his professional hands. Getting the programme in the can meant a quicker return to Cheadle Hulme for his own pleasures.

So Maggie's offer was too good to refuse. He sensed she would be his saviour.

Jimmy Tollan made things difficult for them. The shock arrival of the TV crew outside the bookies set him thinking. If he couldn't discover who had grassed him he could at least change his routine in case the TV inquisitors showed up again.

He was nothing if not streetwise, putting two and two together he concluded that the phoney punter tipping an afternoon winner in the evening racing at Hamilton, was in some way connected with the TV investigation.

So Jimmy moved his operation out of the Black Inn to the Whisky Well, the Rum Do and the Wee Hauf. He was now a moving target.

Unfortunately he made the mistake of telling his terrified wee pal Johnny McPherson and his debt ridden lover Jenny Mullen. The punters had to know where to find him to make the payments. Both eagerly relayed the information to Nigel and his shark hunters who obliged with thirty pounds to each for the crucial information. Easy money.

The hunt intensified. The man who preyed on the poor was now the prey of the rich.

Nigel had a heavily budgeted programme at stake. Jimmy had more, much more, at stake. His freedom and a business, grossing £200,000 a year, untraceable, with no costs other than £1,560 basic wages to his credit controller. Four or five times a year there was a bigger pay-out for 'extras', broken legs, smashed ribs or a scarred face.

It fell to Margaret to catch the shark. She was far from naive when she offered the chance to carry a hidden microphone into the pubs seeking the close proximity of Tollan. The chore was dangerous, difficult but a pleasure. The prize for her was gratification of her hatred.

The sad reports had crossed her desk too many times for her to be unaware of the violence in the darkened recesses

161

of this heartless business. The men carrying the facial scars of their failure to pay were the more obvious signs of the trade. The gut-wrenching fear experienced by women threatened by violence went unseen on the streets. Only a woman could fully understand the intensity of their feelings.

Margaret learnt of their fear from women who turned up at the area office with deadened eyes, begging to be understood as they unburdened their enormous secret.

"I'm intae a money lender. I need help."

Was this simply a manipulative woman trying to con the department out of crisis cash? Or another girl from the nearby scheme who actually was unable to support her children to the extent that she couldn't feed or clothe them properly?

In the comfort of the open plan office she shared with five other social workers Margaret appraised the increasing number of reports from clients pleading poverty at starvation level. The girl from the country decided to find out for herself. The desperate clients were recalled to the area office for a second interview. They came eagerly, delighted with a second chance to raise some cash. Maybe the 'social work' would relent and make a crisis loan or even better give them a few hundred pounds to get them out of the trap.

It was a busy week at the area office, with Margaret muttering obscenities about the government, the system, the cutbacks, Thatcher, Fowler, and the useless Labour party trying to woo the middle classes a million miles away in Essex. At home her patient loving husband listened as she threw Dickens at him . . . poorhouses, thieves, Fagin, Oliver Twist.

Margaret was distraught. None of the women who bared their shame by unburdening their stupidity would name Tollan. Not that it would have made any difference. For the report on each client was totally confidential. Social workers were there to help families, not to remove Tollan and his like from the scheme by involving the police. These matters were confidential, only talked about to husbands and parents.

162

Margaret was struck by the number of mothers who had turned to the loan shark for ready cash in a crisis. Money for clothes, gas and electricity bills, and often to pay up a Provident debt or catalogue debt. According to the tearful girls sitting opposite her in the interview room, they had paid him hundreds of pounds for loans of between fifteen and fifty pounds. They simply failed to make regular weekly payments and in consequence their debt rapidly rose above their meagre subsistence allowances.

She was mystified by the women's lack of anger over the exploitation. Nobody would ever have mistreated Margaret or her mother or her granny for that matter, without receiving retribution. Surely a few would go to the police if only to have him removed, and enable them to escape his relentless grip.

The reason behind their refusal to name the loan shark emerged from the broken sentences of a twenty six year old woman begging for cash or, even better, help in being re-housed in another part of the city. "I've got to get away. We cannae stay in the hoose."

Margaret prised gently. "Surely you're safe in your own home."

"It's no that. Ah need tae get the kids to another school."

"Why?"

"Because every day they've got tae get from the school back tae the hoose."

It was like drawing wisdom teeth. Margaret felt such a fool when one trembling woman finally overcame her primeval fear.

"The bastard telt me he can have ma kids dealt with at school. Some big wans punched ma youngest wan. The oldest wan got a right doin." She blurted the information out.

Every interview was laced with obvious truths supplemented with half truths. The facts were held back. The exact amounts, the whereabouts of benefit books and the names of the men involved remained a secret.

The identity of 'the bastard' remained a tight-lipped tearful secret. He was in their minds a darkly dangerous fear. A shark.

Margaret Hazlewood strove to picture the man who made his money from mindless extortion. She dug deep below the clichés of greed, ruthlessness and evil, but found nothing. How did he talk? What did he look like? What was he? He was an ex prisoner regularly visiting the same building. He was a case for another senior social worker in the office above hers.

If only Margaret had known where to look. They had passed each other several times. Jimmy in a hurry to get the chat out of the way. Margaret preoccupied with the problem of whether or not to authorise a one-off payment to a mother who, after paying the loan shark was left with only ten pounds for the week.

They would meet again. At his place of work.

Then she would know him. He would talk to her briefly without ever learning who she was or why she was there. Margaret stepped up her work, as an unpaid aid to the TV crew, by drinking regularly in The Wee Hauf.

18 Too close up

IF JENNY MULLEN could have seen the way they treated her in Studio Ten she'd have been mortified. Indeed she almost was killed off in the heat of an argument about her voice.

Johnny McPherson lost his identity completely. Most of it had already disappeared under a cake of putty, make-up and hair. His cackling voice was next to go.

By the time the editor finished with them they were unreal.

Their only consolation was that they were out of it now. Back in their own worlds . . . for richer for poorer.

Jenny had made two hundred and fifty pounds selling her information and half-hidden face to the TV mob. Johnny made only two hundred pounds by recounting his amazing tales of bone-crunching baseball attacks. He also enjoyed a few drinks on the house.

They kept Jenny alive because she was the only prostitute they had on tape, the only whore brave enough to open her pretty mouth. It was her mouth the viewers saw. Moist, trembling lips, liberally coated in bright orange lipstick, breathing out her sad words.

Riveting stuff. The lips quivering with fear. Her tongue moving between clean white teeth.

They caught her sexy strong beauty in profile, showing only the right hand side of her pale face with a strand of her dyed auburn red hair lying on her cheek. Barely four square inches of her face with that mouth as the centre piece.

The same six images beamed out of the six editing screens on the wall above a young editor brought in for his first effort on a major documentary. He had gained his experience in news editing, but this was more sophisticated. There was time to perfect the end product and so create a polished seamless programme.

The words were the problem. Their meaning was

perfect. Exactly what they wanted. Jenny was too good to jettison. "I'm on the streets because I went to a money lender. I only borrowed one hundred but now I owe more than six hundred."

They had agreed to reduce her debt by two hundred to put Tollan off the scent. A little red herring. There were plenty of them going round.

The voice was the problem, in both Jenny and Johnny's case. It was a give-away.

Eddie was concerned. "I don't want her talking. I know it's her. So anybody else, who knows her, will know it's her."

Nigel wasn't budging. "We're going over the same ground again and again and again.

"We got to this stage at ten o'clock last night. It is time to move on," he said wearily. The weariness was more of an act than anything else. A bit of a joke.

They moved on. Eddie reserved the right to win the battle later. There were another two days to go before the four hours of tape were boiled down to a sauce to serve the viewers.

They had plenty material. Jenny's case was only one of a myriad of harrowing images. Floor to ceiling misery. Girls in tears. Men in fear. Women on the streets. Men on the run. A house on fire. A blood-smeared baseball bat. An ambulance. A bloody face. A surgeon at work. The lengthy queue of tired faces at a post office. The images were so bleak. Dark, drab and unhappy, any colour faded into grey dirty pictures of people struggling to eke out an existence on a basis of jobless failure.

Happiness for the editors. Success for the researcher. Grotesque. The truth as seen through the eyes of the camera. The obscure faces talked about money, the lack of it or the size of their debts. What they owed . . . in unpaid gas bills, fivers to the neighbours, hundreds to the Provy, to the catalogue collector, and to the government for loans taken out on the strict rule that they be repaid.

Their voices, dull, devoid of any hint of exuberance,

flat and even-toned as they reluctantly repeated their sad stories of abject miserable poverty, filtered out of the screens.

There was a hint of shame that they tried to pass off as stupidity, and a lot of fear when talking about the debts. Human beings bereft of dignity, but clinging to a vestige of humanity beneath a thin veneer of anger, fear and forced mirth. Some were beyond that point, reduced to suicidal thoughts. There was no horizon to their poverty. No exit from the worsening debt resulting in electricity cut-offs, little food, a constant lack of bus fares. Fear of violence to themselves or even worse to their children, pushed them to the edge. Mothers suicidal in their daily desperation for a fiver for the power card. Wall-to-wall misery.

Millions of capable working families would soon be aware of the realities when the grim tales were relayed into their comfortable homes. The information would arrive down the tube in a form designed to entertain. So the edit was crucial. No point in allowing the camera to linger too long on any one subject. Pack in the information and keep the pace up.

Most of the horror would be pushed into the nation's front rooms. Not all of it. Just enough to 'get the picture'.

Some tales were true. Others were inventions of the streetwise poor, cunning enough to give the researcher exactly what he wanted . . . at a price.

The patchwork of televised poverty glittered across the wall from the neatly stacked TV screens linked to a mind-boggling array of control panels. These were designed to animate the deadened faces and voices when necessary, or when required, reduce the voice levels, deepen the voice tones.

Nigel and the team sweated in the magic room, where the switch of a button, the turn of a knob, could enlighten the dark world they had penetrated in a two month blitz on the city's poverty blackspots. They had the technology to develop the truth, to direct it in whatever manner they wished.

Now was the time to turn the rough images, secured

in what had seemed like endless negotiations, stake-outs, tips-offs, and manipulative deals, into a fast-moving TV documentary lasting exactly twenty six minutes and twenty seconds.

Time to splice it together, so that nobody would see the joins.

The room buzzed with enthusiasm, anticipation and professional know-how. Ahead lay two more days in which the hours of filmed depravation would be boiled down. Tasty, and strong enough for the viewers to appreciate.

Editing was never fun. It was always fraught with tensions when decisions were bullied through, compromises reached and personalities clashed, however politely.

Eddie was no longer a key figure. The research was over. The long nights in dark, wet, fear-filled streets were thankfully a thing of the past. Forever. He had made his mind up to get the hell out of this game but first he would see that the promises he had made to vulnerable families were kept.

"You won't be recognised. We'll cut the bit about you meeting him at the bookies. Don't worry. Don't worry Jenny, we'll give you two children. The bit about offering him your TV won't be used. No. Don't worry. We won't say that your pal knows him. Your face will be in total darkness."

So Eddie hung about the room, respected by the technicians for his ability to communicate with the punters featured, keeping a watchful eye on the proceedings. Unfortunately he was powerless.

He would have to rely on persuasion or generated anger to impose even the slightest control on the finished product. He had started in the exposure game and was now in the protection racket, for all the right reasons.

Nigel was in the driving seat. Indoors this time, in a state-of-the-art technical studio, demanding results from men who understood the equipment, while he insisted on the end package.

The producer wasn't sure of exactly what he wanted.

Only that that the end product have the stamp of authority through authenticity. First he mapped out the sequences.

"We will open casually. With a song. About loan sharking."

The assembled company sniggered internally. Nigel could almost touch their unspoken rejection. He forged on.

"Done the right way, in a sleazy club with a struggling unknown singer who has been on the circuit for years. It'll work."

Silence.

"We want the viewers to realise that illegal money lending is a way of life in cities throughout Britain. A song catches that."

Silence. To a man they had rejected his off-the-wall idea. Nobody said so. They had heard the conviction in his voice.

Nigel went to the toilet. Mike, the fresh-faced editor, waited until he was out of hearing in the corridor and burst into song.

There's no business like show business,
Like no business I know.

The others laughed nervously but Mike continued.

Everything about it is appealing,
Everything that Nigel will allow
Nowhere can you get that frightened feeling,
When he is stealing an extra bow.

There was an edge in his voice. Mike hated the idea of launching a loan shark programme with a song. Eddie saw the danger in allowing the editing team to drift away from any commitment to creating a quality programme. Without everybody's input it would fail.

"Don't cop-out. When he comes back express your feelings by all means but don't cop out. What's the point of throwing everything on him."

Mike was still angry. "Because that's the way he wants it! Fuck him. At the end of the day I am paid to cut where he wants it cut. I'll do my job to perfection. If he wants to fuck up that's his problem. Not mine. God knows what he intends to do with the shots of the baseball bat attack stunted by you. Where you get your legs smashed outside the pub," he said with a sneer.

Eddie paused, looked round the assembled technicians and sought support. He included himself in the team of Nigel doubters. "We're getting our knickers in a twist over nothing. Nigel's got a good track record. Give him his position. Argue your corner where you feel strongly about something."

Out of the corner of his eye Eddie saw Nigel returning. The pep-talk to the rebels ended.

While having the pee Nigel had also been reviewing the situation. He knew that they had rejected his decision on the opening shots. He had two choices. Be reasonable in seeking support for his decisions or demand the technical changes he knew were best for the programme. Nigel chose to be his usual smarmy self.

"We will try it my way with the song. If it doesn't work we'll try something else."

They ran it through several times cutting the song tightly to four verses, with a fade-in and fade-out of high rise blocks in the rain against a dark sky, dubbing in applause from the audience. Then the problem of . . .what next?

The baseball attack.

The prostitute victim.

The loan shark's face.

Which one to slot in after the song?

The controlled anger in Tollan's face would grab the viewers' attention. But it was too early to bring in their baddie. Let the evil deeds be revealed before Tollan was caught by the intrepid investigator.

The baseball attack would illustrate the violence within this ruthless business. All they could show here was a close-up of the bat striking a leg; a man collapsed on the pavement.

170

Then the shots of the ambulance with its siren sounding.

There was agreement that the prostitute talking next to the car park was 'atmospheric, informative, shocking.' With no need for a voice-over either. It introduced the depths to which people sunk when forced to pay a loan shark.

"We'll go with Jenny at the car park."

The editor ran it through. It was too long, three minutes in which she explained too much about herself.

"This has to be cut severely," said Nigel.

Eddie was pleased. "Good. We can get rid of that stuff about her wee girl and the holiday. Tollan could work that one out. That helps a bit!"

"What do you mean, helps a bit?"

Eddie was wrestling with a bigger problem. Jenny's face was unrecognisable in the dark recess of the concrete overhang. And the close up, shot in the studio, four square inches round her lips, wouldn't identify her either. That was fine.

The problem was that her accent gave her away. It was a mixture of lyrical Highland and guttural Glasgow. He explained.

Nigel was irritated beyond control. "You could have thought of that before we filmed her," he muttered.

"Sure," said Eddie, "there were hundreds of whores queuing up to go on camera. I just chose the wrong one," he said evenly.

This was a real problem. There was no getting round the fact that they only had one prostitute on film. A young mother forced to sell herself. Too good to lose. She would have to be salvaged one way or another. There were twelve million viewers to consider. Their feelings were important to the ratings. Their anger, their sympathy, their social awareness must be activated on transmission night.

The nation must go to work the next day with one question on its lips – "Did you see that programme about loan sharks last night? God!"

Impossible to imagine what the viewers would have

171

thought of Jenny's efforts to escape Tollan's clutches by sleeping with him. For Jenny was not a character to be explored or explained. She was part of the package. Unfortunately few would look beyond the plight of Jenny or Johnny or for that matter Jimmy. They only added weight to the sledgehammer in the living room.

So Jenny's presence was an essential ingredient to generate a national interest in the programme. Nigel was in a harsh contest himself – the ratings race.

Eddie faced up squarely to the moral question. "The girl will be identified by Tollan if we let her talk. Her voice is the problem."

Nigel played it fairly. "True. We'll work on it Eddie."

"Thanks. I gave her my word that she would not be recognised."

"I'm on your side. Nobody wants her recognised. And she is not recognisable. You can't see her face."

"She may not be recognisable but she is identifiable."

"I am not saying that we will use her voice. We'll work it out."

They were politely tussling. Enjoying the natural clash of professional interests which, in this case, reached an inevitable conclusion. Jenny's interesting voice was edited out.

In the privacy of her home, Jenny was the first to complain about her change of voice. "That's not me speaking," she said aloud in the empty flat.

The voice was June's. The make-up girl, trying to inject some authenticity into her smooth deep but neutral sounding Glasgow voice, spoke out on the consequences of borrowing from Jimmy Tollan. "I'd no choice but go doon the toon. It gave me peace of mind. My wean won't get a doing. I can make enough to pay off the loan shark. I borrowed sixty pounds and I now owe six hundred." They changed the debt from eight hundred and the loan from one hundred to sixty.

They dubbed the voice perfectly to the movement of Jenny's voluptuous lip movements. Unfortunately the jargon didn't quite fit the culture in June's voice.

Millions were moved by the prostitute's words, a crushed mother, flaunting her sexuality in a tight leather mini skirt, outside a bleak rain-sodden concrete car park. How sad. The images and words moved so quickly that the viewers were given no time to fully absorb or question the situation.

The truth was that Jenny was a prostitute, working the cold wet dangerous streets for one reason and one reason only. To pay off an eight hundred and eighty four pound debt after borrowing one hundred pounds.

The truth was that she wanted off the streets for fear of meeting another psycho who might do more than blacken her eye and bruise her hip. The next time she could be left for dead. She couldn't face another rape.

Fear had driven her into the welcoming arms of the TV team. They now had a problem in deciding how much of her they could use. They settled for virtually nothing. Her long legs, leather skirt, profiled face and her hair blowing in the wind whistling through a concrete car park. And four inches of her face, centered on her lips.

It took them a long time to compromise. Nigel sat upright in his centre spot chair, dominating the small room, script in hand, concentrating on every syllable.

"Have you got a note of her voice at the bottom of page twenty one?"

"Yes. And it is coming up again on page twenty two.

"I want it to stop on page twenty one. Only her saying 'I had to go doon the toon to pay him off.'

"Where she says that she got used to being on the game quite quickly. That's out. She goes on to say that she is frightened by some men. Keep that in."

Mike ran it through the tape, stopping at the point where Jenny, using June's voice, said, "Some of them turn nasty. I have been attacked and I have been raped."

The four men in the editing suite were ashamed of their thoughts. How could a prostitute be upset about being raped?

Mike ran the film through again. Jenny was now saying, "I had to go doon the toon to pay him off. Some of them turn nasty, I have been attacked and I have been raped."

Adrian spoke all their thoughts – "That doesn't make sense."

"Obviously," said Nigel. "We'll make it make sense, with a voice-over from you."

They wrote the voice-over and Russell went into a sound room nextdoor to read it out while Mike ran the film of Jenny standing next to the concrete pillar supporting the car park.

He read it with voracity in his voice. "This is one woman who paid the full price of borrowing from an evil loan shark. In her own words she tells of her life of prostitution and the vicious attacks that come with the profession she was forced into after borrowing just sixty pounds from a loan shark."

"That's fine," said Mike. "Give me five or six minutes to put her second two sentences in after Adrian's voice-over."

Johnny McPherson got similar treatment. They gave him Eddie's voice, as most of the researcher's friends were quick to point out to him after transmission.

There was disappointment as each part of the jigsaw became more contrived. To have a broken loan shark victim on tape talking about baseball bat injuries and then use another voice was a compromise, verging on failure.

The boxed basement studio packed with high tech equipment was overloaded with creative tension. Each sought release from the present by contemplating the future.

Adrian had his mind on the next glory run. The target was gun runners from Russia. A researcher was already working on that one, travelling across Europe in a massive truck ostensibly to deliver concrete mixers to Rostov on Don where he would make it known to the right people that he was in the market for machine guns destined eventually for the IRA. An exposé of international proportions. After that a book to tell the public a few home truths about rip-offs, government failures, big business scams and backstreet deals. All in the perfectly worthy cause of campaigning truth.

Nigel's thoughts were of a more homely nature. The cottage in Cockermouth. First home to Macclesfield, pick up Louise and the kids, up the M6 in the Range Rover, along the twisting A6 and down into daffodil land. They'd put on their walking boots and head for the hills, clambering over stone dykes before returning to tea and coarse brown bread in front of a log fire. The joys of their country cottage. The urban man goes back to nature. At the weekend. Nigel understood his own fantasy and hoped through careful investment to retire early to the Lakes.

Eddie had made his mind up that this was the last one. Get out now. Get behind a desk and have some other mug find the fodder for these exciting, socially correct documentaries.

Strictly speaking the programme was of his making. His idea, his work and his effort had created the concoction being stirred to perfection by the skilful use of new technology. You can't stop progress. Especially when it moved so fast. He had had some personal matters to sort out – a marriage that simply wasn't working, a house to sell, lawyers to deal with, and most important, a new job to find. He was putting on the weight, which meant buying a new suit. Fuckin hell. He should have followed his father into the joinery business.

Slaves to computerised technology, Eddie, Nigel and Adrian had nothing in common other than their work. They shared the pressures and little else. They had less in common than the Jimmy, Jenny and Johnny, who sadly were shackled to Tollan, without the strength or financial independence to escape.

"Let's eat," said Eddie

They were hungry after six hours concentration.

"I'll buy. Salad sandwiches on brown bread and mineral water for you Nigel, two hamburgers and Coca

Cola for you Adrian . . ."

"Chips as well, please," said Adrian with a smile.

"Right. Salt but no vinegar. I can't stand the smell of it. The stink stays in the studio for days. No vinegar."

This was their time for friendly communication, when their professional relationships could be put aside for a few brief moments.

Soon they would be in conflict again as each tried politely to impose his concept on the documentary. Mike paused at his array of knobs, shoved one forward to silence the voice-over, and said, "I'm sticking to my diet. A banana and a black coffee, please."

They ate without talking, preparing themselves for the battle ahead. Frozen on the six screens above on the wall stood Jenny. The street light shining on her black leather skirt. Nigel was studying her intently.

"Have you ever been with a prostitute?" he asked Adrian.

The media star responded casually. "Who says I have? I've driven past them a few times though."

He took a slug of Coke and returned the question in a slightly different form. "Have you ever slept with anybody since you got married? "

"None of your business, pal."

"Back to work chaps," said Eddie, "It's after eight."

Nigel allowed himself his monthly joke. "Time for your chocolates?"

Eddie responded flatly. "I want out of here by midnight."

They ran the Jenny scene through again, agreeing that it worked well enough, then moved on to the baseball bat attack. A close-up of the blood-smeared bat smashing into Walter's leg. It had been his bright idea to buy the bat at the Sportsman's Emporium, so he was elected to receive the treatment in a mock attack.

Again they needed a voice to cry out, "Ah'll pay ye next week. Gie us a brek."

Eddie obliged with the obvious joke on the first take.

"Ah'll pay ye next week. Gie us a brek. No pun intended."

There were plenty of shots to argue about. They had problems with one of a distressed mother in the park with her two children playing on the shute with the swings in the background. It was a nice sequence taken from the top of the slide with the children slipping away. The kids had been told not to look back when they reached the bottom. Their mother, interviewed sitting on a park bench, talked hysterically of her fear for the weans, of the loan shark and the family's hopeless future. Her face was never revealed as she walked away from the camera, along a path beside flower beds and out of sight behind a statue.

"I'm not too happy with that," said Eddie apologetically.

"You're never happy," said Nigel without the rancour he felt. "What's the problem, Eddie? We aren't showing her face or the children's faces."

"I know."

"But what?"

"Anybody who knows her would recognise her from her clothes. They'll recognise the children from their clothes. You can hear the fear in her voice. That tells it all. Let's drop the shot of the kids and their mother walking away holding hands. We could do a close-up of a woman's hand holding a child's hand and a voice-over."

Mike and Adrian exchanged knowing looks. An explosion was coming.

Nigel's voice edged. "We could run and get actors to play it through. There's plenty of them on the dole. You could go back to radio! Even better why don't you go back to bloody newspapers where you can write whatever you want to write."

"At least they told the truth . . ."

"The truth!"

"Certainly more of the truth than . . ."

"This is the truth. Thousands of people are so poor that they are borrowing from money lenders every day. We are, here and now, in perspective, showing the public what is happening in their rundown, clapped-out bloody country."

Like a newly married couple they started to score points. They weren't shouting yet.

"The public know that already! Go into any town in Britain. Liverpool. Birmingham. Glasgow. There are thousands of people who know what's going on. Social workers, policemen, lawyers, post office staff, taxi drivers and . . ."

Eddie let his wisdom sink in . . . "so do all the people that are borrowing from money lenders. And their relatives. And their neighbours in the street. Everybody knows."

He leant forward, totally out of control and spat the words out at Nigel. "Nobody. And I mean nobody, gives two fucks. So why are we . . ."

"Beecause we don't have a World War at the moment. And this public would get bored with that.

"Beecause . . . we have millions of thinking and unthinking couch potatoes who must be fed.

"Beecause . . . this particular programme is on the schedule.

"And beecause . . . you, nobody else but you, put the idea forward."

Eddie out-matched him in the control stakes.

"Correct," he said, instantly dropping out of philosophy mode. That was for the pub or conversation at a party. The shot of the family stayed in.

Bit by bit they pieced their sixty eight thousand pound effort together, defying the problems with astute linkages, fade-ins, fade-outs, graphics and slices, until they reached the point where Tollan was caught on camera inside the Wee Hauf.

The half-baked proof that he was a loan shark was that he ordered Kenny to "send her across tae me."

The girl trudged across to the bar where Jimmy climbed off his stool to tell her. "Now are yi sure yi can manage thirty, hen? If yi cannae don't take it. Ah'm giein yi good advice. Ah don't want yi getting intae difficulties."

178

"Perfect. That tells all," said Nigel. He was actually clenching his fist, revelling in the moment they had striven to capture over five arduous days. The moment that made the rest of the work worthwhile. The moment made possible by the courage and commitment of Margaret Hazlewood, whose anger matched the violence of her bold red hair. There she was, wired for sound, standing next to the brutish loan shark, smiling as he glanced her way. Cheeky but friendly. What a performance.

"Cool, calm and collected," was the involuntary comment of Eddie as he gazed intently at the wall of TV screens, before stating as a matter of fact. "She's got to come out."

Nigel erupted.

"No! We can't take her out without taking Tollan out. They are together. It is impossible to split them. There is no cut we can make. She's in the shot. For Tollan to stay in she must stay in."

Eddie threw the job he intended to quit, on the line. "She is out or I go to a lawyer on her behalf. We told her we would protect her in the editing. Leave her in and she is in serious danger."

Nigel tried a softer line. "How could she possibly be in any danger? She's a professional woman, working for the Social Work Department."

Eddie explained. "Exactly. Margaret has clients whom she has met regularly, in Garthill! They'll recognise her. The word will spread fast. To Tollan. Glasgow is a village. Garthill is part of a village. They'll murder her."

Nigel argued, "She agreed to help us. She volunteered. She wouldn't want us to drop Tollan. The chances of her being identified are a million to one."

"Are they? And if she is identified, you won't hear a word about the consequences for her. You'll be in a cottage somewhere in Cumbria counting sheep on the fucking hillside."

Mike turned from his array of knobs to calm them down. "Now now, lads. No squabbling."

He had the obvious solution to the problem at hand but out of sheer devilment he kept it to himself, allowing the argument to heat up. It did.

"Yes, I probably will, while you're trying to sort out your marriage."

"Fuck off," said Eddie, bending down to take a cigarette packet and lighter out of his jacket.

Nigel allowed him time to click the lighter before saying smugly, "No smoking in here."

Eddie lit up, walked out of the editing suite, out of the building and into the nearest pub, where he drank a long cold pint. Ten minutes later he was back in the editing studio where the solution to Margaret Hazlewood's identity was being applied by Mike.

To darken the screen leaving only Tollan's face in light. The impression left was of a spotlight on the loan shark.

"Not new, but most effective," said Nigel with a friendly peacemaking smile. Their personality clash was over until the next hurdle.

Mike elaborated on the solution. "Margaret is left in the dark. We can see her because we know she's there. We know where to look. The only person you'll see clearly at the bar is the loan shark."

A bit like any day in Garthill. Everybody saw Jimmy and tried to stay back in the shadows.

There was nothing new in the trick. In the heat of the argument they had forgotten the power at their fingertips. The power to protect those brave enough, or greedy enough, or desperate enough, to participate in their TV jigsaw.

In this case, the power of life or death.

19 To see yourself

IT HARDLY needed a TV documentary to reveal that Jimmy Tollan was a loan shark. The locals knew already. The man was obviously doing very nicely as he cruised his territory in an upmarket car, dressed in the obligatory leather jacket, and sporting a round-the-year tan acquired on regular holidays to Spain and his caravan in Fife. He was on the dole yet there was no mystery to his wealth.

His family were ashamed of his achievement. They lived with the stigma, conveniently overlooking his activities, preferring to take the occasional hundred pounds he pushed their way and dismissing him, behind his back, as 'a stupid bastard'.

Only the blinkered in the scheme were unaware of his sordid deals. The rest lived in resentful collusion or righteous indignation at the cancer in their community.

The colluders passed on messages, held money for him until he arrived to collect, and generally supported his questionable status. Amongst his unpaid supporters were the barmen in four pubs, two girls in the bookies, former classmates who tipped him off about the whereabouts of creditors, the mechanics in a backstreet garage, and a couple of unlicensed taxi drivers.

There were others who knew of his activities but were unable to stop him – policemen on the beat, the lollipop-lady at the primary school, assistants in the post office, housing officials, social workers and his son's teachers.

There was no secrecy about his operation, his collectors, his enforcers, or his obscene interest charges. Not that anybody except the Trading Standards officers ever bothered to work out the exact rate.

How could he keep it secret when there were two hundred and eighty four names in his tally book?

Tollan was the new breed of loan shark. A man of the nineties. Where once the loan sharks operated outside shipyards, they now cashed in on the unemployed, the nouveau poor, recipients of income support, housing benefit, invalidity benefit, family income support – the masses shunted around and tagged the underclass. They danced to the fashionable political song.

Ripe pickings for Jimmy Tollan.

Within two months of his release from prison they all knew he was back in business. Two hundred and eighty four men and women signed on.

His power in the scheme more than equalled that of any bank or building society manager in the bought houses of bountiful Bishopriggs and Bearsden. Those people carried a mortgage. If they lost their jobs, they lost a lot. Their holidays, cars and eventually their homes. Sometimes they threw themselves into bankruptcy.

Very few Tollan clients had jobs, houses, cars or wages. To call in his outstanding debts it was necessary to break a few legs. The only collateral he held was DSS books.

Nobody noticed the injustice. Jimmy easily convinced himself that he was helping the poor. Then again, didn't everybody else who charged extortionate rates for food, cash and clothes and electricity. They paid for their poverty dearly in interest and in insecurity. They smiled in gratitude, then grimaced in fear when he turned the screw. They apologised to him for missing payments.

The arrival of the TV mob at the bookies spread elation amongst the righteous in the scheme. Tollan was going to get shat on.

Fearing that they might have evidence that would mean a return to prison, Jimmy was worried. Equally he feared exposure as a worthless human being.

Jimmy and the scheme were waiting for the big night. Transmission night. He was the main man. Not the star. But the main attraction.

He was to be stripped naked, exposed as an evil greedy ruthless bastard, exploiting the old, the disabled, the poor, the addicted. Jimmy had no illusions about the impending programme.

There would be no Godfather glory. Nor would they give him the Goodfellows treatment. Di Nero and Pacino and Brando. They brought the gangster image into his living room. The music. The colour. The courage, the brains and the bottle to be a gangster.

"They'll crucify us," he told Rita.

"Us!" she cried. "You! Ya bastard."

This was not the way to speak to Jimmy Tollan. Rita didn't care. She was more terrified of the consequences of the programme than of Jimmy's anger. The trailer was unavoidable. She had seen it four times. It popped up after Coronation Street. Again before the news on Tuesday. A couple of other times too. Her sister was in the house on one occasion.

"Adrian Russell confronts Scotland's most evil loan shark. The shocking truth about poverty and illegal money lending."

Jimmy wasn't the country's most evil loan shark. He was the one they had caught on film and was hardly in the position to ring up and claim he was only the twenty second most evil loan shark in Glasgow.

There was a shot of the Black Inn. A blurred shot of Jimmy climbing into the Audi. And a shot of a sobbing girl.

Rita was standing in the kitchen doorway screaming at him. "Crucify us? What's it going to be like for Matt at school? Christ all fuckin mighty."

She was out of control. Matt was curled up on the couch watching a kiddie's video cartoon. He was worried. What next?

Jimmy offered a solution.

"Rita. Tomorrow you go round tae yir sister's. Me and Kenny'll watch it here."

Rita burst into tears. "What difference will that make. They'll be watching it at their house."

She was sobbing between sentences. That irritated Tollan. If only she would cry properly rather than inducing it between her attacks on him.

It got worse. Rita started whining. "You send me

183

round there as though there was a match on. Fuck that. I'm staying here."

She was relentless. "What exactly are they goin to show? Your face? Ma house?"

Jimmy was asking himself a more serious question. What did they know?

That was uppermost in his mind and he tried to hold her emotions down to allow space for his own concerns. "Take it easy Rita. Matt. Up tae the bedroom and watch yir own telly."

"Ah've no video up there. Ah'm watching this," he said foolishly. He was only a child.

Rita saw the anger flash in Jimmy's eyes but wasn't quick enough to prevent his attack on the boy. The loan shark grabbed his son by the arm, hauled him off the couch and threw him toward the door. "Do as yir fuckin telt."

The boy bolted upstairs.

Jimmy turned to Rita. "Ah'll get yi a video fur his room tomorrow. Nae problem."

Rita sat down in the armchair. "Switch the video off Jimmy. Let's talk about tomorrow. I'm no goin round to ma sister's. To have them talk about it in front of me." Tears welled in her eyes. The five week long delay between filming and the transmission had drained her.

Jimmy pressed the remote control once to stop the video and a second time to switch off the telly.

"It would be handy if Ah could switch everybody's telly aff tomorrow. Just staun on the veranda and switch aff every telly in Glasga." Beyond the boundaries of Glasgow was outside his domain.

"That's just fuckin stupid," she said.

The pressure was taking toll, turning their words and thoughts into farce. Neither of them noticed.

Rita tried to haul the conversation back onto an even keel, stating her stance on the problem of the impending programme. "I've told you. I'm no staying here tomorrow. And Matt's no goin tae school after it's been shown. He's staying aff school for the rest of the week."

"That's up tae you. You're his maw."

Her blood pressure rose. "And you're his faither. You got us intae this."

Jimmy himself was tired. The TV people had caught him on camera five weeks ago. He was unsure of what the programme could prove. He had no control. He was afraid of the unknown. Without realising it Rita was offering him the excuse to run. To go away and rest.

First though, he would try to placate her.

"Taggart did that thing on loan sharks. It wisnae a bad wan either. They nearly got it the way it is."

"Jimmy. You're fuckin crazy," she screamed. "That was bad for me and for Matt. My sister mentioned the Taggart one. She was fuckin at it. I just said that I never saw it. I'm no goin through that crap again."

"It was forgotten after a few days."

"No Jimmy. You forgot it after a few days. I didn't. Anyway this is gonnie be different. You're on the telly. No some fuckin actor. You!"

He gave up and offered the obvious solution. Jimmy always seemed to be seeking a solution after a discussion. An old age pensioner begging for cash, a mum to feed her weans, a man to pay the gas bill.

"We'll take a wee break. We'll go tae the caravan in the mornin."

Rita was instantly pleased. Her eyes softened in gratitude as her voice warmed. "Thank God for that Jimmy. I hate tae run frae it. I'm only wantin tae save Matt."

Crail. The sea. Peace and quiet. Away from this nightmare. The only drawback was that Jimmy was coming along too. He could never manage to be nice when they were up at the caravan.

Never mind.

"Thanks Jimmy. I just can't face it here. I'm no havin wee Matt sherricked by the ither weans. They'll no let him aff the hook, and it's fuck all tae dae wi him."

At mid morning the next day they pulled in at a lay-by past Kincardine Bridge while Rita phoned the school on

185

the mobile and talked to the deputy headteacher. Matt had been sick throughout the night and would be off school for a few days, she said without much conviction.

"That's a pity," said the teacher, "We will see him next week then. Thank you for calling Rita." The voice was laden with sympathy.

In Anstruther they pulled into the carpark of the first restaurant they saw. "A funny name, eh? The Craw's Nest. Looks nice. Thae bastards back in Glasga will be hivin a drink in the Black Inn. Hard cheese on them. This is class Rita," said Jimmy.

The lounge was empty but they were made welcome as the first guests of the day, ordering a pot of tea for Rita and coffee for Jimmy. They said little looking absently at some Russell Flint water prints displayed for sale on the restaurant walls.

It was too quiet for Rita. She broke her sad thoughts. "That's a nice painting there Jimmy. I like the way the women are staunin next to the pillars. The colours are nice and soft."

"No ma cup of tea," he said curtly.

Jimmy was quite irritated when the waitress failed to return with the bill. The receptionist was warmly polite, with an open smile and a friendly chat. "That will be two pound ten."

He gave her three pounds, told her to keep the change and asked, "Ah want tae buy wan of yir paintings hen. The wan in the restaurant on the right hand wall next tae where we were sittin."

"I don't know where you were sitting. Was it a Russell Flint or a Monica Anderson? She's a local painter who hangs her work here."

Jimmy looked at the girl without answering.

Rita moved to a small stand displaying postcards where Matt was studying pictures of puffins perched on rocks beneath a rugged cliff. He had a postcard of the Isle of May in his hand. She put it back in the stand, took her son's hand firmly and made her way to the door saying, "Jimmy,

I'll see you at the motor."

She kept going through the door as he raised his voice. "Rita, dae yi want wan of they pictures or no?"

Rita heard but kept walking. He was a bit out of his depth.

He held his temper. "Come wi me, hen," he told the receptionist, making his way back to the restaurant. "That wan there. It's thirty five pound."

He drew a large wad of notes from his inside pocket and counted out the cash. She offered to wrap the painting she had lifted off the wall but Jimmy said he would take as it was. "Thanks a lot, hen," was his parting shot.

In the car Rita was ready with her appreciation. "Jimmy that wis really nice of you. I'll put it in the bedroom."

The first hurdle had been cleared. Jimmy's next move was to make Matt happy. "Where dae yi want tae go son?"

"Tae the beach Da."

He compromised and they went to the harbour in Anstruther.

Matt was first out of the car running out across the long wooden pier. The tide was out and he sat down dangling his legs over the edge studying a strange fat ship which appeared to be stranded on the silt.

In the distance he could see the Isle of May, sanctuary to puffins and thousands of other sea birds. The view out to sea was similar to that from the caravan at Crail. The harbour was different with more people and more cars, but essentially it was the same scene.

Jimmy and Rita leant against the car bonnet and watched their son enjoying the freedom and the fresh air. They weren't in any hurry to go to the caravan, preferring to have lunch in Anstruther, where they could be among the visitors and locals mingling in the daily tourist routines. As long as they stayed in Anstruther they were part of the holiday scene, able to consider the maritime museum, allowing Matt to play on the pier, and later paddle in the open air rocky swimming pool at Cellardyke.

They wandered the day away.

They pushed the caravan and the TV to the back of their minds. They were not really on holiday. They were on the run – from the faces in the scheme, from the people who might, with the help of the TV programme, have the courage to taunt them for their illegal wealth. Or worse, mock their son. The caravan with the television in the corner was their nemesis.

They took a boat trip to the Isle of May. Matt enjoyed the boat trip more than the actual sight of the rocky island and multitude of sea birds. Rita tried to avoid the sea trip but Jimmy insisted they all go.

Back at the pier they eased their hunger with hamburgers and hung about in the village taking a long walk through the narrow streets between the fishing harbour and nearby Cellardyke waiting on the hotel and restaurants to start serving dinner. Jimmy had decided that they would eat out before going to the caravan.

They wandered through the ancient streets amongst fishermen's houses now converted to holiday homes or bought and modernised by the lawyers, artists and architects who commuted to Edinburgh.

Rita could see that this was a million miles removed from the sameness of the yellow grey graffiti-smeared scheme where the shops huddled in fear behind grey-steeled shutters.

"This is another world Jimmy."

"Right hen. But would thae people here hiv the bottle tae cope with Garthill? Ah fuckin doubt it. They couldnae survive in ma world. That's fur sure."

The words unlocked her mind to the impending programme.

Rita responded without anger. "Are we really surviving, Jimmy? Look at us. We're feart tae stay in our own home. We cannae send our boy tae school."

"Jimmy," she said, "we're no surviving. Stop kidding yersel."

Her eyes and voice offered sympathy. Rita was looking

for a debate. A heart to heart that would lead to resolutions and promises and plans for a happier future. Jimmy almost fell in with the appeal.

"Rita. They come tae me and ask fur loans. Ah don't force the deals on them. They know the score."

He was encased in stress. From his childhood to his future. Gazing across the Forth estuary his mind sought justification. "They could do a fuckin programme on hunners like me. It's just ma bad luck some bastard's fired me in."

He stopped talking and gazed out across the sea.

"Ah'll survive. There's naebody in Garthill will grass me. Ah know them. They wouldnae grass."

He was getting it both ways. But he was right in saying that nobody would grass him with hard evidence. There were several who were more than willing to earn a fortune helping the documentary team reflect the grim realities of poverty. There was nobody who would provide the hard evidence that Nigel sought to turn his programme into an award winner.

They sat on a wooden bench watching the eider ducks. A drake and his partner moved between the rocks. The willow warblers that had arrived early, swooped round the bay.

Matt joined some local boys who were sledding down a grassy embankment. They were confident enough to know that you don't need snow to go sledding. Matt soon joined in the fun. Two redshank passed over, their orange legs tucked under as they flew across the calm sea waters.

The restaurant was warm, quiet and the seats were comfortable. Rita tried some fish soup and was delighted to find it so enjoyable. Jimmy and Matt had fun with prawns, mussels and scallops. They had a full meal with all the trimmings. That killed some time.

On arrival in Crail, Jimmy drove down to the harbour to buy three crab salads. They were at the caravan half an hour before the broadcast. Matt was sent down to the beach. He sat on a rock staring out to sea, wondering what life was like for the lighthouseman on the Isle of May. He knew not to go back to the caravan until he was called.

Jimmy and Rita watched the programme in silence. The screen shone in the corner of the compact caravan lounge beneath the expansive window overlooking the rolling sea. A persistent wind tugged at the caravan. Jimmy poured them two whiskies at the chill turn of the evening. He switched on the video to record the programme. As did half of Garthill.

The programme opened with a man in a glittery show business suit, on stage swaying behind a microphone, in full voice.

> *If you ain't got no money,*
> *Come straight to me honey,*
> *I gie ye the dough,*
> *I'll never say no.*

Jimmy was as nonplussed as Rita by the unexpected opening. A sing-song start. Jesus. What the fuck was this about?

They listened carefully as the entertainer unclipped the mike from the stand and moved round the stage.

> *I can help you get by,*
> *There's no need to cry,*
> *For I'm a real friend,*
> *Who'll be there to the end.*

The scene changed with rain-spattered high rise blocks, fading into boarded-up shops scarred with graffiti. Rita broke the silence. "Those shops are nowhere near us. That's down at Barrowfield."

"Shut up, Rita. Wan singer wan song," he added with a forced laugh. The man in the shining grey suit was back on screen with his weird rendition of the loan shark's lament.

> *But remember that I*

Can never rely,
On people who run,
They'll have no fun.

Jimmy took a large swallow of whisky and turned up the volume slightly to catch more clearly the next verse of this bizarre showbusiness invention.

They'll lose everything,
When hit by the sting,
The bat and the knife,
Will sure end their life.

For some strange reason the audience applauded. Even Rita was smiling. This was ridiculous and they both knew it.

The scene switched suddenly to the dark profile of a prostitute stepping out of the darkness at a city centre multi-storey car park. Her face was never revealed while she talked of her life on the streets to pay off a loan shark. The voice was strangely cultured. Jimmy had never heard a prostitute who spoke so well.

"I am working on the streets to save my kids from a beating," she said with conviction. "It is this or my weans go without food. I borrowed twenty pounds to pay the gas bill and then found I couldn't keep up the payments."

Jimmy studied the profile carefully trying to ascertain whether or not it was Jenny.

Rita asked. "Do you know her?"

"Naw. Ah don't think so. She's no wan of mine."

A girl droned on about handing her Monday book over, living on twenty pounds a week, and her fear for her kids. A Monday book spread across the screen, the name blotted out as Russell explained that thousands of families relied on this for food and heat.

Suddenly Jimmy was staring at himself with the fish and chip shop in the background, while Adrian Russell thrust himself onto the screen pushing a microphone in front of Jimmy's frozen face . . .

191

The words stabbed at Jimmy's heart. "Why are you charging such massive interest rates on illegal loans to the poor, Jimmy Tollan?"

Jimmy saw himself replying. "Fuck off. Yiv got the wrong guy."

In the peace of the caravan Jimmy's eyes remained riveted to the screen as he blurted out. " Fuckin stupid."

That was all he could manage as Rita cried out, "Jesus, Jimmy." The cry was saturated in love, anguish and anger.

Like a fireball the programme swept on. Jimmy's face was filling the screen as he strode toward the camera. His face froze on the screen. The round face, dark eyes and thick blackish hair. He was staring into the caravan.

With Russell's piercing accusation. "This is the man who drove a young mother to prostitution."

The images clicked into slow motion action as he was shown running to the bookies, without even a glance over his shoulder. His every movement depicted fear and cowardice.

Russell's voice cashed-in on the image. "That's him. The loan shark running from the truth."

Then the close-up of a Monday Book with the voice explaining. "Thousands of families rely on this type of book for their weekly allowances. Yet loan sharks hold their books as collateral."

There was no release from the fast moving scenes as the programme zapped through the images . . . the prostitute, the loan shark, the single parent mum, the victim of violence.

Then a fade-out to the commercials!

Jimmy was shaken by what he had seen so far.

He had suffered the tension of several serious trials resulting in his incarceration. The experience gained in travelling to and from prison, to the cells beneath the court, before standing in the dock with a hopeless Not Guilty plea left him ill-prepared for the shock of seeing himself cast in the role of an evil bastard.

Arrests and court appearances were adversarial. First

it was Jimmy versus the police. "Whit can yi prove? Ah never done it. It wisnae me."

The detectives came back with their broadside. "We know it was you. You were there at the time. We have witnesses."

Then to court where the prosecution vied with the defence in the contest to decide his innocence or guilt. No matter the result Jimmy need never examine his behaviour. Defeat was easily dismissed as the consequence of having a 'bum lawyer' or 'lying witnesses' or being 'fitted-up by lying cops'.

The verdict was reached on the evidence rather than on any assessment of himself as a human being. In court he won or he lost. That was all there was to it, like a football match, you could be relegated to the cells if the team failed to play to form.

This bastard on the television wasn't bothering with any organised game. He simply branded Jimmy as a greedy loan shark preying on the poor without, as yet, proving anything.

The next fifteen minutes would be crucial.

"Ah'm gonnae sue thae bastards," he told Rita pouring himself another whisky.

Rita was badly shaken by the sight of her man focused as the central point in the sordid scenes being depicted on the screen.

"Pour me one too," she murmured.

He splashed out a large one for his distraught partner. Rita had been buoyed up by a delicious seafood meal in the comfort of the Craws Nest restaurant when Jimmy was doing his utmost to charm the fear out of her.

The whitebait and lemon sole washed down with a bottle of white wine was no cushion for the large whiskies she was gulping, as each new image threw her mind into a grey abyss. Rita held onto the glass of whisky, unable to release it as she drank repetitively. They were both reaching for the bottle.

The adverts seemed to last an eternity. Cars that

crashed safely, insurance policies, and holidays.

The documentary theme music dragged their eyes back to the screen. The title faded to reveal Jimmy sitting at the bar in the Wee Hauf, talking to Kenny. "Send her across tae me," he was telling his collector. Kenny disappeared off the screen to be replaced instantly by a tired looking girl about twenty years of age. Jimmy watched himself climb off the stool allowing the girl, head bowed, to stand next to him.

He heard himself advising the girl. "Now are yi sure yi can manage thirty hen? If you cannnae, don't take it hen. Ah'm gieing yi good advice here. Ah don't want yi gettin intae difficulties hen."

She had her back to the camera. She squared up to him looking into his face, saying. "It's OK Jimmy. Ah can definitely manage OK."

Jimmy and Rita's attention was broken when the door of the caravan opened. Matt stepped in with a young teenage girl in tow. Before Matt could say a word Jimmy let go with a salvo. "Get out. Fuck aff and don't come back fur half an hour."

The boy turned quickly bumping into Jocelyn who was in the throes of closing the door behind her. They turned and stumbled down the steps, leaving the door open behind them.

The cold evening wind swept through the caravan. Jimmy and Rita were instantly concentrating on the TV screen, picking up another girl's words.

They caught the last of them. "I'm intae him for hunners. I'll never get out." She spoke the words without the correct dialect. The words seemed bogus. Old fashioned. Like an American actor failing to make it as a Scot.

Rita put her whisky down and got up to close the caravan door. Jimmy kept his eyes on the screen, which filled with a page of names, dates and cash payments due.

| Jan 10 | Bent Willie | £648 |
| Jan 10 | Jessica | £260 |

| *Jan 10* | *Johnny* | *£1248* |
| *Jan 10* | *Wee Hughie* | *£780* |

It was darkening outside. The wind had softened allowing the sound of waves breaking on the rocks to invade the caravan. There was no commentary as the names of shame rolled up the screen.

"Where the fuck did they get thae names fae?" said Jimmy, gulping another whisky.

"This is fuckin bad. If they've got the names some cunt's talked. That's no ma writin"

More names rolled down the screen.

Jan 10	*Old Eckie*	*£860*
Jan 10	*Sam the Bam*	*£55*
Jan 10	*Aggie McColl*	*£840*
Jan 10	*Aggie's pal*	*£125*
Jan 10	*Shaggy Aggy*	*£1210*

Jimmy saw a face behind every name. Each and every one was pigeon-holed in his mind under categories – unreliable, has to be leant on, always tries to pay, might do a runner.

He saw more than their names. He saw their total situations. Their houses, their drink problems, their children, their attitudes.

The images of his business clients raced past as his eyes soaked in the names. Units in his monetarist world.

Jimmy was staring at his collapsing financial empire. Huge in his mind and in the minds of his clients. The bastards?

Adrian Russell's voice took up a dismal commentary. "These are the victims of ruthless loan shark Jimmy Tollan. Families who cannot survive after the government's social security cutbacks." He punched out the words. "Families trapped by inhuman interest rates."

Jimmy shouted back at the screen. "They cannae survive without fuckin comin tae me. They were all in the shit when they came tae me."

Mercifully the names ended. A slim man without a tie or jacket seated behind a metal desk was talking. "The gap between the rich and the poor has widened under this government. When grants were turned into loans the poor were made even poorer. The repayment of the loans is taken off their benefits at source."

There was no time to introduce him. His name appeared along the bottom of the screen with his title – Welfare Rights Officer, Social Work Department.

The official had little more to say other than to warn the public not to turn to loan sharks for that would only increase their debts.

The images on the screen changed at breathtaking speed. The next was a blood-spattered baseball bat connecting with the leg of a man who collapsed screaming in fear. "I'll definitely pay you next week." No faces were shown.

Then a hospital operating theatre with surgeons, nurses and a bloody wound.

Jimmy was keeping up with the action images that would ignite a thousand short term conversations the following day.

He was lost. Struggling to understand. The programme ended with another shot of his face, a repeat, as he told Adrian Russell to fuck off.

Jimmy took a large swallow of whisky before attempting to lift Rita's sagging spirit. Her eyes reflected her abysmal dejection. She was hurt, angry, frightened and shamed. Broken beyond tears.

The loan shark's next words were stupid beyond belief. "There's nothing in that tae worry about. They hivnae got anything on me. There's nae proof there."

His only concern was whether or not he might go back to jail.

Rita looked away, out of the window across the wave-flecked sea. He tried again, hoping for a response of some sort.

"The cops won't do anything. There's fuck all they

can dae from that."

She said nothing so Jimmy tried the most underhand of moves pouring more whisky into her glass.

Matt's voice carried through the still night above the waves slapping onto the beach. They couldn't hear his words. Only the warmth in his voice as he talked to the girl from the farm. She was laughing.

The little boy's animated voice triggered a terrible response in Rita. She lifted the glass of whisky and threw the contents fully in Jimmy's face, screaming, "You fuck off."

Jimmy wiped the whisky off his face, stood up, took a wad of notes from his pocket, peeled off one hundred pounds, placed the notes on the table and left.

Without a word.

He took the tape out of the video recorder, pulled his leather jacket on and was gone.

She heard the car start.

He had no power over Rita. Without that terrible corruption he had no desire to spend any more time with her.

The Audi eased through the countryside. At the Kincardine Bridge Jimmy's spirits lifted enough to press in the tape.

> *Start spreading the noos,*
> *I'm leaving today,*
> *I want to be a part of it,*
> *Noo York, Noo York.*

The thumping upbeat song with all Sinatra's penetrative musical swing failed to ease Jimmy's troubled mind. He switched the tape off and pressed the Audi on down the motorway. He was moving a fraction above comfortable cruising speed, running from what was behind, domestic distress, racing toward the pleasure of control.

He arrived at Jenny Mullen's flat at 10pm. She was in, having decided to take a night off work to watch herself

197

on TV. She felt sure that Jimmy would have recognised her mouth.

"Did you see it? Ah'm suing the fuckin bastards," were his opening words.

No need for niceties here. He had control over Jenny.

Jenny masked her fear. That he had sussed her presence in the fast-moving documentary.

"Yes. I sent Christine round to her friend's house and watched it here."

"Whit di yi think?"

"It didn't seem that bad. Want a cup o' tea?"

"Yea. Ah'm staying the night."

Jenny protested mildly. "Christine's back now. She's sleeping here tonight. It would be better if you . . ."

"Fuckin shut up. Ah'm staying."

Christine had heard bits of the conversation. She tried to fall asleep.

20 Cowboys and Indians

ANGUS HAZLEWOOD was jumping up and down in the living room, his eyes aglow at the thrill of seeing his mother on the telly. "That was you there mum. At the bar. It was you! I'm certain that was you mum."

His father gently calmed him. "Sit down Eagle Eyes, so that we can all see the rest of the programme."

There weren't any chairs left so he sat on the floor next to his cousins. This was a family gathering with a difference. Callum was out at the Scouts. The rest were here. Granny had come down from Lochgoilhead. The couple from next door were in too. On the promise that they wouldn't breath a word to anyone about Margaret's involvement.

Angus was assured by his father that there would be plenty of time to see mum on screen after the programme was finished. "I'm taping it Angus. You can watch it again before you go to bed."

"That's good. I never saw her," said granny.

"Neither did I. We'll study the tape closely later."

"I could borrow the tape to show to my friends at home."

"Shh. Be quiet mum," Margaret said gently.

"I can't help talking Margaret. You're on the telly," she said happily.

They were sitting next to each other on the two seater couch. Margaret put her arm round her mother and whispered in her ear, "I only have a small part, mum. A character part," she chuckled.

Angus couldn't contain himself for even a few seconds. "Dad when do you appear?"

"I do not appear Angus. So sit down and be quiet. There's only ten minutes to go."

"Dad, why . . ."

"Leave the room Angus."

"I was only asking why you aren't . . ."

"Leave the room now, Angus."

He left. The assembled family and friends watched the remainder of the programme without interruptions. Margaret watched the exposé unfold with mixed feelings. The fear she had experienced came flooding back, as did the disappointment at not being able to secure sufficient evidence of Tollan's guilt.

The investigation had taken over her life for the best part of two weeks. First the lunchtime calls to the Black Inn, the Rhum Do and the Wee Hauf when they checked out the bar, the lounge and the car parks. Then the evening visits.

The cops and robbers game held a greater significance to Walter, Eddie and Nigel than to Margaret, who didn't have the pressure of a deadline. Nor was she concerned about the escalating costs.

They kept at a distance from their prey driving past the pubs in the hope of spotting his red car. Occasionally they actually spotted a red car similar to Tollan's. Such sightings led to interesting diversions.

Walter had the keenest eye. "There's a red car. Could be an Audi. We could see it more clearly from the scheme overlooking the back of the pub."

At their vantage point he pulled out a small pair of binoculars casually remarking, "handy on jobs like this." The equipment didn't bring Tollan any nearer. Purely by chance he avoided them, leaving them endless hours of wasted time.

One day they followed a red Audi, driven by a chunky man wearing a leather jacket. They tailed it all the way from Garthill to Clydebank and into a car park at the shopping centre. The driver wasn't Tollan. Another day they parked at a safe distance from Rita Fullerton's house waiting six hours, but the loan shark didn't show.

Rita took a taxi, which they followed to a house in Cumbernauld. The taxi waited. She came out carrying a large cardboard box. They tried to follow the cab back to

Rita's house but lost it at the Stepps traffic lights.

"Eight hours wasted. God knows what that was about," said Nigel. "We can't even open the box."

Eddie scowled in the back seat.

The investigation had lasted too long. As researcher he was the one-man advance party, living out of a hotel during the endless days of talking to single parents, social workers, police officers, and organising meetings with families who had borrowed from the city's growing army of loan sharks.

He was drained of commitment, emotionally bankrupt, and sick to the back teeth of Nigel Atkinson and Adrian Russell. He had some sympathy for Walter Harvey, whom he considered a fellow traveller, a foot soldier who actually did the real work. The hack's bad luck had happened on his first day.

Eddie had little or no security of employment either. Only a six months contract with the understanding that it would certainly be renewed because he was accepted as 'a good operator.'

A good operator! He considered himself that and a bit more. Digging out punters who were willing to talk about their despairing debt-ridden lives was, to say the least, difficult.

Not for him the simple role of front man, firing loaded questions at loan sharks. That could be dangerous of course. The percentages were however on Russell's side in that it was unlikely the criminals would launch a serious attack. They rarely did. Not in front of a camera.

Eddie's problems were more subtle. He could, and did ask twenty single parent mums if they had borrowed from a loan shark. Eight admitted they had and he was left to wonder how many of them had reported his inquiry to the loan shark. After all the information was worth money.

He was tired from the endless nights of assuring people that they would not be named, identities would be disguised, and yes, there was a payment in it for them. "There's fifty pounds now. The rest later."

Eddie gave his word and stood by every promise he made to the men and women willing to risk violence for a bundle of notes. He let none of them down, for Eddie was as honourable a researcher as it was possible to be in this business. He was bored, his professional edge blunted by years of commitment. He'd been at it too long and was now without inspiration. He lacked any self delusion and worse still, was losing his sense of humour.

Anderson, the man who had made it happen, was a first class professional at the end of his tether and happy to admit it. As far as he was concerned the contest could end any day now. Time to pack up and cobble together a programme that would satisfy the viewers.

Two days surveillance at the pub locations proved fruitless. Cops and robbers had deteriorated into cowboys and indians. They sent their best scouts into the concrete valleys to check every watering hole in the badlands. Paranoia set in to the most unlikely team member. Nigel Atkinson began to think that Jimmy Tollan had outmanoeuvred them.

He snapped on the third day.

They were sitting in the rented Sierra across the main road and up a side street overlooking the Rhum Do when Nigel decided to go back to the Black Inn.

"He won't be at the Black Inn. We know that for a fact. Jenny told us that he's now operating at the pubs we're concentrating on," said Eddie.

Walter agreed. "There's no point in going back there. He won't be there. Two of them have told us that independently."

"Johnny and Jenny could be lying," said Nigel. "After all, they both need the money."

"Yea. I know that. But it is in both their interests to see Tollan off the streets and in jail. Johnny owes him six hundred and forty eight pounds and Jenny owes eight hundred and something."

Walter was convinced that the two Tollan clients were telling the truth.

Nigel wasn't sure. Then he introduced his own paranoia induced theory. "What if Tollan lied to them. He doesn't trust anybody so he gave them bum information. We're going to the Black Inn."

There was a pregnant silence in the car while Eddie, Walter and Margaret digested his theory. Nobody wanted to tell the producer that the pressure was getting to him. He was losing the way.

Nigel started the car and drove to the Black Inn. The red Audi was nowhere in sight. They checked up several side streets and on the derelict land behind the pub. There were no cars that caught the eye.

They drove back to the Wee Hauf without anybody telling Nigel in so many words that he was paranoid. Eddie came closest. "That should restore your faith in the human race Nigel. Jenny and Johnny are sound."

From the back seat Eddie noticed the car first. "Fuck me. He's here now."

The red Audi was parked in front of the Wee Hauf for all to see. There was no time for rehearsals. Margaret was on. Straight into the lion's den with the tape strapped to her back and the mike under her blouse taped into her cleavage.

"Sexy but safe," said Eddie. "Nobody will find it there." The moment was shared in the back seat, while he helped prepare her for the climax of the lengthy investigation. They wired her up in the car round the corner from the Wee Hauf while Eddie was quickly drafted in as a stooge cameraman.

They dare not send in the real cameraman for he had most likely been clocked outside the bookies three days earlier. Anybody who took part in that circus would have to step down from duty at the Wee Hauf.

They placed the small camera in a sports bag, stuffing Nigel's pullover into it and tearing a hole in the side. The lens was carefully pushed into the hole so that it protruded fractionally. They switched on the camera seconds before strolling to the pub with Nigel's reassurance ringing in the ears. "Don't worry. We'll be outside in the car park. Not too far away."

Again Nigel's words carried little or no weight with the others who understood that they could offer no protection.

They were a few strides from the entrance when Tollan and Kenny Watson walked out of the pub. Margaret and Eddie had no alternative but to continue inside, walking straight past their prey.

Nigel was driving the Sierra into the car park as Jimmy reversed the red Audi out from between the other cars, and drove past. Nigel shouted at Walter, "Get down. Lie down."

He crouched down to avoid the eyes of the streetwise shark, who would remember Walter's face from the Black Inn racing page incident.

A complete cock up! The day had turned into another circus without the consolation of any contact whatsoever with Jimmy Tollan. Inside the pub Margaret and Eddie ordered a drink and chatted for ten minutes before returning to the Sierra parked up a side street.

Eddie was seething. He slammed the car door shut and shouted at Nigel. "You and your fuckin paranoia. We could have got him today. He must have done his business while we were farting about at the Black Inn."

"He might have been there."

"But he wasn't. He was here. Why don't you listen to me. I know these people. I know their minds. You haven't a fucking clue what's going on. Tomorrow stay in the hotel. That way we'll get out of this before Christmas."

By the time they got back to the Holiday Inn for another pow-wow, Eddie's anger had abated.

21 The sting

Margaret never forgot that day when the producer elected to go to the Black Inn rather than stay at the Wee Hauf. The day she almost gave up on them totally.

She phoned home from the hotel telling her husband that she would be late as there was a lot of talking to be done to salvage the programme.

Nigel had given up all pretence of reluctance to use Maggie.

"Have dinner with us tonight. Please. You've earned it."

She smiled to herself at the invitation. As if a free four course dinner was something worth earning. Margaret ate when she was ready and had no need of a free meal, no matter how sumptuous. She joined them, more out of sympathy for the team who were beginning to lose heart. They deserved better luck in their loan sharks' hunt.

She gave it one more shot.

She went drinking to the Wee Hauf with Eddie posing as her husband. They both sported wedding rings. They played a dangerous game, cuddling intimately in the public bar to the irritation of the regulars.

They spent hours together supping drinks slowly, giving the regular punters time to accept them. At first there was an imperceptible attraction. Eddie was almost on the rebound from his failed marriage. He was lonely. Margaret was quite excited by the tension involved in chasing a dirty loan shark.

To kill the time they talked. As the stake-out stretched into days Margaret began to philosophise. By the end of the exercise Johnny had lost any sexual interest in Maggie, as he then called her. She was too angry. Nice as she was, she had degenerated into a crazy socialist.

Years later he would still hear her anger – "All they ever get is advice. Drugs are for Mugs. Eat Sensibly. Play

Sport. Don't run in the street. Stay away from Strangers. Don't smoke. They're even introducing sex advice in primary schools to stem the spread of AIDS. Wear a condom. What a disgusting destructive introduction to sex."

While recognising that the age of innocence was shortening with each new decade she was repelled by the necessity to manage childrens' very childhoods.

Margaret hurt for them. For the suffering children. She could see that their empty lives were far removed from the pleasurable disciplines of her own childhood.

Eddie got it all.

"I had a real childhood. At lambing there was always a spare one for me to to nurse."

She rambled through her early years on the farm. "There were eggs to be collected from round the yard. The shells were white and inside them orange flecked yolks."

Her red hair tossed and swished. The spirited talks, verging on lectures, were spoken in an undertone. Her images were real. They had happened. Her father with the clips on his dungarees loosened, his black scuffed boots, relaxing in the armchair talking to mum about bantam hens. Margaret recalled those distant conversations between her parents without any deprecation of her father. He was down-to-earth. He thought straight. And that had helped her to think straight.

Eddie listened. She laid her childhood out like a thick warm carpet. The games, the pleasures, the memories. About the shearing season when the dirty greasy bales of wool were piled up in the shed. Dirty on the outside and creamy white on the inside, where they had been carefully clipped to within an inch of the animals' skins. By day three of the shearing season the bales were stacked fifteen feet deep in the draughty shed. Margaret, William and the other kids from the farm down the road climbed up the old wooden ladders and crawled along the rafters, taking it in turn to plunge into the stacked wool. They could hide in the strangely smelly bales. It was warm. Secretive. Adventurous.

Eddie was in limbo, unable to escape her life, while absorbing the daily goings-on in the pub. The punters had other priorities. "There's a cert in the three thirty. Ah'm backing it on the nose an putting it in a treble."

"I knew Elton John'd split fae that woman he married in Australia. He denied they were splittin."

Margaret heard their idle words, as they nursed their beer and worked their daily tickets. Their culture matched their environment.

Eddie made little comment as she unloaded her mental baggage in the corner of the Wee Hauf.

How she did her homework, grew up and moved on to Aberdeen University to secure a sociology degree, to Stirling as a social worker, and finally to Glasgow as a senior social worker. To what they liked to call a culture shock. She saw it as more than that. She arrived in Glasgow as monetarism began to grab the nation. The market was the force that would create wealth. The sons and daughters of the unemployed would have to stand on their own two feet.

Margaret saw the deprivation as the direct result of government policy. For ten distressing years she tended the wounded – filling out case reports on child abuse, setting up crisis centre for battered wives, creating support for prostitutes facing the threat of HIV, arranging treatment for delinquent teenagers, attending the busiest court in Europe, directing alcoholics to support agencies, setting up heroin addiction groups.

She married a gentle school teacher who saw her beauty and shared her socialism tinged with Scottish Nationalism. They had two sons Angus and Callum. Margaret tried hard to give them as much as she had received from her parents. She was stretched to the limit.

The job. It got in the way of her life. The stress of dealing with families without any purpose in their aimless, jobless lives, left her a bit short in maintaining close relationships with her own family.

Her childhood had not prepared her for the onslaught of human wastage. The case reports were more than just professional analyses. Behind the paperwork were faces and voices. Flesh and blood people. Houses and children. Live people who talked about their damaged loves and about their hatreds. Their fears, as they huddled around colour TV sets, closing the door to an unfriendly outside world, dominated by a powerful money-driven regime.

The women seemed to suffer most. Maybe that was because they were able to express their innermost sufferings more easily than the broken men, who rejected the TV escape without taking any serious political action to change their situation. Not for them sits-in, strikes, or mass demonstrations. That was history. A faded black and white image of the past that seemed to merge with jerky soldiers, sinking ships, bombed cities and old newsreels.

She looked round the dull pub and sighed, "They don't march now. Today is Technicolor time, get the contrast right, bring up the brightness and the colour. Videos and holidays."

Out of control, and unhappy with the state of the nation, her feelings cascaded out in full flood. "What are they supposed to do? Make their little contribution to the economy. Watch TV or march against the Poll Tax. They're only bystanders. Thousands are now invisible bystanders . . . they have disappeared from the face of the earth to avoid paying the Poll Tax. Did you know that? They can't afford to exist. They are unofficial."

She was, Eddie felt, spitting in the wind.

Jimmy Tollan could have saved Eddie from her endless monologues. If only he would turn up. At first she had seemed so happily upbeat. The lovely smile, the red hair, the bounce of her walk, had fooled him. The deception of first impression. In fact, to Eddie she was a bore.

For three long days, an hour at lunchtime, and two or three hours in the evening, they waited for Tollan to arrive. Eddie began to hate her.

Margaret apologised for her crusading words. "I can't help myself Eddie. I'm sorry. It's so stupid. I work in communities where there is no hope There's too much stress on families. Too much fear and hatred. Drug addicts – I hate the word junkies – mugging pensioners, stabbing each other, stealing."

Even her apologies twisted into a continuation of her deep-set concerns. Eddie tried lamely to close her mind down. "The poor have always been with us."

Margaret refused the chance to turn off. "That's true Eddie. Very true. The trouble is, this time they're being used as the commodity. For useless training schemes, to give me work, to make TV documentaries, to staff welfare rights centres, to recycle old furniture."

She was out of control and she knew it.

"What am I doing, sitting here with a tape stuck on my back and a microphone on my chest?"

Eddie tried to simplify things. "Waiting on Jimmy Tollan."

Right on cue, the loan shark sauntered in. The pub quickened in awareness. The barman was first to acknowledge the money man's entrance. "Hi Jimmy. How's it goin? Pint?"

Jimmy climbed onto a stool at the bar, taking his time to answer. The barman waited for the reply. "Ay. And wan fur Kenny – he's parkin the motor."

Eddie's pulse quickened. His right foot touched the sports bag under the table. He bent down to lift it up while keeping his eyes off Tollan. He looked into Margaret's eyes. She was calm but was looking for guidance.

"Sit tight. Just keep talking."

Suddenly she could find nothing to say, so he asked, "Did you see that film last night. I've seen it before. It's good."

"Who was in it?"

"Dustin Hoffman and Meryl Streep."

"Oh yea. Kramer versus Kramer. It was one of those films that are good the first time but not so good the second time."

Margaret was warming to the small talk game. "That won her an Oscar. I think that was her second Oscar. I'm not sure. She's a proper actress, if you know what I mean. She's different in every role."

"So is Dustin Hoffman. Did you see Midnight Cowboy?"

"Sad, sad film. Perfect though. The cowboy should have got an Oscar." She smiled at the memory of John Voight's performance. "You knew from the beginning that New York would be a disaster for him. He couldn't communicate."

Tollan remained perched on the stool, parallel to the bar, noting the punters who were in for a mid-day drink. Kenny had joined him. Neither showed any interest in Eddie and Margaret. Strangers, yes, but just a couple having a drink and a natter.

"What made Midnight Cowboy so all-round perfect was the sound track – Everybody's talking at me, I can't hear a word they're saying. It fitted the film to perfection."

Eddie smiled at Margaret's enthusiastic appreciation of the sad film. He dropped his voice imperceptibly handing her a five pound note. "He's not bothered with us. Get change for the cigarette machine. Switch on the tape."

She walked straight to the bar, standing next to Tollan who was facing her in profile. She was in his space and he took control.

"Tam. Serve the wee lassie."

The barman stopped chatting to a customer immediately to ask, as he walked the length of the gantry, "Whit dae yi want, hen?"

"Change for the cigarette machine, please." She said, handing over the fiver. Remembering that she didn't smoke she added stupidly. "They're for him."

Tollan looked directly at Eddie, straight into the lens of the camera hidden in the sports bag. Margaret stepped up her cunning. "I used to smoke. I stopped, just like that."

The black eyes switched back to hers as he responded. "Ay. It's a waste of fuckin money."

She took the change from the barman but failed to connect for cigarettes in the vending machine next to the toilet at the other end of the bar. The machine wouldn't return her money.

She made her way back to bar beside Tollan to report the loss of her money to the barman. The loan shark was instructing another man to "send her across tae me."

Margaret waited patiently for the barman to finish serving a customer. He was pulling two pints. Perfect.

A girl arrived. She said nothing. Tollan slipped off the bar stool. He was standing shoulder to shoulder with Margaret, she facing the bar and he with his back to the bar. He spoke to the girl quietly but incisively. His voice was clear. It carried within a five yards radius.

"Are yi sure yi can manage thirty hen? If yi cannae, don't take it. Ah'm giein yi good advice hen. Ah don't want yi gettin intae any difficulties."

"No, Jimmy. Ah kin definitely manage. Ah promise yi that."

Margaret could feel the tape grabbing the damning words. Her flesh tingled to the contact of the microphone. She feared that it might click to a stop.

Tollan turned away from the girl, climbed back onto the stool and took a deep swallow from his pint. The girl went back to her seat. Margaret felt Tollan's eyes on her.

She anticipated his question. "I can't get ciggies. The bloody machine's broken. It won't even give me my money back."

"Tam. The lassie wants her money back."

The barman stopped pulling pints, opened the till and returned her cash. Margaret thanked Tollan and returned to her seat beside Eddie.

Eddie played the game. "Where's my fags?"

"The machine doesn't work."

Eddie feigned irritation. "Nothing works these days."

They talked about coffee machines that took your money in return for hot water, or kept all the change. They sat tight watching for the chance of a second bite at the loan shark.

It came when Tollan fired more instructions at the

enforcer. "See that wee bastard, Johnny. He never showed yesterday. See him the night."

"Ay."

He was more conciliatory about a woman who had failed to make her payment. "Don't bother about Mary. She'll turn up on Monday. She makes it every second week."

The tape picked up this juicy conversation while Magaret bought two packets of crisps.

They left the Wee Hauf high on success, loaded with taped evidence and relieved that it was finally over. Eddie could escape her angry socialism. Margaret could return to the arms of her family.

Their relationship was finished. It began in a shared commitment, tickled into attraction and faded out in boredom.

He loved only one thing about her. Her courage.

22 The price of eggs

PETER VEITCH and Graham Scoular had plenty of leads but no touts' tip-offs. They desperately needed a little pointer in the right direction. Solving crime is as much about knowing who are the likely targets as collating evidence.

They were an awesome twosome. A Doberman and a Labrador. One hunted without mercy; the other gently retrieved.

Detective Inspector Veitch liked to solve crime by meticulously piecing together the facts. Signatures, fingerprints, documents, times, bank statements, dates, registrations and receipts were his trade in detection.

Tall and slim, strong in body and in conviction, Peter Veitch was a cop going to the top by the most correct of routes. Protestant and proud of it without being bigoted, he worked conscientiously and often over his hours. And always with the sole intention of upholding the law.

Veitch was handsome and instantly attractive to the opposite sex, although he never succumbed to the temptation. His nights were spent as a Boys Brigade officer, on the golf course, in the garden, or studying for the next police exam which would open the way to promotion. He enjoyed his Saturdays at the Ibrox home of his beloved Rangers FC, in the company of the main stand season ticket set.

Veitch told jokes. "Did you hear the one about . . ." He only told the jokes to the people he respected. He offered no friendship whatsoever to the neds, conmen, thieves and bullies he met in the course of his duties. Violence was to be met with swift controlled arrest. Lies were immediately confronted. He went for their throats.

Veitch made criminals feel uncomfortable with his relentless cross examinations backed with sound evidence. "You're wasting my time lying," he would say.

Detective Sergeant Graham Scoular was quite

different. He never told anybody a joke. But he joked with people and extended a friendly comforting voice to the most unpleasant characters.

He caught criminals by using his infectious personality to win the confidence of those connected with the immoral men he brought to justice. He collected touts. They liked him, they trusted him and they became his eyes and ears. He never conned his army of contacts or double-crossed them.

Scoular was overweight, slightly balding, bubbling with humour. Beneath the easy-going exterior was an equally hard-nosed cop maintaining an encyclopaedic knowledge of the movement and activities of Glasgow's criminals.

His phone never stopped ringing.

"Zat you Graham. McVicar's just taken delivery of a thousand phoney cassettes. They're in a warehouse somewhere off Garscube Road. Have you got that?"

"Swanson is in Alexandria. That bird Angela is back with him. She's driving a stolen red Mazda."

"Reid has bought a big hoose in Pollokshaws. The Building Society must be aff their heids. It's not in his real name either."

"Willie here. I can't talk long. That bastard Rafferty is in the Raploch at his maw's place. There's two shotguns there."

Information poured down his telephone line daily. Ninety per cent of the tip-offs were true. The rest was a malicious attempt to waste the officer's time. To fuck him up. He took those calls in his stride.

Scoular played with his criminal adversaries engaging them in apparently harmless conversation to let them see that he knew where they were living, what they were up to and who were their current cohorts. He was all palsy-walsy.

Neither Graham's method nor Peter's was reaping any dividends in the forgery inquiry. Nothing was showing.

Not the slightest murmur on who was behind the spending spree that stretched across Scotland.

There was no shortage of complainers and most of

them were able to give a pretty good description of the suspect passing the forged fivers. They had times, places and a description. The essential lead was missing – nobody was pointing them in the right direction.

All they needed was a name of their prey or of his associates or even his enemies. That was all. They had checked out all the known forgery specialists and could find no link to the trail of worthless fivers.

Peter lit his one and only vice, a Hamlet and groaned at his partner. "This is fucking daft. We have got everything we need except . . ."

Graham finished the sentence, ". . . the guy who is passing them."

"And he's not that smart Peter."

"Ay. He's doing it upfront. So who the fuck is he?"

They were thinking and talking in unison, their sentences and questions flowing like partners paddling a canoe.

"He buys a four hundred pound leather jacket in Argyle Street, petrol in Kincardine, crab meat in Crail, dinner and a painting in Anstruther where he goes to look at birdlife on an island. And he gets hamburgers at Ibrox during the Aberdeen game . . . what is he?"

"Maybe he's from Aberdeen.

"No. He's not an Aberdonian from the voice description. He's Glasgow."

"So he's a Rangers fan."

"That doesn't make him a bad person."

"Anyway he wouldn't go through Kincardine to get to Aberdeen."

"Right. Let's have a look again at what we've got."

"The guy seems to be a bit of an intellect, maybe an arty-farty type. What do you think?"

"Yea, why not. He bought a Russell Flint print in Anstruther. He took his family out to the Isle of May to see the bird life there. He eats well. Crab and lobsters."

"Yea, but he goes to Ibrox. That doesn't fit in with being an arty-farty type or an intellectual."

They were playing games to fill in while they mentally groped for direction. The conversation was diversionary for they were making no progress whatsoever.

The morning chill had lifted and a strong sun began to warm the office. Peter looked out. "It's a lovely day. We're going to Fife. That's where he has passed most of the stuff."

Criminal intelligence had revealed that the forgeries originated in Manchester. They began at the furthest point in Fife, at Crail, where the red-faced fisherman explained that he had twice dealt with a man from Glasgow who paid for three crab salads with forged fivers.

On a previous visit the man had bought lobsters with, as far as he knew, sound notes. Certainly the bank had not notified him that anything was wrong with the first lot of money for the lobsters. The second lot were forgeries. Yes, he remembered the man, heavily built, dark hair, jeans, and a leather jacket. He had paid cash, fivers, which it transpired were forgeries.

"Catch him and if you're in Crail again, there are two lobsters in it for you," said the fisherman. He insisted they take a bag of fresh mussels which Graham gratefully accepted, ignoring the firm refusal made by his partner.

Did he see the man's car?

"I didn't notice it."

Was there anybody with him?

"Yes. A woman and a wee boy but they didn't come right across to the shop."

Would you recognise him if you saw him again? "Yes. And I am willing to go to court, even if I have to spend the day in Glasgow."

In Anstruther they could feel the presence of their prey. They were so near and yet so far. The youth, a student, manning the ticket kiosk for boat trips to the Isle of May remembered the trio.

"Those Glasgow punters that paid me in forgeries. I'll never forget them," he said angrily. "A hard looking ticket, he was."

Graham smiled. "You sold tickets to a hard looking ticket."

The young man chuckled.

"How do you mean, a hard looking ticket?"

"It was obvious. She said she didn't want to go on the boat trip. But the wee boy wanted to go and the father said that they had four or five hours to kill. She said she would rather go to the caravan than go out on a boat to look at birds. She even offered to walk back to the caravan."

"They stood there and read about the trip," he said pointing at the advert on the side of the kiosk.

Peter and Graham let the youth talk.

"He wouldn't let her get her way. I remember now. I remember him saying it. He told her to shut up and let the boy get his first chance to go to sea. The woman wanted to stay behind and go for a walk round the shops. He wasn't having that. They were all to go on the trip or none at all and the boy was going, so they were all going. He was swearing all the time."

Graham asked the questions. "What did he look like?"

"He looked hard."

"Right. You told us that already. We've got the message. He was hard. What was this hardman wearing?"

"A leather jacket."

"Anything else?"

"Jeans and trainers"

"What's your name?"

"What do you want my name for?"

"So that I can call you by your name. And we might need a statement from you when we find him."

"Oh. I'm Ian Walsh."

"Ian, there must be around twenty thousand men in Scotland wearing a leather jacket, jeans and trainers. Could you give us a bit better description. What age was he? How tall was he? What was his face like? What colour was his hair? What about his eyes? Was he thin or thick set? Did he wear glasses? That sort of thing. Did he have a scar?"

Peter looked out across the silt-laden harbour, past

the stone wall that kept the North Sea at bay and into the distance to the Isle of May.

Ian had been thinking hard. "I would say he was about thirty-eight years old. He was nearly as tall as you but not as fat."

He looked at Graham and added, "Not fat. What I meant was he was quite well built. I would say he was a strong man and he had blackish hair."

Graham resumed the questioning. Did anybody else see him?

"The people on the boat, skipper Anderson and Andrina in the tea room – her nickname's Andromeda – might have seen them. But there's quite a lot of people go on these trips so they might not have noticed them."

"That's right Ian. There are a lot of people go on the trips. So how do you know which ones paid you in the forgeries? It could have been anybody."

"He looked the type. He had a huge wad of notes. He peeled fivers off to pay me while he was arguing with his wife about going on the trip."

"What was the argument about?"

"About not going on the boat trip."

"Could you try to remember everything you can. About the argument. Take your time."

"She kept trying to get out of going on the boat trip. She asked how long it took. I told her that it was at least four hours. That really scunnered her. She asked him for the key to the caravan and said she would walk all the way back. She was in tears. What a scene. She asked him to run her back to the caravan. He refused. She said she had the keys to the caravan. He just wouldn't give her a lift back. She gave up. I felt sorry for her. She even offered to walk back."

"So he paid you in five pound notes?"

"Yes, he gave me four fivers, eight pounds each for the adults and three pounds for the boy. He told me to keep the pound change. Don't tell my boss if you are speaking to him about this."

"We won't. One more question. What caravan sites are within a half hour walking distance of here?"

"One or two. One along toward Pittenweem. There's another at Cellardyke and two on the other side of Crail. They're everywhere. There is one at Elie. There's a right posh one at Crail. You take the road marked for St Andrews and then fork to the right in Crail, doon over a wee bridge up the hill and then doon to the shore past the new houses. The nearest one to here is at Cellardyke. It is right on the shore. A great spot spoiled slightly because there's a pig farm nearby. There's a smell of pig manure. Follow your nose."

They escaped his enthusiasm and went to the Craw's Nest restaurant where Tollan had passed sixty pounds in forgeries for a sumptuous meal after the boat trip. They both felt confident that by the end of a busy day in the Kingdom of Fife they would have at least identified their man. There might be a bonus, they thought with the glee of detectives hunting a criminal. "The bastard might be up here on holiday."

"We could interview him at the caravan," said Peter. Before hitting the caravan sites they would enjoy a bar lunch and a chat to the manager of the Craw's Nest.

The manager was also owner, a sharp eyed individual, who wasted no time in describing Jimmy, Rita and Matt.

"If the guy paid by cheque, or credit card I would have been worried about whose money he was spending. I wouldn't say he was a wide boy. But there was something unpleasant about him. He was too pushy."

"Yeah. We know the type," said Peter.

"I was in the restaurant that evening. They came in early. I like to be here at the start to make sure everything gets off smoothly.

"He helped the boy choose prawns. But he told the woman to make her mind up. She was on edge and complaining about being cold.

"Her name was Rita. His was Jimmy. I can't remember the wee boy's name."

They were getting there. Jimmy and Rita who had stayed in a caravan nearby. They had a sound description of Jimmy from the lobster fisherman, the kiosk attendant and the restaurant owner. And so to the caravan site at Crail, where the trail went decidedly cold.

There were plenty of families from Glasgow using the site but none, according to the site manager, fitting Tollan's description. There were a few called Jimmy, of course.

"Look at that view," said Graham as they drove back from the Crail caravan site. Peter took his eyes off the road and glanced to his left out across the sea to an island.

"That'll be the Isle of May."

Graham had turned his head round to stare out of the passenger's window. He kept looking. "Pull up Peter – there's a caravan down there next to a farm."

They never argued, having earned each other's respect during eight years' partnership. Peter stopped the car and without talking they both got out looking down from the roadway at the isolated caravan.

They looked to the right along the coast to Anstruther and reached the same conclusion, that a woman would take about half an hour to walk from town. And that she could not walk to the Crail caravan site in half an hour. Without speaking they got back into the car and drove down the farm road. There was no need to talk. Their minds were attuned. The farmer heard the car and came out with two collies at his heels. A girl skipped out of a barn.

Peter and Graham got out of the car. This was a serious possibility. What the farmer was telling them meant that they might have struck gold.

Jocelyn had volunteered, "There's a wee boy comes to the caravan with his mum and dad. I know him. I can tell you quite a lot."

"I can't tell you that much about the man," said the farmer. He pays me three hundred pound a year for the ground rent and electric supply. His name is James Tollan and he uses it off and on throughout the year. His wife comes with him. I don't know her first name."

Jocelyn placed a tray with teapot and digestive biscuits and white Cheddar cheese on the table. She covered the teapot with a cosy saying to her father, "I know the boy's name dad. It's Matt. His mother is called Rita. She bought eggs from me and told me her name."

"Do you have his address?" Peter asked.

"No. The agreement is that he pays me at the start of the year and the caravan stays. That's all there is to it. I have a telephone number to contact him if anything goes wrong at the caravan. If it was broken into or damaged by the wind. No address though.

"What kind of car does he have?

"He's got a new one now, a red Audi."

"Do you know the registration number?"

"It's this year's reg," he said with a smile.

"It would be, wouldn't it?" said Graham to Peter. They were pissed off chasing criminals who drove brand new cars.

"Could we have the telephone number he gave you?"

The farmer rummelled through papers in a sideboard drawer. "This could take a bit of time," he said seeming at a loss to lay his hands on the information. "It's in here somewhere . . . I could send it on to you."

"We would appreciate if you could find it now," said Graham. The detectives realised that the telephone number was the sure fire link to tracing the criminal. The phone number was the key. The name might be phoney.

After some minutes he handed the scrawled number to Peter. "Never thought I'd find it so quickly."

There was one more question. "Did they say when they would next be here?"

"They hardly ever talk to me or to my wife . . . only when they buy eggs. They come and go as they please. They could turn up at any time."

The detectives began to wind-up the pleasant interview with the usual police advice. "There is no need to mention to anybody that we were here asking questions. There may be nothing to it. We are only making enquiries."

He changed the subject abruptly. "Your eggs will be

real eggs. Farm eggs. Not the eggs you see marked as farm eggs in shops. These will be the real McCoy. Proper farm eggs."

Peter read his partner like a book. He leant forward, placing his elbows on the kitchen table and looked into his partner's eyes. "We don't want any eggs. I don't care whether they are real eggs, proper eggs, farm eggs or McCoy eggs, or even Easter eggs. You already have a bag of mussels."

He turned to the farmer. "Thank you very much though."

Graham made no response allowing the farmer his predictable words. "Jocie, go and get some of those eggs."

They made their way to the car, reversed round and stopped to ask the farmer one last question. He was standing in the middle of the yard with Jocelyn at his side, poised to wave them away.

Peter asked. "How did he pay you, by cheque or cash?" Before he could rely Graham added, "You can tell us. We are policemen not Inland Revenue inspectors."

"He paid cash."

"For the caravan and the rent of the site?"

"Ay. For both."

They pulled out of the yard with Jocelyn waving goodbye. "Everybody's at it," said Peter.

"Ach. Good luck to him. It's not every day we meet such decent people," said Graham adjusting his feet round the shoe box of straw covered eggs.

They drove back to the Craws Nest in Anstruther where the receptionist and waitress gave a description of Tollan the art lover, which was replicated by the petrol attendant in a small garage near Kincardine Bridge, who told them that it was a brand new red car. He had not taken the registration because the man had paid in cash.

On the motorway they reflected on life's ups and downs. Peter was honest enough to confess. "I'll tell you Graham, if it hadn't been such a nice day, I wouldn't have thought of a trip to Fife."

Tollan was in fact totally innocently spreading duddies round Scotland. If only he had known, he would have been in the position to make some money out of the forgeries, by sending a hireling into the nearest travel agents to exchange the cash for French currency.

The following day another hireling would have been dispatched to change the francs into sterling. That was somebody else's game. Not Tollan's. There was money to be made there by fair means or foul. Big profits when dealing in duddies.

And a steady solid profit when perfectly legally turning real pound notes into foreign currency and back again. It was the banks that made the profits.

Peter and Graham went straight back to the police station calling criminal intelligence on the internal phone.

Graham answered the return call ten minutes later, putting the phone down with consternation on his face.

"There's nothing on him for forgeries. He's an illegal money lender, with a lot of previous for theft, violence, robbery and extortion."

Peter smiled. "He's expanding into the forgeries. They never learn. I can't wait to speak to him. I can't wait to speak to Mr Tollan."

23 A fly philosopher

JOHNNY McPHERSON had, what was for him, a real job. Legitimate because it was hard work. Legitimate because you had to turn up for work every day by nine.

And legitimate because you earned the cash by dint of results, posters pasted to any empty space available throughout the city centre.

In sheer fear for his life he turned to fly postering after a chance meeting with Jimmy and Kenny. They had met as Johnny was coming away from a late visit to his mother. Jimmy saw Johnny standing at the bus-stop waiting on the last bus to the safety of his Nitshill flat. He was alone.

The car pulled up slowly and Jimmy Tollan stepped out with a dirty grin. "Hello Johnny. Where the fuck are yi stayin these days? Where are yi hiding noo?" The questions were hissed out of clenched teeth.

"Here and there. Ah'm no avoiding yi."

The passenger's door slammed shut as Kenny joined his boss at the bus stop, stepping onto the pavement to stand in ominous silence as Jimmy chose to ignore Johnny's obvious lie. The car was always at hand when violence ensued.

"Ah don't like wans that dae a runner. Yi know that. It wiz a mistake leaving Garthill. Where are yi stayin noo?"

Johnny lied, saying he was in a homeless unit, in the town.

"Are yi shy about coming back up here tae see yur old friends? Yi hivnae paid me fur weeks. In fact yi hivnae paid me since yi fucked aff. Hiv yi?"

The questions were both rhetorical and pointless. This was Jimmy Tollan at his worst. Dangerous. Dirty in his thoughts. Exuding violence. No escape this time.

Johnny was petrified. He remained speechless waiting on the attack. His body softened in anticipation of the blows. He had collapsed before a blow was struck.

"Yi know the score. Kenny. Remind him."

Johnny looked past the dark eyes, unthinking, at the high rise flats blinking in the distance. The night was empty.

Kenny stepped round Jimmy and without warning downed Johnny with a punch to his drink-weakened stomach. Kenny carried no baseball bat for this was a chance encounter.

Johnny grabbed the bus stop post and held on when Watson's boot drove into his ribs. Then there was a knife. Kenny bent down and placed the point of the blade under Johnny's upper lip. Kenny Watson was laying on the violence for the benefit of his boss. Matching Tollan's anger.

"Let the wee bastard staun up. Ah want tae see him gettin it," said Tollan.

Kenny drew the knife back, straightened up and stepped back half a pace. Johnny pulled himself up by the post. Tears of pain watered his eyes.

He spoke. "Ah'll pay yi Jimmy. On ma maw's life. Ah'll get it tae yi."

"Will yi?" said Tollan with a doubting shake of his head. The words were more a statement that Johnny would not pay, although all three knew that Johnny McPherson would pay.

Kenny stepped back behind Jimmy.

"There's nae point in putting him in hospital. Safer there, eh? Ah'll see yi on Tuesday, won't Ah, mate?"

In the deepest recesses of his cunning Tollan always asked questions of his clients rather than made demands on them, as though they had a choice in the matter. A bit like the once friendly building society manager asking the customer when he would be able to put the house up for sale to avoid repossession.

There was no room in Jimmy Tollan's psyche for anything other than persuasion. This was not extortion. It was a reminder that Johnny was breaking their unwritten contract . . . to pay every week for the rest of his life. To remain in the community and be contactable. To keep crawling. To submit. To play out his role in the fear game.

Johnny blurted out his response. "Thanks Jimmy. Ah mean that. Thanks. Ah'll see yi on Thursday."

"How much will yi have on yi?"

"Fifty."

"Ay."

The next day Johnny went job hunting. His invalidity money would not meet the fifty pounds demand. His choice lay between finding ready cash or going back to hospital. He went to the only man who might give him a job. Alex Swanson the Prince of Flypostering.

"Jist to get back in the swing of things," he told Alex.

"You're a lucky man. Bobby's just quit on me. He couldnae staun me any more."

The job had the added bonus of being illegal so enabling Johnny to draw his invalidity. The one hundred and twenty pounds for five days mixing glue, slapping it on derelict walls or wooden fences, then brushing the posters on, gave him a nice untaxed one hundred and fifty four pounds weekly income.

There were few risks involved. The cops could pounce if they so chose. That might be a fifteen pounds fine, when the court notice arrived. The worst that could happen was that the cops could confiscate the posters and Alex would drive back to the depot, the back-street garage, where they mixed buckets of paste every morning and stored the posters.

On the whole the job was a winner although it took Johnny the best part of a week to shape up physically to the task. His alcohol-sodden body ached from stirring paste and lugging posters in and out of the old transit van, rattled round the city by Alex in the race to meet the demands of pop impressarios and disco proprietors vying for the limited cash in the pockets of unemployed teenagers.

Johnny found his work enriching both financially and emotionally. Once his muscles stopped hurting his spirits rose considerably.

"Ah'm working," he told his mother with pride. His down-and-out drinking companions mocked him for being mug enough to exert any energy on behalf of a boss.

They sat on the bench in the park on Saturday and gave him a verbal 'doing'.

"Yir gettin conned Johnny."

"How many hours are yi working a week?"

"Do yi know how much it would cost the disco and pop concert guys tae advertise on TV or in the paper?"

"They're rippin yi aff, son."

Johnny retreated into his humorous defence. "Listen, it's me that's rippin them aff," he said with a cackling laugh. "Ah bin them when Ah get a chance."

He was lying of course. Alex wouldn't countenance binning them. Life on the streets with Alex was an education. His boss should have been beside a blackboard rather than a makeshift billboard.

Never a dull moment in Alex's company, who talked in lengthy monologues as they slapped the glue on after ripping off last week's posters. He was thirty years old, single, slim, strong, and without any steady attachments. Sex was for Friday night. No woman could possibly have put up with his constant barrage of homespun philosophy. Alex had an answer, a justification, a motive, and a social base for everything he saw or heard.

"See that TV phone-in this morning. What a con. The oh- eight-nine-oh numbers con. Call in and tell us if you want hanging brought back. What a fuckin joke. That's a good one to get the punters calling in. Anybody that wants hanging brought back is an angry person. You've got to be a mean bastard to want another human being hanged. Anyway they'll never bring back hanging. Parliament won't vote for it. That's a 'no no'. Maybe they'll do it for shooting a cop but no for shooting an ordinary citizen. They wouldn't mind if they hung the wrong man for shooting a cop. That's a risk worth taking? But hang the wrong man for shooting a citizen.? That's too big a risk."

He relentlessly pursued almost any subject, tearing everything to pieces. "They'll never bring back hanging, so why do the phone-ins? I'll tell you why. To make money. I

reckon they'll make ten thousand pounds over the day.
Think about it, thirty-four pence for every call. They get
ten pence or something like that on every call. They just
treat people like mugs."

Alex worked while he talked. That's the type of person
he was. He simply could not be quiet. Johnny eventually
ceased hearing his hardworking partner's endless flow of
philosophy.

"Know what the trouble is? The trouble is that people
are just units. That's all they are. Units to make money out
of. They might as well list human mugs on the stock
exchange. Millions of people to invest in. Get them to do
whit ye want and they'll make you money. Guaranteed
dividends or unit returns or whatever is the financial term
for profit. They never learn. Christ almighty! These phone-
ins are the biggest joke going. Does Maradona play for
Russia, Scotland or Argentina? That's the fuckin level of
the questions."

Johnny responded to that one quickly. It was his
subject. "Ah wish he played for Celtic."

"Ay right. But you take ma point. They are treating
us like mugs. Did you ever see The Third Man? A great
film. Orson Welles. The third man, selling penicillin on the
black market after the war. Did you see it?"

This time he actually paused for an answer. Johnny
had seen it.

"Yea. The zither music."

"Ay, you did. Did you see Welles standing on the top
of the carnival wheel. He looks down at the people on the
ground. Just walking about. Dots. Nuthin. That's what it's
about. Making sure that you don't just become a dot for
somebody else tae use."

He slapped more glue on the wooden fence in Albion
Street. Alex talked to the flow of the brush.

"People get fucked easily. Graham Greene wrote The
Third Man. Orson Welles could write a bit himself. Did
you ever see Citizen Kane? Reckoned to be the all-time
greatest film. Wells was only twenty five when he wrote it.

A classic. A rich man broken by greed."

Johnny had seen it and was keen to prove that he had by blurting out one word. "Rosebud."

"Ay, you did see it. You don't have to be poor to be a mug or a unit or a dot. Where the fuck are we going today?"

"To Clyde Street, then along tae Anderson next tae that pub you took me intae last week."

"No. I mean where are we going as a society?"

Johnny chuckled. "How would Ah know where wir goin as a society?"

"Did you ever read Dickens? Now there's a writer who. . ."

Johnny interrupted. "Gie us a break Alex."

"Tired son? You must be knackered. Go and sit in the van for ten minutes. I'll get this lot up and we'll get a cup o' tea and a bacon roll at Sammy's."

"Naw. Whit Ah meant wis, gie us a break frae yir patter."

"It's no patter. It's fuckin serious. OK. Your ears are sore. That's me. That's the way I am. I cannae help it. Ah think all the time."

He stood back on the pavement and studied the postered wooden fence. "Beginning to look good. Did you ever read Tom Sawyer? Mark Twain wrote it. Now there's a writer that could bring a smile to your face. I like to do the postering right. If a job is worth doing, it's worth doing well. That stops you being a mug. Tom Sawyer painting the fence at his auntie's house. That made me smile. Life is about doing and humour. He had to whitewash the fence as a punishment. Saturday morning and the rest of the kids mocked him for having to work while they played. He outfoxed them. He ignored them and got on with the job. They became intrigued. Eventually they asked if they could paint some of the fence. Know what he did? He refused them! That made them even more intrigued."

He stopped talking. Johnny let Alex know that he was also aware of Mark Twain. "Reports of my death have been greatly exaggerated."

"Ay. You're no so fuckin daft," said Alex with a respectful smile. "You know a lot more than you realise you know. Get me a Barrowland poster, four Tron posters and a one for the Tunnel."

Reports of my death have been greatly exaggerated.

A chill ran through Johnny as thoughts of his own death clicked in his mind. Maybe he should not have tempted fate by getting back intae Tollan. One day the bastard might go too far. It had happened to others. So why not him?

Alex followed Johnny across the pavement and continued his lecture on life. "Tom Sawyer's pals started to buy the chance to work on the fence. They offered him things like a dead rat, marbles, toys, apple cores. They wanted the chance to do something however menial to a decent standard of workmanship. It was the fact that he told them they couldn't do it as well as him. That's what got them."

He followed Johnny back from the van to the half-postered fence, talking. "This was their chance to paint a fuckin fence. Jesus. Mark Twain was one fabulous writer. Just a story about a wee boy in a Mississippi town. That's why I read a lot. TV's not in the same league, son."

Alex lifted the Tron Theatre poster and with the ease of ten years' practice, slapped it onto the fence. Five balanced brush movements secured it in position.

He stood back to admire the poster. "That, Johnny, is the perfect poster. Simple. Clear. And in big letters. The punters can see that from a passing bus. It catches their eye as they walk along the street. See. How simple it is . . . Sharks. Catches the eye. Just like Law as in Denis Law. Short and simple. Law hat trick. Everybody knew what it was about. Best. Best AWOL. He never turned up again."

He warmed to his theme.

"Ally McCoist became Coisty. Jimmy Johnstone, Jinky. Simplify it. That's the secret. The same with posters. See the ones that are crammed wi information, telling you what it's about, what the critics said, who the actors are, and how to get to the theatre? They're a waste of time, space and money. Sharks. Eyecatching."

Johnny studied the poster.

Sharks. Presented by Wildcat. He read the small print.

"Some fishy goings on in the seedy underworld of loan sharks. Wildcat's traditionally hard-hitting style turns its attention to money dealing, finance and crooks! With the usual blend of music and laughter along the way and starring Dave Anderson of City Lights fame."

Alex was off on his philosophical trail. "Same with everything these days, all eye-catching. Look at the news on TV. They hit you with it right between the eyes. And the ears too!"

He moved the paste bucket along the pavement without stopping the flow of words. "Look at the nine o'clock news. Two tiny wee news readers sitting at enormous circular desks. The graphics are fantastic. The world turning round in front of your eyes. Then you hardly get any chance to absorb each bit of news before they're switching to another item and another face. Look at it in the mornin. Women with perfectly dyed blond hair. One minute they're reading the weather forecast, then they're reading the news and soon they are opening supermarkets. Superstars. Jesus."

He got quite angry at the thought of the girls reading the news. "Look at their eyebrows. Dark eyebrows. Then look at their hair. Blond."

Johnny had his chance to ask about something that mattered to him. He was enjoying both the company and the work. The money was going to Tollan regular as clockwork. Johnny was content. He had broken the link to the boredom of an afternoon on the wall behind the Black Inn with his down-and-out pals. They'd given up.

"Sharks? It might be short and simple, but what's it about? Dae yi know?" Johnny asked his vibrant flypostering boss?

"Ay. Loan sharks. They did it three years ago at the Citizen's. It's been brought back by popular demand. It'll no be a show so much as a play. Wildcat specialise in socially

231

aware themes. I like their stuff. They jump from one theme to the next as the Tories hammer us down to nuthin. Unemployment, poll tax, loan sharks. The next one will be water privatisation. Mark ma words. They'll rig up the stage with sinks, baths, lavvies and do a backdrop of Loch Katrine. They get stuck intae Thatcher's crappy ideas for the country."

Johnny wasn't paying attention. He had stopped slapping the glue on and was standing still, thinking.

"Are yi goin tae see it?" he asked.

"Going to see what?"

"Sharks."

"I've seen it. Three years ago with wee Morag that barmaid I used to see."

Johnny wasn't quite ready to go to the theatre on his own. The rehabilitation process was incomplete.

"Dae yi want tae see it again?" he asked eagerly.

Johnny was elated at the thought of going to the theatre. The boundaries of his life were extending daily since he joined up with Alex. It was years since he had been in Sauchiehall Street, or in restaurants, or friendly pubs for steak pie, chips, peas and a pint. Waitresses came to him and asked him what he wanted.

His life had been squeezed down into virtually nothing after he borrowed from Jimmy Tollan in 1986. All he ever did was pay, drink and go to Parkhead on the Celtic bus. Now he was going to the theatre. The prospect was quite exciting. Home to the flat, a bath, a shave, aftershave and his best trousers. He didn't have a decent jacket but felt he could get away with his one respectable pullover, a present from his mother.

Alex remained in work mode insisting, as he did at every site, that all the old stripped-off posters were picked up and placed in the back of the van and that they swept up the pavement before moving on to the next site.

The Prince was proud of his work feeling that he improved the environment with the profusion of stylish posters across the city. He was also a tough man to beat should anybody try to push into his specialised but illegal venture. That day Johnny learnt the hard way that Alex could be as uncompromising as any.

They finished the fence and moved on to Sauchiehall Street, up to Great Western Road, and back to the city centre. They had finished by three o'clock and Alex decided to go for a spaghetti bolognese at Lorettos in Albion Street. He parked the van next to the fence they'd carefully postered at mid-day.

"Christ, look at that," he said to Johnny. "Some bastard's postered over our stuff. Right, back to the depot and we'll get more of our posters."

Johnny looked at the makeshift hoarding and saw that Sharks had disappeared under a poster advertising a cheap booze night for students in a city centre pub.

"What dae yi mean. We're finished, are we no?" said Johnny sensing that Alex was about to undo the rogue flyposter's work, there and then.

"We are not finished now," he said defiantly. "This is my pitch. I keep it right and I keep others off it. Nobody's muscling in on us. The only way to beat these bastards is to cover their posters now. We can outwork them. Anyway we've got more posters than them."

On the way to the depot Johnny questioned the need to cover the fence a second time. "We're no gonnae become millionaires. So why are we havin tae dae that fence all over again. We've done the work already. It's no our fault that some bastard has postered over our work."

"That's not the point. Let them in on our pitches and they'll fuck us up good and proper. See if the bosses of the pubs and clubs we're postering for pass the pitch and see that their posters aren't up. They will soon stop using us. It's all about results and money."

Johnny was slightly on the defensive for trying to wriggle out of the extra work. As usual he turned to his own humour.

They collected more posters, mixed more glue and recovered the hoarding in a patchwork of Alex's clients' advertisements. By six o'clock the job was done.

"Are you still on for Sharks tonight?" said Alex to an exhausted Johnny. There was no stopping his enthusiastic boss and Johnny had caught the new pace of life. "Ay. Can you gie me a run home in the van, Ah'll need tae get cleaned up."

He grabbed a fish supper, eating it quickly on the way from the chippie to the soulless flat, where he spruced himself up and grabbed a taxi to the Tollbooth.

The lights in the theatre dimmed and the stage flickered into light. Dave Anderson burst into song standing playing a piano organ.

On the way out of the theatre they bumped into Jimmy Tollan.

"Whit are yi daein here?"

"Jis seein whit it wiz like. Fuckin shite."

The audience reaction proved his lie. They breathed every fear filled moment, laughing nervously when a young girl contemplated suicide, and cheered when the loan shark was arrested.

They understood. And gave a standing ovation.

24 A hearty breakfast

THEY WERE almost at Rita Fullerton's home when Jimmy sauntered out of the close.

The worn windscreen wiper left a smeared curve. "Is that him?" said Peter leaning to the side, peering through the distorted glass, as he pulled the car into the kerb.

Graham had a clear view. "That's his car. That'll be him getting into it." They were forty yards from Rita's home.

"Let him go. We'll follow him," said Peter, allowing the loan shark time to start the Audi and cruise down to the shops. Peter and Graham were in crime-busting mode. That meant self-generated anger fuelled by a concern for the decent hard working people who were left with useless money dumped on them by an uncaring ned. The policemen were human beings with all the requisite emotions. And the same boredom thresholds. Years of chasing criminals blunted their enthusiasm.

If only they had known that Tollan's clients had suffered horrendously for their folly in taking a loan to see them through the week. That Jessica an innocent girl had taken her own life. That Johnny, a harmless karaoke singer had been hospitalised. That Jenny, a decent good-looking mother had turned to prostitution. The knowledge would have generated even more commitment to putting him behind bars.

Tollan bought rolls and a paper and returned to the house.

"Let's talk to the man," said Peter, the adrenaline rising like a boxer going into the ring against an opponent admittedly weaker but capable of defeating him by cheating. The detectives closed in for the interview and arrest knowing they were dealing with an experienced hardened criminal who would lie, twist, and deny.

Tollan answered the knock. Graham made the introductions.

Jimmy was curt. "Whit dae yi want?"

Peter answered simply. "We want to find out where you are getting your money from these days?"

No trick was intended.

"Is that any of your business? Are yi charging me with anythin?"

"No. But you could help us. We are trying to trace the source of your money. Will you come down to the station."

A mild wind drafted through the close. The dank elements were moving into the warm hallway. Jimmy sought an escape back inside, however brief.

Before they could inform him that their inquiry was about forgeries Jimmy asked if he could finish breakfast.

"Yes," said Peter. "You better get something in your stomach. You've a long day ahead of you. We'll come in while you eat?"

"Ay," he replied, morosely regretting his request

They sat cosily in the front room, the detectives sharing the settee and Jimmy in the armchair, tray on lap cutting his sausages. The meal had lost its taste.

Graham prodded his antagonist gently. "That could be your last supper."

All three laughed, Graham and Peter because they were confident of making the charge stick, Jimmy because he was confident that he wouldn't be charged with illegal money lending.

The detectives gave little away. The vital questions would be asked when they had him at the station, in the interview room, next to a tape recorder.

Tollan was not concerned about them gaining entrance to the house without a warrant. There was nothing incriminating in the house. The DSS books and the tally book were at Kenny Watson's home. They could turn the place over and find nothing.

Rita came downstairs, excused herself quickly and went to the shops convinced that Jimmy was going back to jail. She was numb with despair.

Not again. Why had she stuck by him the last time he went to jail? Her mind raced through the mess of previous cases. Visiting him on remand in Barlinnie, then down to the court on the final day as he twisted his head round offering that emotionless smile from the dock. Then a second look up as he turned round after the sentence.

She took the bus to her sister's to unburden herself. It was a waste of time but something to do. Her face felt dead. Her mouth was dry, her legs weak.

The only consolation was that he would be out of her life for a few years. There would be a rest from the tensions of living with Jimmy's double-edged lifestyle. She felt sure that by the time she returned Jimmy would be at the police station for the night. She rented a video tape on the way home. A good sexy thriller to escape from her depressing thoughts.

Jimmy took his time over the remains of breakfast. Thinking time. He assumed that the TV publicity had triggered a police investigation. He tried to take the initiative away from the detectives. "That programme was a lot of shite. Fuckin crap. Ah'm suing them."

Palsy-walsy Graham took advantage of Tollan's assumption that they were there to question him about illegal money lending.

"What are you talking about Jimmy?"

"Don't give me that crap. Youse saw the fuckin programme. They got it all wrang. They can call me a loan shark because of wan conviction as youse fuckin know. They knew that when they did the programme. They know it's difficult fur me tae sue them when Ah've got a conviction. Cunning bastards."

Jimmy was trying to be equally cunning.

Graham was his usual self. "Yes, I see what you mean Jimmy. You've no reputation to protect. That's your problem. You're trying to get your life going after doing time for illegal money lending and along they come to ruin your efforts." There was no hint of sarcasm in his voice.

Jimmy ignored the detective's shrewd comment,

finished his sausages and egg, and offered them a cup of tea.

"Listen, Ah'm finished giein oot money. Even when they keep askin me fur it. They still dae and Ah refuse them."

Graham and Peter had plenty of time. If this ned wanted to deny he was an illegal money lender, when they all knew he probably still was, then let him continue.

Peter got serious. "You stay here most of the time, don't you?"

He assumed they had a warrant. "Go ahead. You'll find nothing."

The evidence was at Kenny's, under the third step on the hall stairway. The bastards would find nothing here.

The detectives were having fun. "How many old age pensioners' books have you got under the bed Mr Tollan? Beside the Monday Books?"

"There's nuthin here."

"Were are they?"

"Where are what?"

"Just answer the question?"

"Ah don't know what yir talking aboot?"

"You don't know what we are talking about?"

"No. Ah fuckin don't."

It began to dawn on Tollan that they weren't pressing him for answers to any factual questions.

"So how do you like being on TV Jimmy?" said Graham.

"Ah told yi. Ah'm suin them."

"Did they give you the appearance money, Jimmy?"

Jimmy just smiled back. His mind was stretched to the limit as he sought some pattern to their questions. He would not be questioned seriously until they took him to the station. But what was it all about? They were playing games. They had no facts. They had nothing.

There were no Trading Standards Investigators along. Not like the last time when he quickly realised that they had him bang to rights. Three years ago he held his hands up.

This time they were struggling and he knew it.

Graham changed tack with his questions. "Do you like Russell Flint?"

"Who the fuck is Russell Flint?"

"Are you interested in birds? Puffins?"

Tollan couldn't see where the questions were leading. His thoughts were centred on benefit books and baseball bat attacks. His mind was clicking through the names in his tally book as he fiendishly searched for the man or woman who might have grassed.

The next question was just as obtuse.

"Do you like lobsters?"

"Ah've only had them a few times. What the fuck does that hiv tae dae with money lendin?"

They ignored his assumption.

"What about crabs?"

Jimmy was finding the chat somewhat confusing. This wasn't the routine the polis followed. They were too casual.

He remembered the last time he was arrested. The sad day he was caught with thirteen DSS books in his jacket. That would never happen again.

Those fuckin books. It was a Friday morning three years ago almost to the day. He was giving Rita a lift to the shops before going on up to the Garthill post office to hand the books out. He was watching her walking away from the car. There was a knock on the driver's window and he turned to face a plainclothes cop. There was another one at the other window.

He stepped out the car and glanced over to Rita, to see if she had made it into the shop. Two more detectives were talking to her outside the newsagents.

His woman had to be protected. She mustn't suffer any aggravation. Not from the polis.

He had shouted across the pavement. "It's got nuthin tae dae with her. She's no involved."

The game was up from the beginning. He wasn't exactly confessing, just conceding that his woman should not be pressurised. The code of the criminal. Later he would plead not guilty. At that moment, the point of arrest, Rita had to be protected.

He had heard the cop telling him that he was being detained under the terms of Section Two of the Criminal Justice (Scotland) Act 1980, and that he was under no obligation to answer any question other than give his name and address. The words fluttered on his ears for he was concentrating on Rita's situation. Two officers were escorting her to another car. He was being taken firmly toward another police car.

He twisted round, repeating his plea. "She's got fuck-all tae dae wi it. Let her go. It's down tae me."

They pushed him firmly into the back seat.

Jimmy leant forward. "Don't take her tae the station. Ah told yi, she's got fuck-all tae dae with it. She disnnae . . ."

The cop responded. "We'll let her tell them that. She's a big girl."

The extra comment turned his fear into anger. "Fuckin smart ass."

On the way to the station they asked if he had any DSS allowance books in his possession. So formal. "In your possession."

It was a waste of time denying it and he could see no way of unloading them. He took them out of his leather jacket and handed them over.

Trading standards officers had been tailing him for three weeks. They had times, details, names. They probably had photographs too, of him chatting to the punters . . . Jean, and Willie and Tam and Johnny. Gladys and wee Ernie. Some of them were still with him now, back on the books after his release. He had only been doing them a favour.

In the station they made it seem so criminal. Jimmy tried desperately to explain that he was merely the man the poor came to when they needed help.

Why was he in possession of thirteen DSS books belonging to other people?

"Right, Ah'll tell yi the truth. Thae punters came tae

me. Beggin fur money. The word got roon that Ah wiz holdin money. Ah got a big win at the bookies."

The lies were wrapped in sincerity.

"Whit wis Ah supposed tae dae? Ignore their pleas fur help. They were fuckin desperate. Honest. Whit wid you dae if somebody came beggin fur money?"

Jimmy was asking questions again.

They ignored his question. Their question about being in possession of thirteen DSS books was still unanswered.

This was not a matter for discussion. This was a statement made under caution, tape recorded, to be sent to the procurator fiscal and then used in court for a conviction that might lead to a substantial jail sentence. There was no leeway.

The detective knew to play with a straight bat. No devious tricks. Straight questions. That was all. Tollan's lawyer would eventually be studying the statement closely. They did it by the book.

"What interest do you charge the people you lend the money to?" they had asked.

"Ah don't charge interest. They offer tae pay me back more than Ah gie them. They came tae ma hoose with their weans in tow, carryin their books and begging me . . . 'gonna gie us a loan.' Ah'm telling yi the way it is. They bring their books with them tellin me that there's fifty four pounds in the book. They're askin me tae hold their books. They offer tae pay me a tenner on top."

"In other words you do charge interest. What is your interest rate?"

Jimmy was floundering, unable to avoid the fact that he was carrying the benefit books. The fucking books. He was angry with himself, and frightened. It took him several days to come to terms with the prospect of a jail sentence.

"Ah don't charge any fuckin interest. Ah jist agree tae take a fiver or tenner on top of whit Ah lend them."

"So it varies on the amount you lend? Ten pounds interest on fifty. Five on twenty five?"

"Ah wouldnae say that. For fuck's sake whit are youse

trying tae put on me. We're no talkin real profits here. Whit we're talkin is helping people who are so fuckin desperate they offer tae pay me a bit mair. It's no interest, it's just somethin for helpin."

The detective resisted the temptation to say that it was fucking downright robbery. He dropped in a few names, to let the loan shark know that they had more than just thirteen benefit books.

"We have a statement from Angelina Thomson. We have spoken to Willie Edwards. Angelina says that she gave you her Monday book three months ago. Why have you kept it for so long?"

Jimmy was angry that two bastards had talked. His anger broke his concentration. "That woman owes me mair than . . ."

He almost said, "three hundred."

"Know how much she borrowed? Fuckin months ago. She wis desperate when she came tae me. Four kids in tow. Ah helped her. She haunded me her books."

"We have talked to her. To be honest she's not saying a lot. But you have her book. And twelve other books."

Jimmy scowled.

The woman had had little choice but give the Trading Standards officers a statement when they came to her home. They had traced her through the post office where Kenny was cashing her book.

"Ah don't want to talk about it," she had said in fear of Tollan. "Ah won't have to go to court, will Ah?"

She was told that there would be a much better chance of avoiding a court appearance as a witness if she gave them a full statement. The more statements they had the more likely Tollan would plead guilty.

Her statement had read,

Four days before Christmas I borrowed £80 from James Tollan. I gave him my book which is worth £52 a week. He told me I will get it back the first week in February. I can identify the accused.

There had been several other statements from victims whose sad stories were translated into the language needed for a conviction.

Jimmy had seen the scenario only from his side of the fence. The cops questioned him on specifics. Not about the culture in his community.

"And Willie Edwards? Why do you have his invalidity book?"

Jimmy composed himself, giving the detective a truthful answer supplemented with a justification of his position.

"He's an alkie. Hiv yi ever had an alkie beg yi fur money? He was at school wi me. Ah couldnae refuse Willie. If Ah didnae take his book Ah'd hiv got nuthin back."

Jimmy paused, staring blankly at the black tape recorder remorselessly taking his words. The detectives were impassive. Jimmy hadn't bothered to get a lawyer to the station.

The detectives allowed a silence in the windowless room.

"The fact is that Ah gie oot money. But Ah'm no a money lender. Women come tae me when they need money. Ah've never offered anyone a loan. They come tae me. Ah don't double up their money if they don't pay each week."

The core of Jimmy's case was, "they come tae me." The mitigation was the truth.

The memory of the arrest, interrogation and conviction flashed through Jimmy's mind, cutting and scraping at his soul.

Jesus, surely to God, it was not going to be repeated. He only had one life to live. At forty one he deserved a break from the loneliness of prison. He felt insecure, even unwell. There was little consolation in the knowledge that he had plenty money stashed away.

Graham Scoular and Peter Veitch were relaxed. Confident that Tollan would collapse when finally confronted with the fact that he was passing forgeries.

"So you've given up being a loan shark?" said Graham

glancing round Rita's sumptuous living room at the massive TV, the deep leather suite, and thick Wilton carpet. "You've decided to enjoy the good life without committing any crime, Jimmy. Draw your dole money and drive about in a brand new Audi. Good for you, son."

Graham's blue eyes twinkled. The voice was genuinely friendly and his plump body relaxed back into the comfortable suite. Relaxation was the name of his game. Palsy-walsy. "And you were a TV star for a while."

"Whit's that got tae dae wi anythin."

Peter Veitch wasn't so pleasant. He sat on the edge of the settee, bolt upright, waiting to pounce, his eyes hardened, drilling into Tollan's dark brown inexpressive eyes.

Peter stood up to his full six feet. "That was just a wee chat while you finished your breakfast. Now we'll go down to the station. Leave your car here and get your coat. It's raining."

Jimmy smiled. "Ah'll leave it. Ah'll get a taxi up the road."

"We'll bring you back up from the station," said Palsy Walsy. An offer he'd refuse. Jimmy wouldn't be seen dead in a police car, certainly not getting out of it in the scheme.

Peter came clean about the reason for taking him to the station.

"Mr Tollan we'd like you to come to the station to question you about operating a forgery ring."

Jimmy smirked. The smirk enlarged into a smile that spread from his mouth to his eyes. They saw the stress fall away from Tollan like leaves in late September.

He shrugged his shoulders. "Let's go."

"Yiv got nothin on me," he chuckled.

He had no need to deal in forgeries. There was plenty of first class cash flowing virtually directly from behind the post office counters into his pockets.

"Are you coming voluntarily."

"Ah'm no exactly volunteering, but Ah'm no makin an issue o' this."

The questions in the station were informal. He was after all helping the police with their inquiries. The inquiries were bizarre. "Where you're getting your money from these days? Our information is that you collect it in Manchester. A nice wee trip down the motorway in your Audi once a fortnight. When were you last in Manchester last?"

Jimmy smirked. "Christ Ah can't remember that far back. It wisnae last year. And it wisnae the year before. Ah can prove that. Ah wis in the jail. Check it out if yi hivnae already."

"You can't remember. You will remember when you were last in Crail in Fife. Were you there on April 17 this year?"

The question disturbed Jimmy. This was the first fact presented to him. The day trip to Fife was a day he would never forget. The day they broadcast the loan shark programme.

"Ay. Ah wis up in Fife round aboot that time. Ah cannae remember the date exactly. But Ah wiz there. Whit's this all aboot?"

"Did you take a boat trip from Anstruther to the Island of May?"

"Yea. So fuckin what?"

"Did you have a meal in the Craws Nest that day?"

"Ay. Dae yi want to know whit Ah ate?"

"Who was with you?"

"Nobody," he replied, refusing to even mention Rita or Matt to these bastards. They had nothing to do with whatever this was about.

"Nobody?"

"Nobody that would interest youse."

"Everything about your trips to Fife are of interest to us. Who was with you on April 17?"

"My girlfriend and my son."

"What are their names?"

"Rita Fullerton and Matt."

Peter knew their names already. It was simply one of those little questions cops threw in to upset criminals. He turned the screw ever so gently. "I'll tell you what you ate," he said. "Rita had fish soup, followed by lemon sole. Your son had prawn cocktail and deep fried scampi. You had smoked mackerel for starters. Then you had fried fillet of Pittenween haddock. Later you all had fresh Crail crab salad in your caravan."

Peter delighted in giving such detail.

Jimmy said nothing. He was thinking. That they had targeted him for money lending. That they were totalling his expenditure. The next question would be how he could afford the grub on his income support. Nae problem. They'd get the stock answer. The bookies.

"Did you buy a painting in the Craw's Nest hotel in Anstruther on April 17?"

"Ay. It's in the bedroom."

"Can I see it?"

"Yi don't hiv a warrant, dae yi?"

"No."

"Look at it if yi want."

Peter threw another red herring into Jimmy's confusion. "It's a Russell Flint isn't it? Worth a lot of money."

Jimmy fell into the little psychological trap. "It's no stolen. Fuck me. Whit's it worth?"

"What did you pay for it?"

"Thirty five pounds. Rita liked it."

"Where did you buy your petrol that day?"

"Jesus Christ all fuckin mighty. Any mair stupid questions. Is this an interview or a wind-up. You cunts are wasting police time!"

"Did you buy three crab salads in Crail on April 17?"

"Yea."

"Did you pay cash?"

"Yea, Ah don't have a bank account."

"The money you paid was forgeries. Four five pound notes which were forgeries. Where did you get that money from?"

Jimmy paused. "The bookies."

"Right. On the same day you took a trip with Rita Fullerton and your son to the Island of May. You paid for the trip with four forged fivers. Where did you get the money?"

Jimmy paused. "Ah'd a big win at the bookies. A treble. It wis money Ah won at the bookies."

"How much did you win? If you remember it was a treble you'll remember how much you won surely?"

Jimmy stabbed at an answer. "Aboot ninety pound."

Peter's face remained deadpan. "You had a dinner in the Craw's Nest Restaurant in Anstruther that day. That cost you sixty pounds. You paid cash. Where did you get the money from?"

Jimmy played for time. "Whit is this?"

"It is a serious question Jimmy. Where did you get the money from?"

"Ah still had some left and Rita gave me some of hers. She gets her social at the beginning of the week. Ask her?" he said, gambling that Rita would read the situation.

"So how much money did you have with you that day? How much between you and Rita Fullerton?"

Again Jimmy took his time in answering the detectives' expressionless faces.

"Ah would say we had about one hundred and five pounds."

"Right so you spent eighteen pounds on the boat trip, thirty five on the painting, sixty on dinner, and about seven on the crab salads. That's one hundred and twenty in one day. Not bad for an unemployed man. Where did you get the money? Some of it must have been invisible. According to the figures you were left with minus fifteen pounds."

Jimmy ignored the mathematics and answered the question.

"Ah telt yi. The bookies and Rita chipped in."

Peter remained deadpan. "Did you buy any petrol for your new car Jimmy?"

"No."

"How much petrol did you buy in Kincardine? The

man in the petrol station remembers you buying twenty four pounds worth of petrol on the night of April seventeen. He drove a red Audi. The description given fits you."

Jimmy was cracking. "Whitever yi say."

"I don't say so. The witness, that's what he's going to be, says so. Where did you get the money to buy the petrol?"

"Ah don't know about this."

"I do. On the way home on the night of April seventeen you stopped at a garage in Kincardine. You filled the tank. Where did you get the money from?"

Jimmy was tiring. "Ah don't fuckin remember. Maybe Ah didnae go hame that night."

Peter closed in. "You remember going to the Craw's Nest in Anstruther that same day, where you admit you had dinner."

"Yea."

Jimmy was rattled. "Ay. And the fuckin picture. Yous tell me where Ah got the money fae."

"You got it from Manchester?"

"Did Ah?"

"Just answer the questions. Did you get the money from Manchester? You told us you got it from the bookies and from Rita. Every note you spent that day is a forgery. We have the notes. Descriptions of you from reliable witnesses and you have admitted spending the money. You might as well tell who you're getting the forgeries from? "

"God almighty. Ah'm being set up," he cried into the tape, "Some cunt is turnin me over. Ah've never touched duddies in ma life. That's no ma gemme."

It was more a plea than a denial.

Graham, in his best palsy walsy voice with a twinkle in his blue eyes, timed his entry to the interview to perfection. "I believe you might be right about that, Jimmy. Who are your enemies? Who would have any reason to set you up? Give us the names and we might find the source of the forgeries? Give us a bit of help. We want to find the main man. If not, it's down to you."

Jimmy stood up abruptly. "Ah've had enough of this

crap. Ah'm goin hame."

As a voluntary attendant at the station he had that right, unless, they chose to play their next card, which they did. Graham left the room. "I'll be back in ten minutes, Jimmy," he said. "Make yourself at home."

Images flashed through Jimmy's mind. Johnny, white with fear as Kenny downed him. Jenny trying to fuck her way out of debt. Cowardly Jack's nod of recognition after Jessica committed suicide.

Which one of them?

Johnny McPherson. The only one to give him substantial cash. One thousand two hundred and forty eight pounds in cash. How did that wee bastard get forgeries? That story about Criminal Injuries. Crap. His mother forcing him to pay up. Fuckin crap.

Graham returned and smiled, "Worked it out yet?"

"Whit dae yi mean? "

"The next move."

"Yir gonnae charge me."

"Yes."

Jimmy drank a coffee in silence while Peter and Graham discussed his prospects of being released from custody there and then. They might be able to let him go if he co-operated by telling them where he got forgeries from.

He chuckled bitterly. "Ah don't fuckin know."

They took him to a cell. The next day he appeared in court on petition and was remanded to Barlinnie prison, bail being out of the question.

Kenny Watson came to visit. He was given explicit instructions. "I want Johnny McPherson done. Finished. Ah want that fuckin bastard done."

Kenny Watson maintained the normal practice.

"How much is in it fur me?"

Jimmy was keen to have the job done. That equated to big money. "Five hunner. Finish the wee cunt. Ah mean finish him."

"Don't do it the noo. Wait a few months."

Tollan's not guilty plea failed because there was too much evidence against him and he had no defence. The judge noted that he had recently completed a four years sentence for illegal money lending and gave him another three years in prison. The loan shark was jailed for dealing in forgeries.

In the cells beneath the court Jimmy gave the lawyer his parting shot. "Yi cannae trust any fucker these days."

25 A song for Europe

THE BOY from Bellshill was good. The hair was black. The face sagged like melting plastic. And from behind a pair of dark tinted glasses he waited for the famous if trite opening.

> *Dum dum dum dummy doo wah,*
> *yeah yeah yeah yeah yeah*

He hunched over the mike.

> *Only the lonely,*
> *Know the way I feel tonight*
> *Only the lonely,*
> *Know this feeling aint right,*
> *Only the lonely . . .*

He was good but not that good. He fell at the last hurdle, unable to match Orbison's dramatic falsetto finale. He couldn't hold the note. The song collapsed at the death. The applause reflected his weak ending. Pathetic. The punters turned back to their pints. The girls to their vodkas and lemonade.

The compere roused them back into the big game. "Let's have a big hand for a lovely lass from Denny. She's come all the way into Glasgow determined to get to New York. Maggie Anderson. Is that your real name? Not your showbusiness one? Where do you think Priscilla White would have got if she hadn't turned it round to Cilla Black?"

The girl stepped forward, straight into song.

> *Step in – side love,*
> *Let me find you a place,*
> *Where the cares of the day,*
> *Will be car – ried away by the smile on your face,*

251

We are to – gether now and for-e-ver now,
come my way,
Step in – side love and stay
Step – inside love,
Step in – side love,
Step in – side love,
I want you to stay.

She had a fair enough voice. Nearly as good as Cilla's and it had that limp nasal sound. Not untalented in a peculiar Cilla way. But Maggie wasn't going to win. She stood a fair chance of getting a runner's up prize, the big bottle of whisky or the twenty six inch television.

"No bad, hen," was the general verdict. The compere and the packed drinking audience let her soldier on through the three verses. Maggie got decent applause.

The next aspiring karaoke king was ko'd in the first round. An old guy who thought he was a smarter singer than he actually was. He was foolish in his choice of song. Old fashioned, difficult and requiring a subtler touch than he had. And he might have made a better job before the four pints.

Up rose a young man dressed to kill in a carefully tailored dark dress suit, cream silk shirt topped off with a green bow tie. The compere knew the type. "If he can sing as well as he looks we're in for a treat. What's your name pretty boy."

"Sure, my name is Eammon Rafferty," he said with a delicious lilting Irish accent. The women were beginning to take notice. The package up there on the stage was attractive. Eammon smiled. The flash of white teeth grabbed the women's eyes. Their hearts and bodies were following fast.

He was pretty, soft spoken and firm-bodied. He had azure green eyes, was dark haired and, as one lady the worse for drink blurted out, "fuckin gorgeous."

He sang the song perfectly. The beat was slow. The voice was sweetly seductive.

In the pause before his next raunchy rendition the women made their feelings known. One girl screamed, triggering a flood of fun-filled laughter that widened into more warm appreciation. The women were now sharing their lust for the handsome young man. A good humoured desire. A bit of fantasy fun. All eyes were on Eammon Rafferty as his voice slowly caressed them with each line.

Eamon was the star turn, adored by the women for his looks and voice, he was also admired by the men for his quality voice and mannered muscular presence.

Then Johnny McPherson. He lurched up dragging his left leg slightly as he climbed the stairs to the stage. To the audience he was as interesting at the previous contestant was handsome.

Johnny had almost broken the house rules, in that he wasn't even wearing a jacket never mind a bow tie. He was greeted mercilessly. "Are you sure you're in the right place, son?"

His head hung to to the right, as it always did when he was being put down for his appearance. He grimaced a cracked smile. Just to show them he understood the joke.

"Ay. Ah'm sure. This is . . ." he looked round the slickly dressed gathering, " . . .the biggest karaoke championship in Scotland."

"Correct, wee man. And tonight, as you probably know, is big prize night. The biggest prizes in Scotland."

"Ay. Ah know. Yir prizes are amazin mate. A two litre bottle o' whisky," cackled Johnny for the benefit of the crowd. They liked that one. They laughed. The ugly wee runt had a sense of humour to match his dress sense.

He'd done his best, the plastic cream shoes wiped with a wet cloth, matched the brown, verging on orange, trousers. He was lucky in that his only pullover was orange coloured. He'd tucked the worn strands of wool up under the sleeve before leaving the house. The strands were now showing. The collar of a white shirt protruded above the harsh browny orange ensemble.

This was a black and white night, when the girls came

dressed to kill and the men made a proper effort. A big, big Saturday night out. When they came to feel good and to win. Many contestants kept karaoke machines in their homes, practising their songs throughout the week. Their families earnestly supported them advising on the song that matched their voices best. Like mums and dads encouraging their children in their chosen hobbies.

Johnny was transparently a joke entry, a wild card who had somehow gatecrashed the occasion.

He didn't care. He was here to sing. The beat was slow and catchy.

> *Dad, dad, da, ra ra,*
> *Dad, dad, da, ra ra,*

 Johnny grasped the mike from the compere, took a deep breath, exhaled, took a smaller breath and sang.

> *Start spreading the noos.*
> *I'm leaving today,*
> *I want to be a part of it,*
> *Noo York, noo York,*
> *I want to wake up,*
> *Where the sitee*
> *Doesn't sleep.*

The voice was working to perfection. A musical homage to the untold pleasures of waking up in a wondrous place.

The audience were startled by the vitality in the runt's voice. He had them by the throat. Every fibre in their nerve ends tingling. Nobody talked. They put their drinks down and listened spellbound.

He was so good they didn't join in.

He won. The audience returned their cards with Johnny McPherson ticked to the top.

The big bottle of whisky went to the girl from Denny, the giant TV to the pretty boy from Ireland. And the super prize to Johnny. A return flight to New York.

The audience burst into song . . .

Dad, dad da ra ra,
Dad Dad da ra ra . . .
Start spreadin the noos,
He's leavin today . . .

26 When in Rome

PIAZZA NAVONA was a home from home to Johnny McPherson. He was comfortable in the classical square dominated by a Bernini fountain.

The sun shone freely for his ten days in Rome. Twinkle-eyed Johnny was soothed by the endless sound of cascading water from the marble statued fountains. The water swish merged with the soft breeze through the traffic-free cobbled square.

Piazza Navona was Rome at its best.

Johnny a divorced, broken-legged, battered flyposting karaoke king, made the most of his luck. He recuperated in Rome. He revelled in the Eternal City.

He did the tourist bit gazing in wonder at the Colliseum, the Pantheon, the Spanish Steps, the Trevi Fountain, the Vatican, including the Sistine Chapel. His trouble-free eyes sucked in the colour and the lost power.

He battered round the eternal city on and off the trams with the abandonment of a child in Disneyland.

The gnawing fear of a knife or bat evaporated in the heat. He forgot the painful memory of broken bones, the taste of blood and rain, suicidal thoughts, and devious dealing. The clouds that usually darkened his thoughts, while he maintained a bright cheerful front, parted. Blue skies all the way.

He was a free man who had earned the holiday with the song of his life. He was as proud of his achievement in winning the karaoke as he was when Celtic won the double in their centenary year. The competition had been fierce and he won by sheer talent. Frank Sinatra would have been proud of him.

Rome wasn't New York. It was different and for him, it proved to be better.

For it didn't take him long to forget Times Square, the Statue of Liberty, the Empire State, Tiffany's, the Bronx,

Queens, Broadway, Long Island and Manhattan. Those were the Big Apple images he treasured through the songs and movies that mattered in urban Glasgow.

Rome halted his dreams. The fantasies faded as he began to look at himself and his relationships.

The process happened quickly as these things often do on holiday. Here he was among the rich. Johnny shared the splendour with Japanese, American, German and English tourists armed to the teeth with camcorders and cameras and cash and credit cards.

He picked up a few words that he would spray about when he got home to Garthill. Alti and Avanti from the traffic lights. Va Benni from the waiters.

Home is a feeling of reciprocal acceptance. Of comfort. Johnny felt most at ease in the Piazza Navona watching the unemployed men sip wine at an improvised card table strategically placed in the shadows cast by powerful statues.

He slowed down and saw – the tousled kids queuing up to thrust their open lips under a tap while pumping cold water to the thirsty – the tourists refilling their litre size plastic bottles with water – the mothers perched round the sparkling fountains, chattering in the sunshine, oblivious to the beauty that flowed into their eyes at every turn – the lovers, face to face, caressing, kissing, touching, playing. He didn't speak to anybody and yet he was not alone. Johnny was more than happy. He was content.

Piazza Navona, the haven he found for rejuvenation, was within walking distance of the hotel Trevi, his prize for singing Sinatra.

Third prize was all he wanted. That large bottle of Grouse. Instead he won. His reward for being a decent man, willing to sing the song, to take a chance. To give of himself. The courage to face the crowd and sing, even though the heart was heavy with sadness. With fear. His mind overloaded by debt.

In Rome Johnny McPherson found himself. Amongst the ruins the tired little man stopped laughing at himself long enough to take stock. He was out of the race to pay

Jimmy Tollan. For ten relaxing days Johnny took it so easy that thoughts of a cerebral nature developed without being driven. They just happened.

In Piazza Navona the pace of life and love was much slower than in Garthill. There was nothing hectic here.

He chuckled with pleasure at the sight of an elderly lady enjoying the almost rural peace of the piazza. The lady was slightly fat, sitting on a small fold-out canvas seat. He had watched her carry it from a house in the piazza and place it carefully behind a lamp post.

After a few minutes she stood up, lifted the chair and moved it six inches to the left, then squeezed herself back onto the sagging canvas.

In the next hour she went through the ritual six times. He was intrigued enough to walk across the square for a closer examination of the strange procedure. She smiled at his interest and demonstrated the move pointing at the shadow cast by the lamp post and placing the chair in the shadowy relief from the harsh Italian sun.

Johnny looked into her dark eyes, gave her a thumbs up sign, and said with a chuckle, "Good move." They exchanged nothing tangible. Just unspoken, relaxed friendship. Johnny lurched back, past the painters and ice cream salesman, to his seat beside the Bernini fountain.

The simple things caught his eyes. An elderly lady festooned in pigeons. They clustered on her lap, shoulders and thighs, patiently taking turns to eat the oats she was taking from a bag at her side. She was obviously a little eccentric, maybe lonely. The pigeons ate until they were bored, to be replaced by others fluttering clumsily off the glistening marble statues and through the fountain spray, landing at her feet.

The lady talked to the birds, encouraging them to rise and land on her body. The tourists noticed her loving game. They turned their cameras and camcorders away from the famed Bernini fountain to bring a human touch to their holiday record. The old lady gave a shy smile of encouragement to the strangers from round the world.

Nobody gave her money for although she was dressed cheaply they sensed she was better than a beggar.

Johnny just absorbed the changing scenes. The backdrop in Piazza Navona was sublime. He could hear the constant drone of the city from the busy thoroughfares behind both sides of the Piazza sharpened occasionally by the polizeira sirens and the harsh pitch of continental car horns.

His mind drifted. His mother. His ex-wife. His sister. Even his father. Jimmy Tollan, debts, violence and the next drink drifted to the back of his mind.

If only his maw had taken the free trip. She could have gone to the Vatican and maybe seen the Pope. No, she didn't go to Mass any more but she still prayed for him. She never told him in so many words. He knew because he often said, "Say a wee prayer for me." Her eyes told him she was constantly making that effort. The rosary beads were still around.

"Son, it's kind of you to want me to go. I appreciate the offer. I do," she told him. He knew that she wasn't going to make the effort to prise herself away from the house.

"While you're away Ah'll tape Take the High Road for you." That didn't work.

"Your sister could do that for me. That's not a problem. I just don't want to leave the house. No for a fortnight anyway. Blackpool for a few days is enough for me. With my wee pal Betty."

He tried again, with the Pope as the carrot. "Yi could go tae the Vatican. Yi might even see the Pope. He comes out on the balcony once a week, jis like her across the street."

Mrs McPherson was sitting in her favourite chair, the deep black plastic armchair with John Paul smiling benignly into the living room from the yellow framed picture in the alcove behind. The glass in the frame was cracked and sellotaped.

"If I knew for certain that I'd meet the Pope I'd go, John," she said. "But all the way to Rome without a guarantee? No thanks."

An outside chance wasn't enough. It had to be on a plate. Outside chances were not to be counted. Johnny knew that the only person in his family likely to be landing in Rome was himself. He indulged in a little humour, taking the ticket out of his pocket and studying it carefully.

"Wait a minute maw," he cried excitedly. "The ticket says 'Rome return, three star hotel, visit the Vatican and the Coliseum, and meet the Pope.' All inclusive. And it's costing us nothin!"

Her smile was as big as the room. "That's it then. Everything is perfect. Away doon the toon and get me a passport. I'm on my way to Roma. Arivi derci Glesga. Spaghetti for you tonight John. There's a tin in the cupboard."

They laughed as one. Fun. Mrs McPherson was bursting with the pleasure of Johnny's good fortune. He tried to explain that it wasn't luck – he really was the best karaoke singer in Glasgow. She remained unconvinced.

What did it matter? Johnny was going to enjoy the Italian sunshine. Something good was happening to him for a change. He had more than earned a break in his troubled life. All those beatings. The boy never complained. Jesus, he was brave and stupid and kind-hearted. She loved her only son for his weaknesses. He was still alive and she thanked God for that.

Johnny could sense her feelings. His blue eyes glowed. He smiled and the scars converged on his coarse-skinned face as he leant forward to kiss her on the cheek, murmuring, "OK maw, if Ah see the Pope, Ah'll ask him tae say a prayer for yi."

Johnny had given up. He simply could not get rid of the free trip to Rome. There was no way out. He had considered selling it or giving it away to one of his drinking companions. He knew nobody who could afford more than twenty pounds. That wasn't enough, even for a man like him with pressing financial problems. When it came to the crunch the idea of giving it away to a relative stranger was too much to swallow.

He got a passport and flew to Rome.

The fates, in the form of a smart opportunist, decreed that he go to the Eternal City. The super efficient salesgirl in the travel agent conned him out of his trans-Atlantic flight. The Bronx, Forty Second Street, the Empire State, the Statue of Liberty, and Manhattan faded slowly.

The details of New York never entered his mind. Only the vague feeling that the Big Apple was the place to be, to go to, to experience. A challenge. A dream. An unreal reality.

He'd sung it often enough in the playful karaoke chaos beloved by Glasgow punters. With Frank Sinatra's voice echoing in his head Johnny entertained the last of the real drinkers. New York was in his heart.

The fantasy passed swiftly out of his life when he lurched up to the counter under harsh lights in the city centre travel agent's office. She wore a light blue blazer, flashed a white smile, and watched his mangled face from behind a mask of perfectly applied make-up.

Johnny wore his one and only pullover, the brown coloured plastic shoes. He smelled of last night's booze and today's aftershave.

Connie, for that was the name inscribed in red on a white badge pinned to the lapel of her eye-catching blazer, bided her time.

He explained his good fortune in winning the free trip to New York, giving his name and hoping that she would know something about it to save him the problem of contacting the organisers of the competition. He was not well-versed in dealing with matters outside of the Social.

The white teeth flashed again above the startling blue blazer. "Yes, Mr McPherson, we have your name already. The brewery notified us that you have won the free flight. They told you it was to New York? That surprised me. In fact you are going to the Eternal City for ten days. To the city of Seven Hills. You lucky man. Although from what I hear, there was no luck involved. You are a singer of some renown. A karaoke king goes to Rome."

She was overdoing it a bit.

261

Johnny hardly noticed her insincerity. He was swallowing his disappointment. New York was the dream. The cherished destination.

His words faltered out, "Is there no chance maybe of . . . if Ah went later in the year . . . could Ah . . ."

She was ready. "Not during the period of the free flight offer, Mr McPherson. If you don't fancy Rome we could arrange for a weekend in Amsterdam."

Johnny gave up. New York, the capital of loan sharking, was off his agenda. The Big Apple went unbitten. He went to Rome and plucked oranges from the trees.

Life, he had discovered, was for now. If not forever, at least for today.

27 Death in the drizzle

JOHNNY CAME home from Rome to the news that had spread through Garthill faster than a bush fire in the Australian outback.

Jimmy Tollan was off the streets, in jail. He was gone, like an obnoxious smell, cleared by the wind. He'd been bust by the cops. The word was that they had fitted him up for forgeries.

Damned by duddies.

The important point was that he was out of circulation and out of business and soon he would be out of mind. The scheme breathed a mighty sigh of relief as fear evaporated from more than two hundred households.

Their financial trap was released. Like animals caught in a deadly device they limped out of the jaws to nurse their wounds.

Jenny Mullen took her daughter to the pictures. Johnny McPherson sang with renewed vigour at the karaoke.

Alone and isolated in the community Rita did a runner. There were too many who took the brave pills and were open in their disdain for the expensively dressed mum and her son Matt. She could cope for herself but not for Matt.

She packed enough belongings for a long stay and took the train to St Andrews and a taxi to the peace and quiet of the Crail caravan. Jimmy heard nothing from her. He was left without prison visits or even a letter. They disappeared. She kept her whereabouts a secret from her family, only telling the headmaster.

Life was settling down for everybody. It didn't last long. Just three weeks of happiness as Garthilll escaped from the darkened shadows of Tollan.

Soon they wished he was still around. They needed money. And in a curious twist, they needed the fear. They needed stress. They needed to be deeper in poverty. Without a job and the means, the middle course was barely tolerable.

Living in the money-driven world without any money is boring.

Johnny McPherson was relatively rich. He went back to flypostering. Everything was coming up roses. The smell was intoxicating. He lifted his head and breathed in the cleanliness of work, freedom and hope.

He laughed with more pleasure for himself. He had always laughed, the carefully disguised mirth of a man whose only alternative was to cry. Or commit suicide. The laughter of defiance.

He was a new man. The body was the same, a broken, slow-moving, jerking hindrance. The mind was where the change crystallised. It was unshackled. He was better, able to float through long hard-working days on a carpet of contentment. His clawing crab-like walk became more of a strut as he straightened up to look the world in the eye, fearing no one.

Garthill opened its tired arms to Johnny, welcoming him back into the fold for his obvious friendly quality. The scheme was no longer Injun country and he could return at the weekends from his Nitshill refuge to his known haunts. The Black Inn, his maw's home, the rail outside the bookies for some idle serious talk with his pals.

He was out of the cage running free, working, eating and sleeping where and when he wanted.

With Tollan off the street Johnny had choices. He could, if he wanted, quit the hardship and disciplines of fly postering to go back to life on the dole for real. He could return to daytime drinking. His pals were waiting.

So was his mother, with a barrowload of insistent advice.

"He's gone. This is your chance to sort out your life. Go and get a decent job. You've got the qualifications."

There was a slow smile in his reaction. "Maw, who're yi kiddin. Sort out ma life? Do yi no think it's a bit late fur that noo?"

"Why not son? You're still a young man."

"Do you mean, go back tae sea? Run fae the fun here?"

"At least you were happy at sea."

"Ah wis happy when Ah got home. Yi jist thought Ah wis happy all the time. Ah wis pleased tae get hame tae see yi!"

She sustained her argument. "You had a job then. A good job.

"Maw, they don't take sailors back after ten years. No guys that cannae even staun on land."

The jokes remained in character.

His approach to life was changing. Johnny was seriously thinking about retaining his short-lived lifestyle as a glue man to a well-disposed boss. Alex kept the job open while Johnny experienced Rome. The money was good. So why not hold onto the good life he had found.

There was no longer any necessity to pay the loan shark from Johnny's abundant weekly rewards. He was drawing invalidity allowance, including an allowance for the rent. All that was missing was free beer, a bus pass, and a complimentary ticket to Parkhead.

He thrived on his new freedom, chatting to his pals in the lamplight without looking over his shoulder, joining them at Parkhead to lift the ailing Celtic and generally making himself at home again in his own crumbling community. Everybody closed out the deprivation, the empty steel-shuttered homes, the fortressed shops, and the violent hardened children. It remained home.

He was a fixture in the Black Inn, going straight from his work to the pub for a pint with the regulars. Pride and friendship, responsibility and control were rekindled in the karaoke kid. He was strong enough to hold his own in pub conversations. No matter how heated.

He surprised even himself the first time he lost his temper. He was in the Black Inn supping his third pint after a hard day at the postering.

The argument was raging. Did great players make bum managers? Or did average players make great managers?

Wee Tam was trying to have the last word. "It disnae make any fuckin difference. Jock Stein wisnae a great player.

He wiz wan thing and wan thing only, the greatest manager Scotland has ever seen. Best widnae have made it as a manager. He couldnae turn up fur training never mind run a serious training session. Look at the Charltons. Bobby won England the World Cup. Naebody else did it. Look at that goal in the semi final. And the quarter final. He was something else. And whit about the European final against Benfica. Wor Bobby scores again. Then he retires and whit happens. Failure. Manager of Preston North End. Failure. Now let's turn our attention to his ambling fuckin brother. Jack the Lad. Average player in anybody's book except Alf Ramsay. Revie nearly sold him at one stage. What a manager Big Jack turned out to be. He turned Sheffield Wednesday round. Then Middlesborough, and look at what he's done with Ireland."

Johnny was in agreement with Wee Tam but felt that there were exceptions to the rule.

"It disnae always work that way. Kenny Dalglish took Liverpool to . . ."

Wee Tam refused to give ground. "Kenny's an exception. What about Jim McLean at Dundee United? Celtic should have gone for him on a three year contract instead of Liam Brady.

"Liam fuckin Brady. Exactly. There's another great player cannae do it as a manager. If Jim McLean can find all the players he's found, and win the league with them, and regularly get a run in Europe, how the fuck does Brady spend millions and get nowhere. Because Brady was a great player. McLean wisnae."

Kenny Watson walked into bar. He ordered a pint and sat down ignoring the discussion. Nor was he invited to join in, for although he had a sound knowledge of football, he was cold-shouldered since Tollan's exit to jail.

Kenny was there for a purpose. To do Tollan's bidding, to kill Johnny McPherson at the agreed price of five hundred pounds – the price the loan shark was more than happy to pay to obliterate Johnny. To finish the man he firmly believed had dumped duddies on him. The man he thought had put him behind bars without even grassing him.

Kenny waited and watched.

Johnny was there for a purpose. To get right into the chat. He finally got his two cents worth in. "What about Cruyff? He's got to rank wi the all-time greats. Wi Pele, Puskas, Bestie, Jinky, Baxter. Cruyff's a great manager. Whit about Beckenbauer? Two World Cups."

Johnny was pushed out by the barman's intrusion into the debate. "These guys are just part of the Continental system. They're groomed fur the job. The whole set-up across there is geared tae keeping continuity. The way they dae at Liverpool."

Johnny wasn't having his point squashed. "Wait a fuckin minute, Tam. There's mair tae it than just a system. Beckenbauer and Cruyff huv tae pick the right team. They huv tae adapt tae new tactics. They've got tae move wi the times. Tactics change all the fuckin time."

Wee Tam jumped in. "Stein didnae bother wi tactics. No defensive tactics anyway. He made the other side worry about their tactics."

Johnny lost his temper. "Shite. Yir talkin shite. Celtic played defensive under Stein. It's a myth that they always attacked."

"Ah never said they always attacked."

By closing time they were slurring their words and trying to stay upright, hardened drinkers reeling to their destinations on a well-worn track, home to trouble, home to sex or home via the fish and chip shop. Johnny was last to leave, his mind static, blitzed by booze, his stomach repelling the eight swilling pints he had consumed in what had been a 'good night, good crack'.

Kenny Watson's seat at the dark table in the corner was empty. He was outside, waiting in the dark.

Johnny swayed under the half-open shutter. As he straightened up he felt the urgent need of a piss and staggered round the back of the pub, stretched his left hand out to support himself on the roughcast, unzipped and relieved his body. After an eternity his bladder had emptied to the point of comfort. He almost smiled at the relief as he zipped up.

He was being watched. From only seven yards away Kenny studied the paralysed condition of his prey.

The enforcer was comfortable with the job, for Kenny had always been a man without a conscience. Without thinking he did as he was told. This job was easy and the money was exceptional. Five hundred pounds to put Johnny McPherson in the mortuary. He was following Jimmy's instructions to the book. He did it in the knowledge that he himself had dumped the duddies on Tollan. For there was no way out. Should it ever dawn on Tollan that he, Kenny Watson, had passed the forgeries, he would be the man murdered.

So in a farcical act he obeyed the orders issued from behind the visitor's window at Barlinnie. "Make sure the wee fucker knows why. He's got tae know. If Ah wisnae in here, Ah'd torture him tae fuckin death."

Kenny appeared from nowhere, stood squarely in front of his swaying victim and took a firm hold of both Johnny's forearms. The wee man was staring incomprehensibly at the ground. He heard Kenny's words. "Staun up Johnny."

His eyes swivelled upwards focusing on Kenny's face. "Christ Kenny, it's you. Cheers mate. Ah'm no sleeping here the night."

Kenny rarely wasted words. This time he did. He tried to explain to Johnny the reasons for the impending assault – that he was being punished for paying off Jimmy in duddies. Johnny would have to pay the full price.

Kenny's lie to himself was more than self-deceit. He was taking out an insurance policy against Johnny surviving the blows.

Johnny was too drunk to absorb information properly. He tried lamely through a fog of incomprehension to respond to the false accusation. Again he found Kenny's eyes as he blurted out, "It wisnae ma money. Ma maw got it fae the baker. Dough fae a baker. Eh?"

Kenny shook his head in despair. "You and yir pathetic fuckin jokes. Yir fuckin jokin days are ower."

He released the little drunk's forearms and stepped back for space to lever a vicious uppercut into the stomach. The clenched fist drove straight into the solar plexus forcing wind upwards. Johnny collapsed breathless. He lay motionless on the ground, vulnerable to a kicking and unable to cry out. Helpless as a baby seal at a culling.

Drunk, and without the air to beg for mercy, Johnny McPherson was less than two minutes from death. Kenny Watson was about to become a murderer. A pointless killing, carried out without anger or emotion.

The enforcer stepped away from his victim, striding across the filthy overgrown backyard. There was little chance of any witnesses for the two storey flats were mostly empty, the windows steel-shuttered. In the homes where a few families had defied the odds to stay put, the occupants were in the front room watching TV. A soulless place where people stayed indoors except when venturing out to the chippie or video shop.

In the darkness at the back of the concrete pub Kenny bent to pick up the weapon he'd earlier placed carefully in the long grass next to an empty beer crate. A baseball bat.

Johnny was defenceless, his face in the weeds, his eyes on a discarded lager can. Trying to recover his breath he turned his face round to suck in air like a swimmer seeking oxygen for another few strokes underwater.

A grey light filtered out of the window bars dropping on John Edward McPherson's broken face. A lapsed Catholic boy with an absent Protestant father. It was difficult to tell whether he was grimacing from pain or smiling out of his mangled face.

Kenny looked down at his target, measuring the distance to the head. He stepped back to take a solid stance. Like a baseball player he prepared instinctively for the killer blow. If Johnny had to go, he had to go swiftly. The killer was operating on physical instinct, without thought. Stupid.

The voice cut through the night with total command.

"Whit the fuck are yi daein?"

The stranger came at Kenny from the darkness, striding over Johnny's body and growling. "Wait a fuckin minute, yi cunt."

The knife came up from nowhere, held vice-like in the stranger's right hand. A long jagged weapon that slit through Kenny's stomach, under his lowest rib and into his lung. Kenny saw the stranger's hatred as the knife was dragged back out of his body. The baseball bat fell from Kenny's hand as the stranger plunged the knife in again. The second insert pushed Kenny over. He rolled in the dirt, his life draining away as his lungs filled with blood. He died slowly, staring into Johnny McPherson's pulped face.

Exploding out of control, the stranger explained to the dying man the injustice inflicted on himself.

"He's mine. No yours. Ah bought him and another two hunner in Tollan's book. Five fuckin grand the book cost me."

He stuffed the bloody knife into his inside pocket.

McFadzen, the Maryhill loan shark, stepped round Kenny's blood-seeping body, to place his strong arms under Johnny's armpits dragging him erect with the comforting words. "It's awright mate. Ah'll get yi hame."

Without a glance back he half carried, half dragged Johnny to a black BMW, shoving him in the back seat and drove slowly away from the scene.

Johnny slumped in the leather seat, absorbing the gentle movement, unaware of the passing streets. Sickness oozed into his mouth. He swallowed, dropped his head and fell almost unconcious.

He resurfaced to confusion. Gazing out of the car window at the lights on McDonalds burger joint in Maryhill Road, he tried to push his alcohol-deadened senses into gear. He failed. Drunk, sore and disorientated he had no clear recollection of where he was, what had happened, or even the attack. He was alone in the car. Cold from wetness in his clothes. His hands were dirty.

The driver's door opened and McFadzen leant into

the back seat thrusting a packet at him. "Ah got yi a Big Mac. Eat it and we'll talk."

A Big Mac was the last thing Johnny wanted. He had to know why a night out in the Black Inn had ended in McFadzen's car outside McDonalds.

"Tommy? Whit am Ah daein here. Ah don't owe yi nothin. No as far as Ah know."

A cloud of fear overwhelmed his booze-befuddled mind. He placed the Big Mac, still wrapped, on the seat beside him. The words came out slowly and slurred. "Ah definitely paid yi aff. Ma maw saw tae that."

McFadzen wasted no time in explaining the current financial set-up. Johnny walked home.

28 The old man and the sea

MATT WAS more than intrigued, he was fascinated.

At first he had only seen the general picture, the gulls hovering and swooping, the slashes of breaking white as the sea tore over the dark rocks. A pretty and comfortable sight which made no demands on his eight-year-old mind.

Then he noticed a large jagged dot disappearing. It was behind the strip of rocks stretching one hundred yards out to sea. There were three of the long protrusions, known as the Skerries, linking the savage sea to the shore.

This was a transient home or stopping place for the abundant bird life. But Matt wasn't to know that.

He could smell the ozone, the salt and see the white of waves crashing on the rocks. The seagulls, more often than not, fulmars or gannets, were an ever-present. But not that black disappearing jagged blob on the undulating sea.

Matt concentrated. He was breathing easily, enjoying the peaceful freedom of the place. He clambered across the rocks to get closer to the subject of his concentration.

And he got lucky. He was looking in the right area when it popped up again, close to the orange-coloured buoy, a marker for fishermen returning to the harbour.

This time he focused on it. A large back bird, with a long neck and an ugly head. The bird was on the surface now moving toward the strip of broken rocks, where it left the water to walk undignified across the rock and drop into the more sheltered waters on the landward side of the Skerries.

Again it dipped under, first arching its long neck and then upturning to flip below, its webbed feet showing at the last movement.

The sea surface was empty. Matt understood that it would come up again. But where? In the distance a red boat was making a beeline for the harbour. Matt tried to prevent his eyes from drifting to the boat. He failed. While shifting his gaze, the bird was back on the waves. It had been underwater for a long time.

For some inexplicable reason the little boy was embarrassed by his lack of knowledge. He couldn't understand why the bird was able to remain under the sea for so long or why it was repeatedly going underwater.

He went back to the safety of the grass walkway, where thousands of healthy backpackers had trampled the coastline enjoying the bracing air and uplifting sights.

He sat down on the turf and watched the bird dive again. He looked round to see if anybody was coming, taking a sixth sense glance along the worn pathway.

There was a man coming, pushing an old black bicycle with a basket tied to the handlebar. The man was old. In his sixties, weather-browned, without an ounce of fat on his angular face. A small man, he wore black Wellington boots, a worn black oilskin coat and faded brown corduroy trousers.

The character stopped. Matt glanced up at the old man and their eyes contacted.

"He got nowt that time. He's reet persistent. He'll go down again," said the old man with a chuckle.

The chuckle was to be shared and Matt responded. "It keeps goin doon. Ah cannae catch it comin up again."

"Appen you'll see it t'next time, lad," said the man, leaning the bicycle against a thick gorse bush at the side of the walkway.

They had instantly struck up a trust. Matt moved over to watch his birdwise companion carefully untie the wicker basket from the handlebar and lay it on the turf. His curiosity moved to the basket.

"Whit hiv yi goat in that? Fish?"

"Nay. I doot you'll nay have seen what I have here," he said. His bright blue eyes shone from behind thick horn-rimmed spectacles.

The old man had assessed the boy quickly and easily. That he was from Glasgow, that he knew nothing of the

273

coastline, that he was basically ignorant of the sea and that he was consumed with curiosity. He sensed the boy's insecurity.

"I'll show you," he said, undoing the buckle on the basket, turning the lid back and inviting Matt to look inside. "You're in for a reet surprise lad."

Matt peered in.

"Crabs! Fuckin crabs."

The old man gasped inwardly at the obscenity from one so young.

"Nay, better than crabs. Lobsters. They are worth a lot more."

He lifted the lid gently as Matt got down on his hands and knees to peer into the basket.

He saw a patchwork of glistening dark blue and purple shells. And a tangle of twitching claws.

"They're all sort o' colours."

"Reet. They are. They turn red when cooked," said the old man, taking one out of the basket and laying it belly down on the tightly woven sea turf. The lobster's two claws jerked about erratically.

Matt said nothing gazing at the jerky blue-shelled creature. The old man took another lobster from the basket, laying it beside the first. Its shell was different in colour, darker, though also mottled. It was almost metallic in the nature of its colouring.

"Where did yi get them?"

"Oot there. Reet oot at the end o' t' rocks. I keep four lobster creels."

Before he could explain the workings of the creels Matt was firing in another question.

"How many hiv yi got there?"

The old man answered without thinking for the boy. "Twenty pounds worth. I was lucky today."

"Can Ah see the rest o' them? Any bigger wans?"

Soon there were five lobsters twitching on the turf, two cockles and a pile of dark-shelled mussels. The old man was explaining that he could sell the lobsters and make a delicious soup from the mussels.

Matt looked up at the caravan, bright cream amongst the dark gorse bushes in the inshot overlooking the rocky bay. Maybe his ma could make this mussel soup.

"Where did you get they wee wans? Ah mean they wee black wans. They wans yi make soup wi."

"You find them sticking to t' rocks. They are reet easy to collect. You twist them off the rocks," he said demonstrating with his right hand grasping and turning.

The young Glaswegian and the expatriate Yorkshireman had very easily struck up a rapport. Neither made any enquiries about their backgrounds. They accepted that they were both in the one place at that time. That the rolling waves and their own voices were part of the easy afternoon. They were part of the scene, an important human presence.

"You'll get them when the tide is out. The tide's turning now. The best time . . ." His voice petered out and he rounded the boy to take a few quick steps down onto the pebbled shore.

"Look. Over there," he said, pointing to a square chunky rock half way along the Skerries. "A heron."

Matt stared but couldn't pick up on what he was expected to see. His eyes moved along the jutting rocks. The sun was behind him shining out to sea, catching the rolling waves, highlighting the white spray. The old man gave him more time to spot the heron. Matt could see the gulls, some grey, some white, and some black and white. The heron remained unseen for it was standing still, peacefully grey, waiting.

The old man crunched over the pebbles, up the turf and stood beside Matt to guide the boy's vision.

"See big orange plastic can. Look reet over it to the rocks. Left o' where t' waves are breaking through that gap. It's to left."

The boy let out a cry of relief and delight. "Ah see it."

And almost in the same breath added. "It's takin' aff. See."

The heron eased forward its long slender neck extended and its pencil-thin legs draping elegantly behind. With a slow motion sweep of its wings the bird gently eased thirty yards nearer the shore landing feet first in shallow water. The wind, the waves and gulls became unseen backdrops to the heron's activities, as Matt remained motionless. The old man said nothing.

The heron's head turned majestically in slow motion. For fully fifty seconds, a long time for a little boy's concentration, the heron stood. Then it moved, lifting its legs carefully out of the water and purposefully moving five yards forward in the grey sea.

Again it paused with dignity, before thrusting its head into the water, withdrawing the long neck with what appeared to be an empty beak.

The old man broke the silence. "See that. She got nowt."

The boy was in tune with the Yorkshireman's strange tongue, for they were sharing a minor experience. They both wanted the bird to catch a fish. In a strange quirk of nature they were on the heron's side.

The bird regally moved another five or six yards forward in the search for food. Again she waited patiently surveying the location from the height of the long snake-like neck.

This time Matt broke the silence with an astute observation. "It must hiv fantastic eyesight, eh?" Eyesight was not a word he had ever used before.

"Yes, it will have reet good eyesight. Oil coated so that the water doesn't obliterate t' vision."

They waited and watched for five more minutes as the bird continued its dignified search for passing fish. Eventually it struck successfully and Matt saw the fish momentarily as she gracefully plucked her prey from the water. The heron then turned seaward, rose out of the water, winging off in slow motion. The entertainment was over.

The old man bent down to lift the lobsters, returning them to the basket which he tied on the crossbar. Matt didn't let him go without checking out the whereabouts of the creels.

"Where di yi keep yir lobster creels?"

From behind the horn-rimmed spectacles, his blue eyes riveted into Matt's. "I told you, lad. Out at far end of the rocks. Too dangerous for you. Far too dangerous."

Matt gave him an impish Glasgow smile that said it all. "Ah widnae go near yir fuckin creels. Honest, Ah widnae. Whit dae Ah want lobsters fur."

The old man knew a lie when he heard one. He now had to take action to prevent the boy's curiosity resulting in death by drowning. The lobsters weren't that important.

He put the bicycle down. "Is that your muther at caravan window?"

"Ay."

The old man walked swiftly up the hill through the gorse bushes to the caravan. Before he could knock Rita opened the door to get the first word in. "He isnae givin you any trouble. Is he?"

"Nay. He's OK."

Rita stepped down to absorb the fresh blustering air and the view.

"It's really beautiful. Anither nice day."

They shared the vision. The waves racing to the rocks. The sunlight grabbing the white spray.

The old man got down to business. " T'lad's interested in seeing lobsters in t' creels. He's reet keen. I think he might try to find creels himself and that would be dangerous. There's nought I can do to stop him. He's reet curious. I made mistake o' telling him where t' creels are . . . reet oot at end rocks there."

Rita interrupted. "Ah've telt him no tae go all the way oot there. He disnae always listen tae me."

"They never do. There's nought that'll stop them making t' mistakes we made."

Rita laughed louder than the comment warranted. The old man took a closer look at her, absorbing her untold troubles.

277

Down on the pathway Matt had unclipped the basket and was looking at the lobsters again. This time he put his fingers between a lobster's claws, quickly pulling his hand away when the half-dead crustacean reacted.

Rita saw her son's actions.

She screamed into the buffeting wind. "Leave that alain."

Matt straightened up to shout back. "The man disnae bother. It's awright. They're lobsters ma. They're still alive, ma."

The old man smiled. "Tomorrow t' lad could get some himself. He can come wi me in t' morning. Lad 'll be safe." It was all said as a polite reassuring question.

Rita took a closer look at the tidy, shaved, respectable old man in the worn clothes. He had established a comfortable rapport with her and his decency was transparent.

"Ay. Awright. Come for him about ten o'clock."

"That's too late. T' tide'll be in by then."

He left that one hanging in the air for a moment and then added. "T' lad will need to be ready at five thirty."

Rita sat down on the caravan step to absorb all that a five thirty start entailed. She had no alarm clock in the caravan. Nor did she have a telephone for an alarm call.

He was looking at her with those bright blue eyes, a friendly twinkle and the suggestion of a smile on his lips. He was old, but she liked the man.

"Ach, we'll go tae bed early. Matt can get me up tae see him aff. If we're no up, bang on the door."

Matt was up, warmly clothed and ready to go at five twenty. The red sunrise was pushing out from behind a bank of slow-moving clouds.

They saw the old man pushing the bike along the pathway and Matt went down to meet him. Strapped to the crossbar was a pole with a hook which the old man unclipped, handing to Matt. "You carry that, lad."

And off they went out along the slippery Skerries, carefully negotiating the slimy wet seaweed, to the anchored lobster creels dotted along the rocks. They pulled up the creels collecting four lobsters.

Along the rocky Skerries, they talked. About what they saw. The old man was a fount of knowledge. The flood of information began when Matt asked about an immaculate black and white bird. There were two of them, fifty yards away and what first caught Matt's attention was the long orange beak. Then he saw the birds' legs, slender pink yet strong.

"Whit's that wan?" he inquired.

"An oystercatcher."

"Whit's it daein?"

"Getting breakfast," said the old man as a tease. He expected the next question.

"Whit's it gettin?"

"Nay oysters, anyway."

Matt left the question of what an oyster was, for later. His immediate interest was in what the bird, bigger than a blackbird but smaller than a chicken, was doing strutting and stopping to poke its orange beak into the sand. The second one was over in the rocks searching the crevices.

The old man explained. "There's nought safe from it, mussels, limpets, cockles, sand worms, shrimps. The oystercatcher feeds reet well. He gets them all. They can't move, and his beak chisels the shells open. Then he eats the flesh."

"Ay," said the boy in shocked amazement. "No nice. Mind yi, it's beautiful. Looks good Eh?"

"Certainly does, lad."

They stood up and the oystercatchers took off flying directly along the coast. Matt saw the broad white wing bar and heard their shrill call . . . peec, peec, peec.

They made their way back along the jagged line of rocks ahead of the incoming tide. The old man gave Matt two lobsters and they sat in the still morning looking out to sea. The sunrise was easing away. The pink orange and white that grew from behind the dark clouds had faded. The sun was now in power.

From the caravan Rita, who had not been tempted back to bed, watched her son communicating with the lobster man. She hoped that Matt was keeping his father's business secret.

Rita put on her coat to walk down the hill, joining them as the sunrise was fading. The old man twisted round and she greeted him. "Whit a mornin. Worth gettin' oot ma bed tae see the sunrise."

He nodded.

"Look ma, he's geid me two o' them," said Matt pointing at the lobsters lying on the turf, "an Ah saw two oystercatchers."

She laughed. "Could yi no catch a single nugget or a ninety niner?"

The old man refused the offer of bacon, egg and sausages. Breakfast was toast and honey with a cup of tea which he had taken before the early start.

Before moving on to sell the lobsters in a Crail hotel he made a point of explaining about the disappearing dot – the diving seabird that had brought them together the previous day.

"Twas a cormorant, nine parts bird and one part fish. They dive for fish. In the sea they can move like a shark. Like a shark," he cracked out the word to impress on the lad the cormorant's power and speed beneath the waves.

"Anything small enough goes straight down their gullets. They can stay under t'water for three minutes at time. That's why you never know where they are going to pop up They move around down there grabbing whatever they can get."

Matt was excited by the information. He looked out to sea.

The old man was struck by his own words. "They're greedy blighters. They eat more than a pound of fish every day."

Rita and Matt watched the old man pushing the bike along the grass pathway. He looked so small yet strong. They warmed to his strength. He disappeared from view between the boulders on the far curve of the bay.

The day that had started well. They went for a walk along the pathway with the wind, the waves and clouds for company. They spoke little. Rita sat on a boulder and smoked a cigarette while Matt crunched across the heavily pebbled beach to the water's edge. He stood for a long time thinking. At times he was close to tears, grappling with inexplicable emotions.

She finished her cigarette.

"Come on Matt. Time to go back." Her comforting voice sliced through the sea air.

Matt turned. Profiled against the foaming waves gurgling through the rocks, he called out, "Ma, can we go and see ma Da?"

Rita replied instantly.

"Yes. We'll go to Glasgow and see him at the next visiting."

She had made her mind up while she watched her son grow that early morning. She would tell Jimmy. That she was finished with him.

29 Thanks, but no thanks

DAYLIGHT BROUGHT a few home truths to Johnny McPherson. He went straight to the site in Argyle Street where Alex Swanson was hard at work scraping off wet posters.

Alex was relieved that Johnny had turned up. The rain was pelting down and there were six sites to be postered. In the wet that entailed taking off old posters, slapping on the new ones, and then going back round all the sites to check that they were holding. The debris had to be cleared up off the pavements. Left behind it attracted police attention.

Alex's body was already feeling the pressure. The cold wetness on his neck was sneaking down his back. The rain incessantly dotted his glasses.

He was irritated but strong enough to be without anger. "Thank God you've made it Johnny. Drinking?"

"No, really. Ah had a few swallies. Ah'm feelin no bad."

They had almost finished the day's work when Tommy McFadzen arrived at the small Clyde Street site. Johnny was facing the wall. He recognised the voice instantly.

"So this is how yi earn yir livin. When dae yi get paid?"

"End o' the week." He replied looking to see if Alex was watching. He wasn't. He was in the back of the van mixing another bucket of glue.

"Ah'm no waiting that fuckin long."

"Kin we talk ower there," Johnny asked, nodding at an empty shop entrance.

"Ah don't give two fucks if he hears every word," said the killer.

Johnny caved in and talked.

"Ah've got it. Ah missed yi last week and the week afore. Yi wirnae there, no at the usual place. Ah went up tae Maryhill Road, tae the bookies. Then Ah went roon tae the pub. Ah even went tae ootside yir hoose. Yir motor wisnae there . . ."

"For fucks sake, gonnie no make a cunt o' me," he leered. "That wiz last week and the week before that. Ah'm lookin fur three weeks now, no a fuckin guided tour of where you couldnae find me. Ah'll find yi in five fuckin seconds. Ah'll be roon the night."

Johnny's hand was grasping a roll of notes inside his pocket. "Ah'll gie yi it the noo."

He held the roll out. "There's three weeks there."

McFadzen didn't even comment on Johnny's sly effort to hold onto the money.

He counted the cash and smiled. "Thir's a wee bit extra here."

He left as fast as he had appeared, crossing the street to the BMW parked on a yellow line. Johnny watched him unlock the car with a press on his remote control. He climbed in. The car remained motionless. Through the rain Johnny watched the loan shark counting the money, greedily double checking the amount. Alex poked his head out of the van. "Come on Johnny, get the rubbish intae the bag."

Johnny heard the car start and to his surprise saw it U-turn, pulling up at the pavement close to where he stood.

The window purred down.

"Want anythin Johnny?"

With the rain, dripping off his broken nose, Johnny replied carefully.

"Thanks, but no thanks."

What he meant was, "Fuck off."

It was the first time he'd ever said that to a man offering him money.

Argyll

publishing

If you have enjoyed this book you might be interested to read other fiction titles by Argyll Publishing.

Me & ma Gal Des Dillon £6.99

A stunning first novel about the friendship of two ten year old boys. Superbly entertaining and at times hilarious work, Dillon gets at the essence of growing up in the modern world.

quite simply spot on *The Big Issue;* a novel Scotland has waited a long time for *Mentor Magazine;* a brilliant debut, filled with ironic revelation *The Scotsman*

Angels of Death Howard Wilson £5.99

New York prostitutes are being murdered. Clues point to the work of one person — a serial killer with a mission.

Private eye and ex-cop Brett Grant comes across a religious cult who call themselves the Angels. They appear as none too angelic and to help out his old buddy in Homicide, Grant starts asking questions.

a gritty crime thriller *Daily Record;* tough, uncompromising, extremely well-written *The Herald;* ingenious, satisfying, I simply could not put it down *Inside Time*

Second edition, Koestler Award winner

Everwinding Times Mary McCabe £6.99

Ailie Lorimer suffers a strange affliction. Her memory loss, her sense of dislocation, her feyness – all lead her to seek medical help. Yet at the same time she appears to cut to the core of all life before her, now and in the future.

Mary McCabe is a novelist (with) real speculative ability. I'm impressed. *Books in Scotland*

An Anger Bequeathed Bruce Leeming £6.99

> Harriot Murray drives herself to compete energetically
> with men – at work, and in her relationships at play . . .
> But what is driving her? In this novel of lust and high
> ideals, Hattie enrages and delights by turn as she battles
> against entrenched male power. Bruce Leeming has
> created a character of our times – vibrantly triumphant yet
> darkly tragic, fighters for equality like Hattie Murray can
> come to pay a heavy price.
>
> > pretty steamy stuff *Financial Times*
> > Leeming may be trying to prove his New Man
> > credentials. *Sunday Times*

Argyll titles are available in bookshops or by Mail Order

Order the above titles or send a self addressed A5 envelope
with a 29p stamp for our free catalogue

To Order complete the following

Name_____

Address_____

_____

Postcode_____

No		Total
___	Me & ma Gal Des Dillon £6.99	_____
___	Angels of Death Howard Wilson £5.99	_____
___	Everwinding Times Mary McCabe £6.99	_____
___	An Anger Bequeathed Bruce Leeming £6.99	_____

Post & packing (add 10% in UK; 20% overseas) _____

TOTAL _____

Send your cheque/P.O. made out to Argyll Publishing to:
Argyll Publishing, Glendaruel, Argyll PA22 3AE Scotland